ROCK STAR ON THE VERGE

LARA WARD COSIO

ROGUE PUBLICATIONS

Copyright © 2020 by Lara Ward Cosio

All rights reserved.

This is a work of fiction. Names, characters, businesses, places, events and incidents are either the products of the author's imagination or used in a fictitious manner.

Cover designer: Chloe Belle Arts

Also by Lara Ward Cosio
Tangled Up In You (Rogue Series Book 1)
Playing At Love (Rogue Series Book 2)
Hitting That Sweet Spot (Rogue Series Book 3)
Finding Rhythm (Rogue Series Book 4)
Looking For Trouble (Rogue Series Book 5)
Felicity Found (Rogue Series Book 6)
Rogue Christmas Story (Rogue Series Book 7)
Problematic Love (Rogue Series Book 8)
Rock Star on the Verge (Rogue Series Book 9)

Full On Rogue: The Complete Books #1-4
Rogue Extra: The Complete Books #5-8

Hula Girl: A Standalone Romance

ROCK STAR ON THE VERGE

"Think about it. But think fast. This is the chance of a lifetime. Let's go chase an adventure together."

Growing up as the son of notorious rock star Martin Whelan, I've enjoyed both the perks and the ridicule that come with his fame. Now, I've got my own bit of Instagram-ready celebrity, including some harmless pranks and a starring role in the local Dublin club scene.

When, on the eve of my eighteenth birthday, my guitar god uncle Conor Quinn suggests I go on a motorbike road trip through Europe to shake up what he calls my "sheltered" existence, I tell him *I'll go if you go.*

I never thought he'd take me up on it.

But, he's got it stuck in his head that if I get some "real life" experience, I might just be able to jump-start my own musical ambitions.

Only thing is, he's not exactly his usual cool and controlled self. See, in the middle of his surprise fortieth birthday party, he gave his band mates of twenty years some shocking news no one was ready for, least of all me.

With that revelation, it seems this road trip could be a disaster before we've even started.

Or ... it could be the adventure of a lifetime.

Rock Star on the Verge is a coming-of-age-road-trip-through-Europe-finding-your-inner-rock-star book!

1

FELICITY

The drive won't take long. Still, the silence grates at me.

I should be used to it after these last few months, but a part of me thinks that if I accept this non-communication it will mean I have given up. Given up on Conor ever coming back to himself. Given up on our marriage. Given up on the stability and happiness we've had in the seven years since we overcame the toughest hurdle we had known in our relationship up until that point—my trouble coping after our daughter was born.

But I refuse to give up. I will fight for him—for *us*—with everything I have. That includes, it seems, going as far as organizing this surprise fortieth birthday party for Conor.

While our son and daughter are with the nanny, we're on our way to Haddington House in nearby Dún Laoghaire under the pretense of a charity event for which I promised Conor's attendance. He'd told me to get him out of it. He'd told me there was no way for him to put on a happy face, that his participation would be a drain to the cause rather than a boost. But I claimed my hands were tied, that the marketing was done, and surely, he didn't want to disappoint such a worthy endeavor.

And so, my good-hearted husband found it within himself to dress in a Valentino suit that conforms to his incredibly fit body and is now driving us to an event I probably should have never thrown together. I did so in a fit of panic, to be honest. Once it became clear that Conor's justified depression over his father passing away was not letting up, but in fact, worsening, I cast about for a way to focus his attention on something positive. The idea was to bring all his friends and family together in celebration and to maybe, just a little, counteract the darkness he's been dwelling in since the funeral.

The sun won't set for hours and the late summer day has been unusually warm. The venue is on the waterfront, and the party starts with drinks outside. It should make for a lovely event.

But turning to look at Conor, I worry again about this evening. He does not look remotely interested in being here. In fact, he looks rather like a man forcing himself to fulfill an unwanted duty. There's the same grim set to his jaw that he's had for months. He's focused on the road ahead, giving me a chance to examine the fine lines at the corners of his eyes that have begun to set a bit deeper. His black hair is short and still without a trace of gray. His father had only a light sprinkle of gray hair at the temples, so I suppose Conor will follow the same pattern one day. Always one for good posture, he holds his spine and shoulders with more stiffness now. He's wound tight, recoiling from my touch more often than not. Beyond all that, though, he's retreated deep into his own head, his mind occupied by things he won't share with me.

This behavior is all the more upsetting because he hasn't picked up a guitar or sat down at the piano since his father died. He hasn't spent any significant time with Gavin or his other friends. He has no release from his troubles.

The only bright spot, the only time I see a genuine smile and connection from him is when he's with our kids. He drops his walls and becomes intensely present with them. Romeo and Ella are both seven years old and thriving, thankfully unaware of the true depths of their father's troubles.

"You're staring at me again."

I blink and take in a sharp breath at Conor's words. It's a relief to hear his voice. I'm so thirsty for it, craving the sexy cadence of it. That's another thing to have changed. We haven't had sex in months. For the first time in our relationship, he's completely lost his desire. In the absence of real communication, I've taken to examining him when he's not looking, hoping to discover some clue for how to help him. I hadn't thought he'd noticed. He's never acknowledged it before, anyway, always seemingly lost in his own thoughts.

"How long must we stay?" he asks, ignoring the fact that I hadn't responded to him as he turns the Tesla into Haddington House's drive.

"Em," I start, and my mouth goes dry.

There are two valets, one at each of our doors, pulling them open before I've concocted an answer. To keep Conor from sliding out of his leather seat, I grab his forearm and he turns to me.

"Sweetheart," I say, forcing a painful swallow. "Promise me you'll enjoy tonight."

He raises his eyebrows. "You know I'd rather not be here, honey. How am I to promise I'll enjoy this?"

Biting my bottom lip, I wince. "It's not exactly a charity event."

There's a long pause where he's the one to examine me

now. And then he sighs and lets his head fall heavily against the back of the seat, closing his eyes.

"Happy fucking birthday to me, is that it?"

"Surprise?" I whisper.

For a moment, he doesn't react. He doesn't open his eyes. He doesn't move a muscle.

Then he puts a hand over his eyes and laughs.

A beautiful smile transforms his face, lighting up his features to cast aside the morose expression he's had for so long. In its place is the gorgeous guitar God who, to this day, still elicits uncontrollable screams from the crowds at Rogue's concerts. And when he drops his hand and levels his deep-blue eyes on me, I feel a tingle rush through my chest and settle between my legs because that is the same look that has earned him the declaration of *Sexiest Man Alive* by an American magazine on three separate occasions.

I can tell by his knowing expression that he sees the effect he has on me. I stopped trying to hide what he could do to me with just a look a long time ago.

In the not too distant past, he might have acted on that attraction. He would have at least tantalized me with promises of what he would do to me the second we're alone.

But not tonight. Instead, he asks with a nod of his head toward the building on our right, "How big of a deal is this thing?"

I shake my head helplessly. "I kept it small. Maybe a hundred people."

"Fuck me," he groans.

"I just—I just hoped to bring something light and positive to your life. I just wanted to see you smile."

"That's what you and the kids do for me every day."

"Not lately." I think better of that and add, "Not me,

anyway."

"Fee, you know I love you. You *know* that. Right?"

I nod. "I do." We sit in silence for a spell but it's not long before I blurt out, "I was just desperate to see you happy, sweetheart."

His eyes go dark, back to that same sadness he's been carrying around for the last couple of months.

"We'd better get to this," he says with a sigh.

All this time, the two valets have been standing a respectful few feet away. Once we both step from the car, they swoop in, one to close my door, and one to drive the Tesla off to a parking spot.

I fuss over the Zac Posen dress I'd picked especially for the occasion. Not only does it make my blue eyes pop, but it pairs well with Conor's suit. The dress is royal blue, covered in large sequins, has capped sleeves, and falls to mid-thigh. I may be close to forty years old myself, but I'm in the best shape of my life thanks to the combination of regular swims in our indoor pool and frequent Pilates sessions with Sophie and Lainey. As a result, I catch Conor eyeing my legs appreciatively.

Out of relief at the sorely missed attention, I almost blurt out, "Oh, thank God" but catch myself. Still, I'm thrilled to see that spark of desire in him again. I've missed him in so many ways, including having his physical affection.

"Shall we?" He offers his arm and a brave face.

Wrapping my arm through his, I lean in close so I can feel his body heat. We take a few steps toward the front door, but then I stop us. He looks down at me expectantly.

"Con, I'm sorry if this was the wrong thing to do. But just remember that every single person in there is someone who loves you and wants to see you happy."

Instead of speaking, he reaches out and cups my cheek in his hand, stroking the pad of his thumb over my freckles the way he's done for years now. It's a reassuring gesture, and I close my eyes with the pleasure of it.

"Thank you for standing by my side, Fee," he says softly.

I open my eyes to meet his.

"You've been patient and given me time to grieve and I know I've been insufferable—"

"No, that's not true."

"In any case, I appreciate that you've waited me out."

"Until now," I say wryly.

"Yes, well, it's a good reminder that there are still things to celebrate in this life."

Reaching up, I squeeze the hand he still has cupping my cheek. "Yes, there are," I whisper urgently.

When he leans down to kiss me, I drape my arms around his neck and press my body to his. He might have meant it to be a quick peck, as that's all I've gotten from him lately, but I don't release him until the kiss has sparked something between us. It's the spark of our old connection. I've never been able to resist the heat of his mouth on mine or the way his lips draw me into a sensual rhythm. I rise on tiptoes to better meet him, cursing the timing of us finally finding this desire at the worst time.

I don't want our kiss to end, but when it does, I press my face into his neck, inhaling his intoxicating scent.

"Let's not go," I whisper. "Let's run away. Together, now."

He laughs and holds me to him, wrapping his strong arms around me until I'm folded deep into his chest. I can hear his heartbeat. It's steady, strong, just like he's always been. He's always been so stable. When I was first falling in love with him, I feared giving him my heart because I thought he was an immature rock star who couldn't possibly give me the predictability I craved. While it's true that we don't have a conventional married life because of how much time he spends away when he's touring, he has in all other ways been the true partner I wanted. He's never wavered in his love and support of me and our relationship.

I pull away enough to look up at him. "How about just the two of us go away for a little break from everything? Your ma would love to have the kids for a week. We could go to our place on Formentera. Or somewhere else? Let's leave first thing tomorrow."

"Fee," he says, "we can't go anywhere right now. You know that. We've got the anniversary gig coming up."

How had I forgotten? I've been working seven days a week on the upcoming enormous celebration of the band's twentieth anniversary. It's a free concert for over 80,000 fans at Croke Park in Dublin with ticket distribution through a lottery given out first to those in the official Rogue Rockers fan club, and then through open petition. It will also be live-streamed through YouTube, Twitch, Facebook, and Rogue's website. The band is scheduled to start in earnest on rehearsing and deciding on the setlist in three days.

"Oh, of course, you're right," I say. "After then. Let's plan something for after."

He lets out a sigh. "We're set to go into the studio after that."

It dawns on me then the pressure he's been under. For so many years, his life has been a constant cycle of studio time to create an album followed by media appearances and extensive time on the road for touring. It hadn't occurred to me that what has always been a welcome routine focused on the thing he loves—making and performing music—might have turned into something more oppressive as he's been grieving. I thought that the escape of music would be helpful, but the look on his face now tells me it's become just the opposite. He's not eager to do this big gig. He's not ready to go to the studio with the lads. But I don't know how to help. It is, in fact, my job as the band's media manager to push him into doing these things. As his wife, however, I want to do whatever I can to protect him.

"It's okay," he says. "It'll all be okay."

A veil seems to have dropped over his eyes as if to fortify himself for the obligations he knows he can't get out of. He's always been the responsible one, the one who will show up and do the work without failure. He's never snapped or been so selfish that he would let anyone down, including me. Neither has he ever done so with the band. He would never want to disappoint Gavin and the lads by saying he wanted to push the studio time back.

But maybe I can.

"We'd better go in. I've got to get my surprise, don't I?"

"Thanks for not being cross with me over this," I say.

He wraps his arm around my shoulders and we start toward the entrance once more.

Just before we get to the door, he leans down and whispers to me in his sexiest voice, "I'm not cross, but that doesn't mean you won't be getting a spanking later."

That's my Conor. I look up at him with a smile and his hand drops from my shoulders to my backside where he gives me a good squeeze.

"Just remember, sweetheart, I give as good as I get," I say, falling into our usual repartee.

He laughs. "Don't I know it."

2

SOPHIE

They should be here by now.

We've all been mingling outside in the garden for almost an hour. Thankfully, the late August sun is shining unencumbered by clouds, its rays bouncing off the blue-green sea nearby. It's a lovely place for a gathering, but the guest of honor should have been here by now.

I make eye contact with Gavin where he stands across the courtyard at the bar, having been waylaid in his mission to bring me a glass of champagne by several of the guests here at Conor's surprise party. He gives me a helpless shrug. He's never known how to slip free of inconvenient conversations. Letting interactions with strangers or acquaintances go on longer than most people would is his way of making the person he's speaking with feel as if they are the most important thing to him. It's part of why he's such a magnetic person. Who doesn't want to feel important? Especially to a man like Gavin who has spent the last twenty years baring his soul in music and earning both adulation from fans and acclaim from critics for it.

But to me, he'll always be that boy I met in school. The one who was bursting with confidence to cover for the emotional wounds he struggled with. The one who was romantic and ambitious, and most of all, dedicated to me.

All these years later, and the last part is still true. His wounds have healed over, albeit in a messy, should-have-gotten-stitches-but-didn't-fashion. He's come through it all and become a better, stronger man. And god, I still love him just as desperately as I did back when we were teenagers.

A cool breeze comes off the sea and sends a shiver down my spine. I watch as Gavin's eyes leave mine and drift lower. His always sensual mouth twists into something wicked. Glancing down at myself, I see that he's fixed on the way my hardened nipples are pressing against the silk fabric of the dress he picked out for me earlier.

I'd been lingering in our walk-in closet, trying to decide on the right dress when he joined me, wrapping his arms around my waist from behind and resting his chin on my shoulder.

"Can't decide?"

"No, I'm just not loving anything."

"May I?"

I smiled when he pulled away and began running his hand over the garments hanging neatly before us. He's never cared much about fashion—neither for himself nor for me. That's not to say that he isn't vocally appreciative of my appearance. But choosing a dress for me isn't something he usually does, so I watched with amusement as he pulled out one piece and then rejected it before selecting a shimmery, amber-colored silk dress.

"This," he said simply.

I wrinkled my nose. "It's too much for the occasion."

"I thought the invitation said cocktail attire?"

"That's true. But this dress is ... more than cocktails. It's more like *after-dinner drinks*."

He smiled at what that suggests. "I think that you, my supermodel wife, can pull this off. What do you say we try it on?"

I haven't modeled seriously in years, having scaled way back to the odd campaign here and there so I could instead focus on earning my degree in art history. After I graduated, and just before having our fourth child, I opened my own art gallery in Dublin with a focus on emerging artists. Still, I enjoyed his attempt to flatter me with the nod to my past modeling life.

"Well, okay then," I said and pulled open the robe I was wearing. Underneath, I was naked except for a nude thong.

He gently pushed the robe off of my shoulders and then took his time surveying my body. Except for a few stretch marks, I'm lucky that my figure has mostly rebounded after having our last child. No matter what, Gavin always looks at me with appreciation and awe. There was only one period in our long relationship where he stopped worshiping me. But once we got past that difficult time, our connection never wavered.

"Raise your arms," he said.

The look in his blue eyes was pure desire. But there's restraint there, too. He was enjoying this as an exercise. As a sort of game we haven't played with each other before. Because while he's *undressed* me thousands of times, he's never once *dressed* me. And he's found that this has its own pleasures.

I did as he asked and lifted my arms over my head, watching as he gathered the silk of the dress so that he could slip it over my arms and head. It slid down my body like warm honey, molding to my figure as if a second skin. When he stepped back to gaze at me once more, I lowered my arms.

"You know this is the type of dress that I shouldn't wear anything under?" I said. "No bra, no panties."

His eyes locked on mine, and for a moment, I thought his old possessive tendencies might rear up and make him change his mind about me wearing this dress. There was a time when he hated to share me in any way with the world, when it *pained* him that I was photographed for magazine covers that all too often featured me less clothed than he liked.

But I was reassured that those days are long gone when he dropped to his knees in front of me and said, "I wouldn't have it any other way."

"Baby, what are you doing?" I asked with a laugh.

He reached under the dress, his hands sliding up my calves and thighs so that I caught my breath. Those hands of his are strong and assured. They know every part of my body, know just where to tease me. But his mission wasn't to tempt me. He simply wanted to perfect the look he had chosen for me by removing my thong. He used both hands to pull on the straps, dragging the material slowly down my hips and over the length of my legs until he freed it completely.

"Will you pick my heels, too?" I asked, mostly as a joke. Mostly as a way to shake off the heat of desire he generated in me.

But he likes the idea, turning while still on his knees to the custom shelving that holds dozens of shoes. I watched as he considered his options. I have everything from high-end designer heels to ballet flats to running shoes. He selected the pair I had in mind, a metallic gold Saint Laurent T-strap sandal with a four-inch heel. They're delicate and sexy at the same time. They'll also make me a bit taller than my 5'10" husband. Not that he has any ego about that. He slid them onto my feet and patiently wrestled with the tiny buckles until he fastened them at both ankles.

Once done, he stood and surveyed me all over again. I obliged him with one of my old modeling poses.

"Stunning," he murmured.

He, in contrast, was wearing jeans, a white T-shirt, and the same soft-as-butter leather shirt jacket he's been practically living in for the last few months. It's a very *Gavin* look, but it made me overdressed in comparison, and I told him so.

"I'll up it a notch," he said. "For you, darlin'."

His effort to dress up is what I'm enjoying now as I gaze back at him across the Haddington House courtyard while he's still unashamedly ogling my breasts. In a fitted black suit, pressed white dress shirt, and a black and silver striped tie, he's achingly handsome. When he levels his eyes back upon mine, I feel a familiar thrill run through me that makes me smile. And blush. Yes, he still makes me blush.

"All right. Enough of that, already."

Startled, I find that Daniel has joined me—and admonished me.

"What?" I ask.

"I see you and McManus making eyes at each other. Jesus, aren't four kids enough? You're not aiming for more, are you?" he asks.

I laugh, amused at having been caught out.

"No, we're happy with our four."

He shakes his head. "Who in this day and age has four kids, anyway? Everything to excess with you two."

I don't take offense. This is simply Daniel being himself, casually overstepping polite boundaries at will. "I suppose this means you and Amelia are happy to stop with just your two boys?"

"We'll have to be, won't we, since I got the old snip-snip?"

It takes me half a second to realize what he's oversharing. And then I laugh again. "Ah, I see."

"Anyway," he says and glances around. "Where the fuck is Mr. Perfect?"

"That's what I was wondering, too."

There are over a hundred guests milling about here in the garden. It's been setup with lounge areas and fire pits around the perimeter, cocktail tables dotting the center, large multi-colored round lanterns crisscrossing overhead for when it gets dark, and an enormous screen at the end of the garden projecting a loop of rarely seen candid photos of Conor when he has his guard down. They're snapshots of him that are the opposite of his famously cool and controlled image, ones where he is smiling broadly in slices of life with his bandmates, with his children, with his wife. They're a sort of love letter from Felicity to her husband, clearly chosen to depict the tender, human side of him that she knows so well rather than focus on the rock star version of him that most of the world thinks they know him to be.

"Here we are, darlin'."

Gavin's finally made his way to me, champagne glass in hand. I take it from him, smiling my thanks.

"Where's mine?" Daniel asks.

"Over there." Gavin gestures to the bar that's twenty people deep.

"That's not very gentlemanly, is it?"

"You're not drinking, anyway," Gavin says.

"Not alcohol, but a man's still gotta hydrate."

"So, get on with it. We both know you'll use your usual grace and charm to skip to the front."

"Aye, if it's only a spot of fizzy water I'm after," Daniel says, "what's the harm in skipping anyway?"

"See. Knew it."

"You bloody well know nothing."

"Then go ahead," Gavin says, "and get to the back of that line there and prove me wrong."

Daniel pulls a sour face. "I'm not fucking thirsty anymore."

As Gavin laughs, I shake my head at the way they like to go back and forth. *Taking the piss*, they call it. And it never seems to get old for them. They revert to these juvenile exchanges as soon as they come into contact with each other and always come away amused and pleased with themselves.

"You all playing tonight, then?" Daniel asks, shifting conversation into something more neutral.

Or rather, it should be neutral. I fear the fact that Felicity has had a stage set up under the large screen with instruments for each of the members of Rogue may not be entirely welcomed by Conor. She's shared with me her worries over Conor's depression these past few months. Knowing him as I do, I was surprised that she wanted to push things with this party. And with the stage setup. He's not someone who likes to feel out of control. Forcing him to a surprise birthday party is one thing, but then expecting him to play with the band when he hasn't picked up a guitar since his father died is a risky gamble.

"Ah, I dunno," Gavin says. "I think it's just there in case the temptation arises."

"The lighting is shite."

Gavin laughs. "Meaning she didn't have this place consult you on it, yeah?"

"Well, it is my area of expertise. *One* of my areas of expertise."

"You're right about that. But not all lighting gigs need your approval. In fact, I think Con wouldn't mind ignoring the whole thing."

"What whole thing? The possibility of playing tonight or the surprise party thing?"

I exchange a look with Gavin. He's not usually one to hold back and now is no exception.

"All of it," he says simply. "His head is fucked up right now."

"I know that much," Daniel says. "He's been a complete recluse for months now. I haven't seen him barely at all."

"He's having a tough time. Ever since his father passed," I say.

"So, naturally, Felicity thought it'd be the plan to throw him right into the center of all this?" Daniel opens his arms wide to gesture to all the guests and decor.

"I think she was sort of desperate to push him out of his funk," I say.

"Jesus, when will people learn you can't force someone to get well? You think Shay didn't try that shit with me countless times?" Daniel asks. He, of course, doesn't wait for a reply. "And no, it didn't work. Not once. He couldn't force me to get my head straight any more than I could force your man to—" He stops, obviously struggling to come up with an analogy. Finally, he sputters, "To give up being such a bleedin' heart romantic."

"Aye, that bloody romantic nature of mine keeps you employed," Gavin says with a grin.

"You know what I mean. It's going to come to no good, this. If she's after thinking he'll suddenly right himself all because of a party, then she's up for being disappointed, I can guarantee you that."

"Maybe. But it's her right to try, isn't it? She's the one married to him and has to deal with his issues," Gavin says.

Daniel takes that in and then nods. A moment later, he seems to get a different idea, though, because he's soon got a mischievous smile.

"I thought you were his wife, anyway, McManus."

Gavin laughs. "You been trading old stories with Marty, then?"

"Ah, Marty never had to tell me nothing about you and Mr. Perfect. It's clear as day you're secretly in love with each other."

"Makes you jealous, does it? That no matter how good of friends you and he have come to be, he'll always be my best friend and me his?"

"You're off your head with that. I think I will go get me a drink."

Gavin holds up his nearly empty glass of beer. "Get me another?"

"I will in my hole."

Though we all know Daniel's reply was his way of saying *absolutely not*, Gavin responds as if it was just the opposite, saying, "Thanks very much, Daniel."

And just like that, they're back to the banter they so love. The seriousness of Conor's mental state has been glossed over and I'm left wondering just how this evening will play out.

3

MARTIN

I don't see him anywhere. I've scanned the crowd six ways from Sunday and I still can't find him.

"Relax, he's here somewhere."

I turn to Lainey and see she knows exactly who I'm worried about. I don't have to explain to her that it's not Conor, the guest of honor, that I'm searching for. She knows that it's Donal I'm worked up over.

That kid has been in rare form lately, finding every opportunity to challenge and defy me. He's seventeen now and long since became too much for his mother to handle. He's been living with us for almost a year, ever since he came home with a tattoo on the inside of his lip and Celia nearly had a heart attack. It would have been lights out for her if she knew he had pierced his privates, too. I made the mistake of walking in on him after he'd showered only to see the gleaming metal bits poking right through the end of his cock.

Rather than scramble to cover up, he'd just stared back at me with a lopsided smile. He takes after me in size and seems to have all the confidence in the world for it. He's certainly slept with more girls than I ever have and I'm a fucking rock star.

Granted, I got a late start in all that entails, but still. This kid is on a mission to prove something. The problem is, he doesn't know what. He thinks he wants to be a guitar player but he doesn't have the discipline to develop his own sound. He thinks he wants to be a rock singer but he hasn't written a word of his own. At least nothing he's shared with me. He thinks Rogue is shite but it's all he ever practices with his mate, Owen. Their overriding ambition seems to be becoming celebrities of *some sort* so that they can more easily shag girls. Thing is, I don't see that he's ever had a problem with that. The whole country knows my three boys well. Donal and his brothers, Colm and Sean, have long been adored and fairly respectfully covered in the media. But then Donal came of age and has been hell-bent on making a name for himself with the local paparazzi, all too eager to get his photograph taken in the club scene. That's not even to mention the things he puts on his Instagram account. He either shares his inappropriate "pranks" or moans about being bored. As if he hasn't been granted everything he could ever want. He made decent enough marks to go to university, but he's decided against it. He tells his mother that he's taking a "gap year" but I doubt uni is in his future. That wouldn't bother me if he was pursuing something more than shallow Instagram fame.

Lainey's been a godsend. She recognizes in him her own youthful acts of rebellion and has argued for me to give him the space to test his boundaries. He's not hurting anyone, she tells me, so why not just let him figure it out. It can't have been easy to have a famous father, after all. Especially one who had a patch of very public sexual exploits detailed in the press running up to his parents splitting up. That's the part that has made me back off. The guilt over knowing how I fucked up when he was only little. Though, the head scratcher of it all is that we've always maintained a good relationship, even throughout the divorce. So, why he's come at me lately as if we've got this ... *fraught* relationship has me perplexed.

He's supposed to be here tonight. And not because I was insisting. He wanted to be here. Conor isn't just his godfather; he's his bloody *idol*. He's always looked up to him. Hell, Conor's very likely why Donal's first and only tattoo is in a spot not easily visible. Everyone knows Conor would never desecrate his body with ink. Still, the kid can't help but show off the letters F-U-C-K on the inside of his lower lip whenever he can. Of all the bloody things to tattoo. Jesus, I'd have hoped he'd have more creativity than that.

Someone slaps my shoulder before saying, "Can't believe I made it before the man of the hour."

It's Shay. He hadn't known if he'd make it in time for the party, what with flight delays coming out of San Francisco.

"Hey, man," I say and give him a quick hug. It's been far too long since I've seen the guy. But he's here for an extended period now. We've got the anniversary gig, followed by dedicated studio time. I've been looking forward to all us lads really being together again. Us straying apart for too long isn't good for the soul of the band. I imagine it will some time to gel again once we get into the studio.

"Lainey," Shay says, and he leans in to kiss her cheek.

"Good to see you, Shay," she says, "Where's Jessica? And the kids?"

"They made a stop at the house. She'll get them sorted

with the sitter and be along soon enough. Thought I'd better get here for the big moment."

"Good you did." I take a deep breath, feeling better just by Shay being here. I've always felt somehow more … complete with him around. We are a bit of a duo, after all. Can't have a rhythm section without the both of us in sync.

"I'm going to take a wander around," Lainey says, and I see in the uptick of her eyebrows that she's going to look for Donal for me.

"Thanks, honey."

"So?" Shay asks after a lengthy moment of silence.

"So, what?"

He tilts his chin up. "What's the problem, Marty? Why does Lainey need to have a wander?"

Of course, Shay would immediately sniff out that something isn't right. His ability to examine others is legendary.

"Eh, just wanting to track down Donal. He should be here somewhere, but I haven't found him yet."

Shay nods. "I heard a bit about your boy catching some trouble lately."

"The graffiti? Yeah, he's on the hook for cleaning up that nonsense."

"No, I meant the joyriding."

I let my head fall back as I roll my eyes at the sky. Yeah, that's the other thing he got hauled in for—nicking cars and tearing up the streets with them.

Leveling my eyes back upon Shay, I shake my head. "This from a kid who has his own fucking top of the line Range Rover."

There's an apologetic note in his voice when he suggests, "Guessing he heard about me and Gav from back in the day?"

"Ah, who knows? Maybe. But for fuck's sake, your days of it seemed so ... trivial somehow compared to this."

"Maybe because we actually returned the cars to their rightful owners? Last I heard, Donal nearly drove the last one he took into the bloody Liffey."

I had to spend a lot of money to rectify that one. The owner saw euro signs when he realized who Donal's father was.

"Lainey says me trying to reign him in will only set him off worse. Says I should let him be a kid and make his mistakes, as long as he doesn't really hurt anyone. But he's fucking testing my limits," I say with an admittedly bitter laugh.

Shay smiles appreciatively. His kids are only five and three years old, so he's got time before needing to deal with this kind of thing. Still, he's always had a wise word about most things and now is no exception.

"Well, mate, just be grateful he'd rather be like our clean-living Conor than follow in my brother's footsteps."

That was something to take comfort in. As far as I can tell, Donal has no interest in drugs. I know he drinks, but even that doesn't seem to get too out of hand.

Before I can reply, a buzz ripples through the crowd as staff spread word that the birthday boy has finally arrived and is making his way to where we all have been waiting. We're instructed to shout, "Happy Birthday!" and to give our noise-makers a whirl.

"How pissed off do you think Con will be?" I ask.

"Off the charts, Marty. Off the charts."

I glance at him with a small smile, but he's got his usual inscrutable expression. Just past him, I see Lainey at the far end of the garden, near the stage. She's with Donal. I relax a degree and turn back to the doors of Haddington House just as they start to open. The sun reflects brightly off the glass, and for a moment I'm blinded by the glare, unable to see who is stepping out.

It doesn't matter, since the crowd erupts into birthday wishes and the noisemakers go off, forcing a celebratory mood for the man no one believes wants to be here.

4

CONOR

God, I'm good.

At a lot of things, that's for sure. But what I'm thinking I'm good at now is my ability to put aside my own wants and needs to please others. I've always had that talent. Even as a kid. Or at least, I managed it as long as I could when I was a kid and wanted to please my mother. I kept on with violin and piano lessons long after I knew I'd much rather be a guitarist. I did it when, as a teenager, I gave up any chance of wooing Sophie in deference to Gavin. I did it years later when I fell so hard for her that I gave up any chance at real love with someone else just so I could love her from afar—not that I'd change anything about how all that played out. All those mistakes I made with my heart ended up leading me to my wife, the love of my life. I did it again when I put aside mourning my friend Christian Hale in order to ensure that Gavin didn't go off the fucking rails because of the loss.

I've always been the dependable one. I've always made sure I've held it together so that others could fall apart, including when Felicity had her lowest point after becoming a mother.

It was natural for me to be a source of strength when everything around me was crumbling. I didn't mind.

But when my father passed, I couldn't keep up that same routine. I just ... couldn't. And so, I sank into depression for the first time in my life. There was a kind of relief in giving into that darkness. It instinctively felt like a process that I needed to go through, and so, there was a certain kind of comfort in it. I wasn't in any hurry to push through it. I was content to let it run its course.

But that's no longer an option. At least not for this evening. It's my fortieth birthday and I won't be allowed to wallow in the depths, even though that's exactly where I want to be. No, I've got to put on a show. I've got to pretend that I'm pleased to be at the surprise party my well-intentioned wife has put together.

Double glass doors are opened for us so that we can step out onto the main event space. The sun is bright and the late afternoon is still warm by Irish standards. Even before I can absorb the layout of the garden or recognize the dozens upon dozens of people all here to celebrate me, I put on a smile that is a decent facsimile of surprised delight. I'm a performer by trade and it's time to give the crowd what it wants.

The chorus of birthday wishes and noisemakers washes over me but I don't absorb the sentiment. Instead, I focus on shaking hands and kissing cheeks, all the while proclaiming how surprised I was by the party. I even do a good job of hiding my surprise at seeing my mother here. She's been holding up better than I have, if I'm honest, which only makes my own reaction since the funeral all that much harder to bear. If my mother can get through her days with a smile after losing her life partner, then my inability to cope feels like a selfish indulgence. Still, she gives me a hug, wishes me happy birthday, and urges me to go have fun with my friends, saying she won't stay long since she wants to avoid the "debauchery" sure to come. She says it with a wink and it's clear to us both it's a nod to how my father used to not so jokingly live vicariously through what he imagined was my wild rock star existence.

"Thanks for coming, all the same," I tell her.

"I wouldn't miss your birthday celebration, my boy." She looks around at the crowd, her gaze becoming wistful. "I hope you know your father loved you very much."

I swallow back a rush of emotion. "I know, Ma."

She turns back to me and smiles. It's a smile that I know well. It's born out of that instinct mothers seem to have about their children. The one that says she knows exactly what I'm trying to hide from her and that no matter what it is, I'll still get acceptance and support from her. Usually, the smile is all she gives me. Because it says so much. But not this time. This time, she's compelled to speak her mind, too.

"You can't linger in this darkness much longer, Conor," she tells me. "It'll steal your life away. You've got too much living to waste it like that. Your father wouldn't want this for you."

I nod automatically. She's right, of course. I've known I can't keep going this way. I just haven't sorted out how to make the change.

"That's all I'll say on the matter," she says. "Now, go try to have some fun. You only turn forty once, you know?"

Raising my eyebrows at that truism, I vow to her that I'll do my best and thank her again for coming while walking her to the double-doors. She doesn't let me walk her all the way to the car park, insisting that I get into the mix of party revelers. But she does let me give her a big hug.

When she pulls away, she braces herself by holding my

biceps. "Your father never had your level of fitness, but otherwise, you're so much of him," she says with a laugh. She gets a far off look in her eye for a moment. "It's okay to miss him. We can miss him … and still go on."

"Jesus, Ma," I say, "I'm sorry for being such terrible support to you. You shouldn't have to prop me up."

"Ah, no. You don't understand, do you? I'll always be your mammy and it's my pleasure, so it is."

I smile at that. "I'll be by to see you soon."

"Bring my grandbabies, won't you?"

I promise to do so and then watch as she heads inside.

I've only had a moment to take a breath before I'm approached by friends I haven't yet greeted. Slipping back into the mode everyone here expects of me, I charm my way through small talk with a dozen or so friends.

"Thrilled, am I right?" Gavin asks when I finally make my way to him after almost half an hour. He and Danny Boy are off by themselves at the edge of the garden closest to the sea stirring down below the cliffside.

"Absolutely," I reply with enthusiasm I don't feel.

"Ah, you don't have to pretend with us," Danny Boy says.

"I'm not. I am thrilled that my wife wanted to do something special for the occasion."

Danny Boy smirks, unconvinced. And then he makes a show of looking around as if trying to be sure the coast is clear. Satisfied, he turns back to me and says, "Cut the bullshit, man. The people who know you can see clear as day that this whole thing is fucked up."

"Me celebrating my birthday is fucked up?" I ask with phony dismay.

"You can be honest with us about it, is what I think he's

getting after," Gavin says. "We know the timing is less than ideal, that your head isn't in this."

Rather than reply, I take a deep breath and finally survey my surroundings. I watch the slideshow of pictures on the large screen for a minute. They're images that I wouldn't have approved for something like this. They feel too personal. I come off as too much ... myself. It's moments of me smiling at Felicity or at my kids or of me fucking around with my bandmates. I know why Felicity chose them. They make me seem more like the person she knows, rather than the cool, aloof image of myself I've always tried to present for public consumption. Her heart was in the right place. But it doesn't feel right to me given how many people are here. Yes, they're all people I know and count as friends, but it's just too intimate. I reserve that kind of intimacy for a very small group of people.

And then my eyes fall to the stage under the screen. It's set up with instruments, including my favorite guitar. It's the first electric guitar I ever owned, the one my father bought for me. I haven't picked it up, or any other guitar, for that matter, in months. It's shitty timing, but my desire to play or create music has left me, buried along with my father. Whether I like it or not, I'm going to have to play soon enough since we'll have rehearsals for the anniversary gig in a matter of days, followed by studio time after that. I've been trying to psych myself up for that. Felicity knows as much. Which is why I have no idea why she'd think to provide this stage for us to play tonight.

"Fuck me," I mutter reflexively.

"It's not a requirement," Gavin says, reading me.

"The lighting is reason enough to refuse to play. If only

they had brought me in to give them direction on it," Danny Boy says with a shake of his head.

I laugh at his selfish focus before remembering he'd never react any other way. It's who he is and who he'll always be. Still, I love him like a brother.

"I suppose I should make a few more rounds," I say.

"First stop, get yourself a drink already," Gavin says.

"Right about that."

I move on and am stopped every few feet by people from Rogue's organization, other industry friends, and those I've come to know from different aspects of my life. Just as I'm breaking free again, I feel someone link their arm through mine.

I notice her scent first and reflexively inhale deeper to get more of it. It's the same perfume she's worn since she was a student at our Dublin school all those years ago. A lot of women would have left it behind as they matured, but the Chanel fragrance is as timeless as she is.

"This is for you," Sophie says, offering me a glass of champagne.

I glance at her before taking the flute gratefully.

"Happy birthday, Connie." She graces me with a kiss on the cheek.

The feel of her lips on my skin offers an odd kind of peace, if only for a few seconds. There's something about her that has always brought me a sense of contentment. She's got an infectious inner calm.

"Thanks, Soph," I tell her with more meaning than she can know.

"This is a really lovely event."

I turn to her and do a slow blink once I get a good look at the dress she's wearing. It's like sex has manifested itself onto her figure. The rich honey color of the fabric skims so closely to the curves of her breasts, hips, ass, and even her thighs, that it leaves very little to the imagination.

"You didn't have to wear that for me," I say with a small smile. "But, I am very glad that you did."

She laughs and slaps at my arm at the same time. "If you like it that much, you have Gavin to thank, not me. He insisted on it."

"He is a very good friend, indeed."

This "flirting" is more out of habit than anything else after all these years. Still, it's like a secret code that we use now and again to affirm our friendship and our history.

"Oh, believe me, you were the farthest thing from his mind when he was dressing me in this." She runs a hand down her side, smoothing the silky material.

The implication that they'd shared a sensual moment—or maybe even more than that—with each other as they were preparing for the party is a stark contrast to my own experience with Felicity. I'd dragged my feet in getting ready for what I thought was a charity event, spending way too much time in our home gym. The one thing I haven't given up on in this depressed state is exercise. You'd think that would help carry me through the darkness, and maybe it has to a degree, but it certainly hasn't been a cure-all. Felicity had to practically pull me by the ear upstairs to our en suite and into the shower—by myself. Which was just as well. For a man with a lifelong voracious sexual appetite, I have been sorely lacking in that department since before my father passed. I'm just numb to it, unable to conjure enough desire to even take matters into my own hands.

"It's good of you to put on a happy face for this," Sophie

says, taking my arm again as we walk. "But it's okay if you're still hurting too much to stay for long."

"I'm guessing my wife might want to get more out of me than a quick appearance," I say with a laugh.

"Felicity just wants to see you happy. And if being here for a short while and going home makes you happy, then tell her so."

I drain my champagne in time with a server coming by with a tray full of fresh glasses, and I smoothly swap out my empty one for a refill.

"I'm okay, Sophie. No need to worry."

She stops us and turns to me, her blonde hair blowing gently in the breeze. "I know you're okay. Or, I should say I know you *will* be okay. But I also know that you have never stopped moving forward. Not for years and years. You've never *allowed* yourself a break. Now's the time that you should give yourself permission to take what you need for *you*."

When I hesitate, she squeezes my arm and smiles at me in the same way that made me fall for her all those years ago. It's playful and sexy and oddly maternal all at once. It's Sophie's signature of wanting to help someone in need. She was drawn to Gavin for that very reason straightaway. He was the walking embodiment of *need*. Together, they just made sense in that way: she needed to be needed and, Jesus, did he need someone like her to take care of his wounded heart.

"Okay, then," she says, spurred on by my silence. "*I* give you permission. Does that help? You are allowed to do whatever you need to do for yourself without worrying whether it might somehow be selfish."

I want to tell her that that's what I've been doing. That's why I've been hiding away with my family, resorting to my loner tendencies. But it occurs to me that that hasn't been all that big of a concession. It hasn't helped me heal the way I had hoped it would.

But before I can say anything, she tells me, "Think about it, at least."

"I will."

We share a moment of prolonged eye contact where I try to convey my thanks to her without having to say anything. Everyone wants to help. Everyone wants to find the magic words to push me out of my depression. But not everyone has the same history that Sophie and I do, and despite my current inability to tell her how much I appreciate her efforts, I think that sentiment passes between us.

"There you are, sweetheart," Felicity says, joining us. She gives me a quick kiss before greeting her friend. "Hi Sophie."

"Hi. Great job. This is all wonderful."

Felicity looks around and breathes a sigh of relief. "It did turn out well." She turns to me. "I thought maybe you'd found the whiskey tasting station. Have you?"

"Whiskey tasting?" I ask, eyebrows raised. Whiskey tasting will always conjure up one of my fondest memories with Felicity. Early on in our rekindled friendship, I'd taken her on the spur of the moment to Belfast and we'd landed at a pub known for their wide variety of whiskeys. We'd had the good fortune of an impromptu tasting, guided by a wisp of an old man who was both informative and amusing. That evening together had been incredible fun. But it had also been the start of me seriously wondering why I was engaged to another woman when Felicity was so much of what I wanted.

"Yes," she says. "I made sure they have some of those whiskeys we tried that one time. Do you remember?"

I wrap my arm around her shoulders and pull her close to

me. "Do I remember? I remember like it was yesterday, honey. What a great idea."

"As long as we can keep this lot from getting too smashed, anyway," she says with a less than hopeful smile as she surveys the crowd.

I watch her, taking in the lines of her profile I know so well. This woman has been my wife for eight years but she's been a part of my heart for far longer. She's the one who challenges me, steers me to be my better self, the one who walks in perfect step with me as my partner and lover. She's the one who has brought me more joy and satisfaction than I ever thought I'd know.

And here I am, flanked by two incredible women. I should be riding high at this moment, strutting my forty-year-old arse all over this party. But all I want to do is slip out and curl up into some dark corner to retreat into myself.

"Sophie, that dress is stunning," Felicity says.

"It's too much, isn't it?" Sophie asks, twisting a bit so that we can see how low the back drops to show off her smooth skin. "I told Gavin it wasn't suited to the occasion, but he insisted."

"No, it's, well, it's fabulous. Isn't it, Con?" Felicity asks.

It takes a monumental effort to focus on her because I've already started to pull back into my own thoughts. "Ah, yes. It's grand."

I see Felicity give Sophie a pointed look and realize they've probably been talking about me for months. It's why Sophie was so ready to give me permission to do whatever I needed to take care of myself. She had her speech scripted for the moment. I wonder who else is going to try to reach out to me with such intentions. I don't think I can bear another heartfelt conversation with someone who wants to find the key to bringing me out of the doldrums.

Looking around, I see groups of people chatting and enjoying the party. But when I look harder, I see that there are quite a few people scattered throughout the crowd who are glancing my way, their faces telegraphing the worry that underlines this event.

Fuck. Me.

I really don't want to be here.

But I can't do as Sophie says. I can't cut this short and leave. I'm the center of this whole thing, after all. I scramble to think of how I can possibly stay but not have to engage with all these well-meaning folks.

My eyes land on the stage I'd earlier viewed with disdain. Now I see it anew. I see it as a place where I can seek refuge. Because if I'm playing guitar, then I have a legitimate excuse to not talk to anyone.

Just as I turn to tell Felicity that I might toy around with the lads on stage, I see that she's been watching me. Sophie has slipped away. It's just the two of us, which allows an epiphany of sorts. I can see in my wife's blue eyes that she had thought to set up the stage and instruments just in case I needed this pretense of an escape. She wanted me to have this option before I ever realized I needed it.

"Oh, honey," I say softly.

I don't need to say anything more. She just lifts her chin slightly, acknowledging both what I sorted out and my gratitude for it.

"Sophie thought it would be a mistake," she says with a cock of a brow.

"Well, she doesn't know me as well as you do, does she?"

She smiles at that and leans into me.

Sliding my hand into the nape of her neck and wrapping my other arm around her waist, I pull her closer so I can press my lips to hers. We kiss with our own brand of synchronicity, the kind that is easy to get lost in. She is my home, the one who knows me and cares for me better than anyone in this world.

She means everything to me.

Which is why it's so frustrating—for both of us—that she alone can't help me move past my profound sadness.

5

CONOR

I don't make a big play to round up the lads. I don't even search the crowd to try to catch Gavin's eye, even though I know that simple gesture is all I'd have to do for him to understand where my head is. He would join me in an instant, I know that. He's that kind of friend, always has been. The others would, too. But at this moment, I just want to ease back into what it even feels like to hold a guitar. It's been far too long and I worry that it will feel foreign to take that Telecaster in my hands.

That's why I hesitate at the edge of the stage. It's not a big stage but I don't climb the two stairs to mount it. Instead, I just stand there and stare at the guitar, hearing chords in my head that I don't recognize. It's the sort of musical inspiration I haven't had in a long time. I close my eyes to savor the moment, to try to draw it more forcefully to the forefront of my mind so that I might be able to recreate it once I've picked up my instrument.

"Happy birthday, Uncle Conor!"

An arm grips me in a half-hug and I turn to see my godson

Donal. Though, at seventeen, he's tall and has the frame of a man, he hasn't quite shaken an air of boyishness. He's like a puppy with paws that have grown well before the rest of his body.

"Thanks, Donal," I say. "Your own birthday is nearly upon us, amn't I right?"

"In six days, not that I'm counting, yeah?" he says with a laugh.

"Eighteen is something to enjoy, that's for sure. When I was turning eighteen, I was scraping together gigs with your da and the lads in England. We shared a one-room flat with a toilet down the hall."

I've got a smile on my face at the memory, but Donal groans with distaste at the idea.

"Ah, those days were grand," I insist. "Nothing but music, good craic, staying up all night, and this incredible sense of … possibility."

"Yeah, well, I've got a different sort of plan. One that is a little more, let's say, high roller."

I raise my eyebrows at that. "What'll that be, then?"

"I'm going to Spain to see my girlfriend. Take her out to the best restaurant in town, then treat her to a penthouse suite hotel stay with me."

"Didn't know you had a girlfriend, Donal. Bit young to tie yourself down, no?"

"I'm not after marrying her, but she's the one I absolutely want to spend my birthday with."

"How'd you meet her, this Spanish girl of yours?"

Donal hesitates, flushes red in embarrassment, and then laughs. "Instagram, actually."

"Fuck's sake," I say with a shake of my head.

"I know it sounds idiotic, but this isn't just some whim."

"No?"

"We have a real connection. She's ... she gets me, you know?"

"You mean, she gets that you're the son of Martin Whelan? Meaning, all the money and notoriety that comes with that?"

"You wouldn't understand, Uncle Conor. Your days of living by your passions are over, aren't they? Left them back in your one-room flat with your younger self?"

"What? Because I have a bit of skepticism over your Instagram girlfriend really 'getting' you?" I ask with a laugh.

"Well ... yeah, actually. You probably don't even remember what it's like to bleedin' *yearn* to be with a girl. To feel it so deep inside you it's hard to spend even a day without her."

I fight off a smile. If he only knew the kind of *yearning* I've been privy to in my life. Though, I can admit that feeling hasn't been with me in recent years. On the contrary, I've been quite settled in matters of love and lust. That's not a complaint, it's just the truth.

"Donal, have you ever even met the girl in person?"

"Eh, not yet. But—"

I interrupt him with a derisive laugh that I try to pull back.

"But," Donal continues, "I will soon enough. I'm going to fly to Spain in time for my birthday and it's going to be amazing."

"Guess you've got it all sorted, then," I say. "Your da okay with all this?"

"What can he say? I'll be eighteen, won't I?"

"You'll be eighteen with *his* credit card."

"Whatever. Call it my birthday present from him, then," he says with a shrug. "Are you all playing tonight, then?"

His eyes go to where mine had been before he shook me from my focus on the guitar. "Had thought about it," I say.

"Jesus, but it would be good to hear you, though I don't think I can stand to see my da play rock star."

"Why do you give him such a hard time, Donal? He's earned his right as a musician. He's a damn good bass player."

He visibly shudders. "I dunno. Makes me all cringey, ya know?"

I laugh but wonder when my own kids might start to think of me as less of a hero and more of an embarrassment the way Donal does his dad.

Looking around, he seems to notice that Gavin, Shay, and his own father haven't come to the stage. They're still in the mix of the crowd whose chatter has gotten louder in tandem with access to the bars.

"You need me to round them up?" he asks.

"Not just yet. I think I might mess around for a minute by myself."

"Oh, grand. Glad to have a front row seat to that, in fact."

"How's your guitar playing been going?" I know he's long toyed around with learning guitar but he's never felt comfortable with me trying to teach him anything.

"It's, eh, let's say *evolving*."

That answer makes me laugh once more and I realize that these few minutes with Donal have been a welcome distraction from my own darkness. There's something about him that is … weightless. He doesn't carry around troubles the way I do, or for that matter, the way most grown men do. His perspective is refreshing, even if he does slag me off for no longer being young.

"Can I help with anything, then?" he asks eagerly.

"Yeah, can you find a chair? I think I just want to sit with the guitar for a bit, see what comes with that before I get the lads to join in."

"You got it."

In a flash, he's disappeared. He's always looked up to me, to the point where I've worried that Martin might be jealous of it. I figure, though, that that kind of starry-eyed idol-worship is less about me than it is about his need to break away from his father and find his own identity.

He returns quickly with a chair in his hands. "I'll put it here, will I?" he asks, gesturing to the space on stage nearest my Telecaster.

I nod and watch him get to it. And then there's nothing left for me to do but finally pick up the instrument that had always been my comfort and release in times of distress. Until it didn't. Until there was nothing and no one that could fill the void that was left in me when my father died. I wonder if that fleeting moment of inspiration I'd had before Donal joined me will return or if I'll feel just as blank and numb as I have for the last several months. It's a kind of writer's block, I suppose. An inability to hear music, though, rather than tell a story with words as a writer would. Though, I've always seen my guitar playing as saying something. Saying something in relation to Gavin's lyrics, more often than not. I try to create a landscape of sorts to support the sentiment Gavin is expressing. There have been times when I added my own sensibility to it, but for the most part, it's been me trying to enhance his vision. That makes me wonder what it would sound like to be completely independent of that dynamic.

Picking up the guitar, the weight of it feels good in my hands. I slip the strap over my head as a reflex, though I don't really need to do so since I soon take a seat. I flip the requisite switches and the amp buzzes to life. Without looking at him, I can feel Donal's eyes on me. He likely has no idea that I haven't played in months. His only concern is in wanting to see how my fingers travel the fretboard or how quickly I move the pick between the strings. He wants to see his idol perform.

At any other time in my life, I would gladly rise to the challenge. I'd forgo a chair and instead strut across the small stage, making it mine while creating a beautiful racquet with the guitar. But I don't have that in me at the moment.

Instead, the chords I'd heard earlier in my head return. I give them a full minute to play out before I attempt to bring them to life with the guitar in my hands.

6

GAVIN

I'd been chatting with Jamie when I heard the familiar, comforting sound of an amp being turned on. It's the kind of sound that generates Pavlov's response in me every time. My instinct is to get to the microphone, to be a part of the joint effort that our band's music has always been.

But as soon as I set my sights on the small stage at the far end of the courtyard and see that Conor is there, sitting on a chair with his head bowed over the guitar, I know that I shouldn't rush toward him. I know in that one look that this moment isn't about Rogue. This is about Conor on his own, doing what he needs to do.

When he puts a pick to the strings, creating a sound that exposes his heartbreak, I almost want to look away. It feels like he's sharing too much, just the way I've always done with my lyrics. The riffs he's getting into a groove with are searing, aching, raw.

"Finally getting back to it," James says approvingly.

I love our manager. He's practically the fifth member of Rogue. But he can be dense about what's behind the music.

He's more often concerned with getting us to produce than wanting to decipher the meaning of it, which I suppose *is* his job. At this moment, though, his obtuseness about what Conor is doing sends me moving a few steps away from him as I focus on the stage.

The chatter in the crowd slowly dies down as attention turns to Conor. He's oblivious to it, his eyes closed as he rocks his body slightly with each chord change, finding a melody to embody the pain he's been unable to process these past few months.

I've gotten a taste of the helplessness he, Sophie, and others close to me must have felt when I was in my own dark period. Conor has retreated into himself and nothing I've tried has seemed to bring him any comfort. He's insisted on having his own space, not even allowing me to join him in a silent run for the mere company of it. Having an inkling of what he's feeling, I've respected his need to go through this grieving on his own. But that doesn't mean I'm not frustrated by my inability to help him.

"That's some heavy shit."

I glance at Shay before returning my gaze to Conor. We watch and listen without comment for several minutes. There's no crescendo to his playing, no rising to a sense of release. Just unrelenting melancholy.

"I suppose feeling something," Shay says, "even this kind of pain, is better than the complete absence of feeling."

It's easy enough to get what he means. He'd never mourn his own father like Conor's doing. Shay had no real relationship with his parents. His only true family is his brother. And us in the band, of course.

Throwing my arm over his shoulder, I give him a squeeze. "You're right. And Conor's got no choice but to feel it all."

"What, are we supposed to be on?" Martin asks as he joins us.

"Nah, Marty," I say. "Let him be. He'll make it clear if he wants us up there."

And so, we watch and wait and listen. But Conor makes no sign of easing off, doesn't give any signal that he wants to turn this into a Rogue performance. Instead, he keeps his head down, his eyes closed as he continues to pour his grief into the only outlet he seems to have, his guitar.

He keeps playing so long, in fact, that most of the crowd goes back to chatting and drinking. But not us. Shay, Martin, and I stay still, our eyes fixed on our brother, letting his brand of blues wash over us as if that might diffuse the overwhelming feeling of it for him. All I know is that the three of us can't look away, especially not if there's a chance he might look up to catch our eye. He needs to know that we are here, waiting. And we'll do so for as long as it takes.

7

CONOR

By the time I've drained myself of both the inspiration and the desire to play, my fingers feel raw but my chest feels lighter.

Opening my eyes, I'm startled that the sky has gone mostly dark. How long was I lost in that solo jam session?

I hear the applause of one person—a response both so minute and rare that it takes me a second to place it—and see that it's coming from Donal.

"Jay-sus," he says and lets out a whistle. "That was a fucking *masterclass*, so it was."

Standing, I grimace and place the guitar in its stand before throwing the pick to him.

He holds it to his cheek with two hands. "I'll treasure it forever," he says and bats his eyelashes.

Once more, he makes me laugh. There's something about his energy that lifts my mood.

"You all right, then?" Gavin asks.

He, Shay, and Martin have edged their way to the stage. At least half the crowd seems to have gone inside, likely because dinner has been offered. The others still lingering in the increasingly chilly garden include Felicity, who is standing at a cocktail table with the women she calls her Mom Squad. The group includes the likely suspects: Sophie, Jessica, Amelia, and Lainey. Lainey isn't technically a mother, but she's basically been a stepmother to Martin's three boys for years now, so she's earned squad-status.

Flexing and relaxing my hands a few times, I nod at Gavin. "Yeah. That, eh, it felt good."

"For you, yeah," Danny Boy says, joining the lads, "but you scared off half the crowd with that doom and gloom."

"Fuck off," I tell him, but I've got a smile pulling at the corners of my mouth. With that comment, Danny Boy is both being his obnoxious self and trying to make light of my undoubtedly depressing performance just now.

"All I'm saying is, I hope it's out of your system now. No one wants the next Rogue album full of that misery."

"I think it was brilliant," Donal says earnestly.

"Of course, you do," Martin replies with a weary shake of his head.

Donal rolls his eyes at him before turning his attention back to me. "Yeah, it was fucking dark, but it was *real*. No filter, no bullshit. Just raw and … incredible."

"Thanks, man."

"And not overproduced," he adds.

Martin scoffs. "That's Donal's latest kick—slagging off our last couple albums for being 'overproduced.'"

Before anyone can say a word, Gavin throws his arm around Donal's neck and gives him a rough noogie to his head.

"Uncle Gav, get off!" Donal says, though he's laughing.

"This generation of kids," Gavin says with put-on disdain,

all the while still roughing up Donal's hair. "They like to complain well enough, but why don't you show us how it's done? It is your time already, Donal?"

"I can't help it if I like the way Rogue used to sound, back when you weren't ancient," Donal says, tears in his eyes from laughing.

"Getting older is not a crime."

"No, but getting complacent should be! You all wouldn't know how to produce something these days without ten layers added onto it. No wonder it all sounds the same, anyway."

"You think we've just been repeating ourselves?" Gav asks and slowly releases Donal.

"Eh, I dunno." Donal straightens up and suddenly seems to realize that his words have struck a nerve.

We all fall into tense silence, each of us clearly thinking over Donal's unvarnished assessment of the recent Rogue sound.

Finally, Martin slaps Donal on the back. "Go on and get your dinner. We'll see you in there."

Donal hesitates but is smart enough to seize the pass his father has offered him and heads off.

"He's not wrong, you know?" I say.

"The fuck he is," Martin grumbles.

While I appreciate his protective instinct, I can see some truth in Donal's criticism and I admit as much to the lads.

"I've actually been thinking a lot lately about our plans to go into the studio, wondering if we should even bother. Does the world even need another Rogue album? I'm being serious with that question."

"What do you mean?" Shay asks. "It's what we *do*."

"Yes, but that doesn't mean we're obligated to keep at it.

What if … what if we've run our course? What if we've said all we've had to say?"

"And so? You're ready to *retire?*" Martin asks dubiously.

I shake my head. "I don't know."

Another spell of silence comes over us before Gavin, ever our group leader, speaks.

"I get why you'd ask the question," he says. "But the conclusion that we're done is bullshit and you know it."

"I—"

"You fucking well know it based on the last hour of you pouring your guts out into that guitar just now, if nothing else. You might be too far into your own head to realize it, but that should've been a wakeup call. For fuck's sake, you were creating some of the best riffs I've heard out of you in I don't know how long." He pauses, his eyes fixed so intensely on mine that I have no choice but to believe he's being honest. "No, we're not done. In fact, I think we're just getting started on a whole new chapter. Especially if we can all rise to the level that you just showed us on that stage."

I can't tear my eyes away from his. That's his power: magnetism combined with an incredible belief in us as a band. It's always been there, since before we could even call ourselves a band. And he's always had the ability to make us believe it as much as he does. His certainty that we have something to say has been the thing that's defined our lives. It's the thing that has always inspired me to follow him just about anywhere.

And yet, I'm not completely convinced this time. This time, I've still got the nagging feeling that another Rogue album may end up being more of the same.

"Don't say another word," Gavin tells me before I can argue with him about our future. He knows me about as well as anyone in the world, so it's no surprise that he can see I'm still conflicted. "Just leave it for now. Leave it and try to enjoy your fucking birthday, yeah?"

It's also no surprise that he knows my head isn't where it should be to be talking about this kind of thing. He's right. I need to take a breath and save all the deep thoughts for another day. Today—tonight—is about being in the moment, whether I like it or not. I am here at this lovely venue in celebration. I have to, at the very least, act like it.

"I could do with a drink," I admit, and I see relief transform Gavin's face.

"I can help with that," Felicity says.

She's made her way to the outskirts of our circle and now approaches me, taking my arm into both of hers.

"We'll see you all inside soon," she says as she leads me away.

8

CONOR

Felicity doesn't say a word as we walk together across the length of the courtyard. The night has gone cool even though there are pockets of warmth provided by heat lamps as we walk, and I take the initiative to drape my suit coat over her shoulders.

By the time we stop at the far end, we're alone. All the other guests have gone inside to continue enjoying my party.

I see that we've arrived at a custom bar that has been cleverly designed to look like a traditional Irish pub, complete with a frosted mirror behind an ornate carved wood bar top and stools. But there's a rock star twist with a lit-up replica of the iconic Hollywood nightclub Whiskey a Go Go's marquee. This must be the whiskey tasting Felicity mentioned earlier. I never did get a chance to try it out. I should have taken her by the hand and gone right to it when she told me she'd revisited our past this way. Instead, I'd gone to the stage to get lost.

"This is fantastic," I tell her, forcing levity into my voice.

"Looks like the bartender is done for the night," she says with a shrug.

I'm such a bastard. She's been incredibly patient with me, hasn't once pushed me to snap out of it. She's allowed me this time to wallow, but yet still made a point of making sure I had all the little things she knows I usually enjoy, like purchasing new books by my favorite authors and leaving them on my nightstand, giving me the time to work out, organizing outings like hiking the Wicklow Way with our family, and keeping in close touch with my mother. And I've given her very little in return, not even appreciation for her efforts in putting together this surprise party.

Taking a deep breath, I release it and resolve that, at least for tonight, I will be what my wife needs me to be. I can go back to being a miserable wanker tomorrow.

"I'm actually the bartender for this event," I say and step behind the bar. I find a discarded apron and quickly tie the white cloth around my hips.

"Oh, I see. I'm glad I caught you before you close for the night, then." Felicity says with an amused smile as she takes a seat.

"Have you been here before?"

She laughs. "My first time."

"Lucky for me. What'll I pour you? I have a lovely Bushmills 21-Year-Old Single Malt," I say, examining the options. "Or, how would you like the Jameson Rarest Vintage Reserve?"

"I'll have the Jameson. But I can't stay long. My husband will be wondering after me."

"Ah, you're married?" I affect great disappointment, and she laughs.

"I am."

I push a tumbler of the whiskey toward her. "Mind if I join you?"

"Please do," she says with a small smile.

I pour myself a glass, knock it against hers, and take a drink. The Jameson goes down in a trickle that both burns and satisfies. She takes a small sip and closes her eyes with the taste.

"So, what's this husband of yours like?"

Her eyes pop open and she examines me. "He's a wonderful man."

"Why am I sensing a 'but' to go along with that?"

She shrugs a little before deciding to play along. "But he's been having a hard time lately and I just don't know how I can be of help."

"What's so hard about his life? I mean, with a beautiful woman such as yourself as his wife, what could he have to complain about?"

That gets me a raised eyebrow but she doesn't take the bait to veer off into flirty banter. "He's lost in his grief, I'm afraid."

"Ah, yes, that's a hard one. I suppose time is all he needs. Isn't that what they say?"

After a moment of hesitation, she nods. "It's just, I fear it might be troubling my marriage."

I fight off a grimace at that admission. I haven't realized how my actions might be affecting her, and I certainly never thought our marriage might be in jeopardy because of it.

"So," she says after a moment. "I'd guess that you hear a lot of sob stories, what with being a bartender. What advice might you give me?"

"In regard to your husband?"

She nods, her blue eyes searching mine. I can see the anxiety she's been holding back these past months. I know she wants to help. I know she wants my happiness. But how do I tell her none of that is in her power at the moment? I can't do that. She would only feel worse.

"Well, you're right that in my lengthy experience as a bartender, I've heard all kinds of stories. Now, I don't know much about your particular issues, but I can say that there's not a doubt in my mind that you're doing everything right. You're doing everything you can for that man of yours. And whether he's told you or not, he appreciates it to his very core. He loves you even more for the steady way you've managed while he's stumbled and staggered in the darkness." I smile at her when her eyes tear up. "And I bet he'd want you to know that you are the light in that darkness that he's always trying to move toward. Just have faith. Because he'll get there."

"Conor," she says on a breath, a tear falling down her cheek.

I lean over the bar and take her face into my hands and kiss her. I kiss her because I'm out of words. I kiss her because I want her to feel with my lips on hers how much I love her. I kiss her because she's my wife and she doesn't deserve to have any doubts about our marriage.

"I love you so much, sweetheart," she whispers.

I pull away enough to look into her eyes. "I love you, Felicity. More than anything."

Just as I see another tear fall down her cheek, I lean in and turn the next kiss into something more than assurance. I turn it into something we haven't had in a long while: passion. She moans as my tongue tastes hers. Our kisses turn heated quickly. The desire that has been dormant in me now rises with force, my dick springing to life and suddenly aching with need.

"Get over here to this side," I murmur urgently.

"What?" she asks with a laugh.

Looking at her, I see the flush on her cheeks and the way her chest is rising and falling rapidly. And then I meet her eyes and tell her firmly, "Get your fine arse over here right now because I can't wait another minute to fuck you."

Her eyes widen, but she doesn't hesitate. Instead, she stands and joins me behind the bar. Throwing her arms around my neck and the suit coat of mine she had been wearing falls to the ground. Neither of us worries about that as we are soon so invested in kissing and groping that nothing else matters. My hands roam her body, anxious to touch her in ways I haven't in too long as I squeeze her backside, her tits, between her legs. All of this is done over her dress, which is both frustrating and a turn on as it heightens the neediness between us.

Just as she unties my bartender's apron and reaches for my fly, I pull the hem of her dress up. She's wearing silky bikini panties that are damp with her desire for me.

"Jesus, you're so wet," I say as I push them aside and slide two fingers into her.

She whimpers and takes me into both of her hands, stroking me firmly and sending electricity throughout my body. I'm so hard, so eager for a release after all this time. And yet, I don't want this to end. I don't want this to be over too quickly. I put my hand over hers, slowing her strokes, and she looks at me in confusion.

"It's okay," I whisper, speeding up the thrust of my fingers. "I want you to come, honey. Come all over my hand and then I'll fuck your tight little pussy with my cock to make you come again."

She's both surprised and turned on by this talk. While it's true that it's been a while since we've had sex, it's also true that the times before had admittedly gotten a little routine. Now is not the time to return to that way of fucking.

Snaking my hand up her dress, I squeeze her breast before pushing her bra up and out of the way. Her nipples are exquisitely soft in the moment before they harden to delicious points. I wish I could have her completely naked, but we're exposed enough as it is. The party may be inside, but we're still in an outdoor, public area, albeit slightly shielded by the walls of the makeshift bar.

The combination of my fingers alternating between fucking her and stroking her clit while toying with her nipples has her stifling the moans I know so well. They're the moans that are my guide to her orgasm. They're the escalation of her pleasure, telling me that I'm so close to the prize of making her lose herself.

"That's it," she tells me, as if she wants to be sure I don't stop touching her the exact way that I am.

Of course, I wouldn't. I know what she needs. I know she's chasing that peak. I know it by the way her hips buck against me, by the way her grip on my dick has loosened because she can't focus, by the way her mouth drops open just a little as her breath quickens.

"Look at me," I command, and her eyes fly open. "Look at me while I make you come."

The corner of her mouth twitches but her eyes don't leave mine. And then she's off, coming hard, her legs shaking as she falls into me. I don't stop massaging her clit even after the spasm of it subsides.

She gasps. "Con, stop, I can't—"

"Shh. Don't quit on me now, honey."

"What? I can't. I'm too sensitive—"

She stops when I push my fingers back into her to create

the friction she thought she couldn't handle. I know, though, that she's not done. There's another orgasm just on the precipice and we're going to get it together. She's had multiples before and I feel like I'm making up for lost time and I want to give her this again.

I kiss her, taking control in the way that I know makes her weak. Her body and her moans respond all over again. This time, she manages to keep my dick fisted in one hand, pumping in time to the increasingly anxious thrusts of her hips toward my hand. When I curl the tip of my middle finger to reach that sensitive spot deep within her, she grips my bicep with her other hand, her nails digging into my skin through my shirt. This one comes quick, almost as a shock, and she lets out a moan that, even muffled by my mouth on hers, could wake the dead.

Going limp and laughing, she leans into me. "Conor Quinn, what have you done?"

I kiss her temple. "I'm not done yet."

Grabbing her by the hips, I twist her so that she's facing the bar countertop, pull up her dress, and give her a good spanking on the arse before plunging myself deep into her. She leans against the bar top, pushing herself back into me with almost as much force as I give her. And god, she feels good. The heat of her, the tightness of her. I have that same feeling of both wanting to explode and wanting it to never end.

I lean down and kiss the side of her neck, trying to pace myself. But then she twists her hips in a new motion against me and I'm closing in on my own orgasm.

"That gets me every time," I tell her, and I see her smile, her eyes closed. I straighten up a little so I can watch that swish of her arse. "Keep doing that. Keep those hips moving like that, fucking my dick like that."

She does as I ask and just as I'm about to close my eyes and let myself go, I see motion in the shadows thirty meters in front of the bar. There's someone out there that I can't identify. But whoever it is can undoubtedly see us. The lights of the sign above the bar are illuminating us, or at least our upper halves. There's no other movement and I begin to think I imagined it. Even if there is some voyeur out there, I'm not going to let that stop me from what will surely be the best orgasm I've had in recent memory.

9

CONOR

Hours later and I'm still intensely relaxed, which makes me wonder if I've had it wrong all this time. Maybe the cure to this depression has been as simple as a good fuck and I've been stupidly missing out.

I smile at that thought and take a sip of the glass of whiskey I'd filled to the brim back at the tasting bar and brought here to the restaurant part of Haddington House. After putting ourselves together, Felicity and I walked hand in hand back to join the party. We cleaned up in the toilets, and then ate dinner, chatted with a seemingly endless rotation of people, and settled into the booth where I am currently sitting very comfortably.

Part of my comfort might also be due to the fact that I'm alone and mildly buzzed. Felicity has wandered to the other side of the restaurant, once more grouped up with her Mom Squad. Surveying the crowd of people all here to celebrate me, I realize I enjoy having this solitary time more than actually engaging with them. Guess I'm not sex-cured quite yet.

"You didn't mean that, did you?"

Startled, I turn to see Donal standing to my left.

"What?"

"You didn't mean that about breaking up Rogue, right? I heard my da talking to Lainey about what you said."

I'm confused for a moment before it dawns on me that he had been a witness to my questioning the future of the band.

"Sit down, Donal. Join me."

He does so and eyes me expectantly. I try to think of something to say, to convince him there's nothing to worry about, but I still have questions about it all myself.

Instead, I deflect, saying, "What does it matter? Didn't you say Rogue have become a crap band, anyway?"

"So, you'd just give up on it all? Right before your twenty-year anniversary gig?"

"I didn't say that."

"Might as well have."

I study the kid for a moment, wondering why he seems so alarmed by the prospect of Rogue breaking up. And then it hits me that our band breaking up would probably feel like a divorce to him. He's grown up with us four lads as an intact unit all this time. It would be jarring for that to end. Almost, perhaps, as much as was his own parents' divorce.

"It's not anything to worry about right now," I say gently. "No decisions have been made."

His shoulders relax a degree, but I can see his guard is still up. "Aye, tell me more about your Insta-girlfriend," I say to change the topic.

He rolls his eyes. "She has a name."

"And what is it?"

"Valentina."

"Beautiful name. I suppose she's pretty? Must be if you're

going to all the trouble to see her and spoil her for *your* birthday."

He gets lost for a moment, staring into space. "Eh, yeah, she's the most beautiful girl in the world."

I stifle a laugh, reminding myself that despite how quickly Donal seems to want to be grown up, he's still got a lot of that pureness that comes from the innocence of youth. I should be encouraging him to embrace this rather than deriding it with a snicker.

"Hey, how about you make going to see her into something epic?" I ask in an effort at being more supportive of him.

"Like what?"

"Eh, I don't know." I think for a minute. "Like you make this an adventure for yourself, to celebrate your birthday, *and* something special for her?"

"Again, like what, Uncle Conor?"

I shake my head as I consider the possibilities. What would I have done when I was his age if I could? He's got money and freedom and no burning ambition other than to see his girl. But he should work for it. He needs more obstacles thrown in his way, not a first-class ticket and a penthouse suite at a hotel. He needs to get out there and really live. I start to suggest that he hitch his way across Europe to see more of it before doing his high roller routine. But I think better of that. Martin—and Celia, for that matter—would have my head for that. I modify the idea to something that could still be considered "epic."

"Why don't you take that motorbike I got you for your last birthday and ride it all the way to fucking Spain?" I say. "See parts of Europe you haven't. Eat new foods, sleep in hostels, meet new people. Then ride up like a fucking boss in the end to get your girl."

Donal laughs. "Yeah, right."

"What do you mean *yeah, right*? What else do you have to do? You should take advantage of your freedom to do something special. Get out of your cocoon here."

"Like I'm going to spend day after day on a motorbike when I can just get on a plane for a couple of hours? Nah, don't think so."

"Think of all the songwriting inspiration you can get from this. You say you want to write songs. Maybe you haven't yet because you need some real-life experience first."

"And roughing it on a motorbike trip for a few days is supposed to give me that?"

"Listen, anything that gets you out of this Dublin club scene, anything that opens your eyes to the world around you in a new way, can't help but be good for your artistic intentions."

He watches me for a long moment before rolling his eyes. "Sure, Uncle Conor. I'll go. I'll go if you go with me. How about that?"

I sit back against the booth, disappointed by his lack of curiosity and desire to explore the world around him. But then, I realize the fact that he's lived a privileged life has led to this. He's got no motivation to seek out anything on his own because he's always been handed everything he could ever want. That's not to disparage Martin and Celia, it's just to say he's a product of his circumstances. He grew up wealthy. He's a good kid, but the fact that he's never wanted for anything hasn't necessarily prepared him for independence, nor has it stoked his curiosity to understand life outside his own bubble.

"Anyway, I'm happy you had a good birthday," Donal says. "Seems the missus thought of everything with this party."

"Eh, yeah," I say with distraction, my thoughts still on how to persuade him to do more with his opportunities.

"Even got your happy ending before it was all over."

That gets my attention, and I meet Donal's eyes. He's got a knowing smile and an arched eyebrow, making it clear he was the one in the shadows earlier.

He slaps me on the shoulder. "See, this is why you're the one I've always looked to. You're a fucking rock star. Shredding that guitar and then shredding your—"

"Stop right there," I say sharply, and he goes mute. I eye him silently, trying to think what to say. It's clear from my tone just now that I don't want him to say a word about Felicity. But, am I to acknowledge the fact that he saw me fucking my wife?

"Don't worry," he says with a laugh, "I already know a shit ton about the birds and the bees, so I'm not traumatized or anything."

"Well, Jesus, how long did you stay to enjoy the show?" I can't help but ask.

"Only long enough to get a sense of what was happening. I suppose it's good to know that older people such as yourself can still have a good time."

Despite myself, I laugh. "How about we say no more on this? Ever again, I mean."

"That we can agree on."

He grins at me and I can see admiration in his eyes. It's a look I'm familiar with. I assume Martin would love to have that gaze leveled up on him, but once Donal hit puberty, he decided his own father couldn't possibly be cool. But somehow, *I* could be. And so, I have become someone he looks up to. If only I could parlay that into getting him to do more with his life.

Just then, Donal's mobile chimes and his face lights up in sheer delight when he looks at the screen.

"I suppose that'll be your Valentina?"

"Aye, it is." His focus goes to the mobile, a smile tugging at the corner of his mouth. And then I've lost his attention as he starts a rapid-fire text exchange.

His instant absorption in connecting with this girl is another reminder of how removed I feel from so much of my life lately. Though I have been tremendously blessed with a wonderful wife I love, beautiful children, and a band that has been successful beyond all imagination, I have found myself wondering if this is all there is. Have I come to the point in life where the best is behind me? Will I ever have that spark, that fire that Donal has with his girl? I miss it. As much as I love Felicity, I miss the way we were with each other at the start. Back before we had kids and a routine sex life. Our quickie at the whiskey bar was a nice reminder of the intensity we used to have.

This vague discontent and nostalgia have carried over into Rogue, too. I meant what I said, wondering whether the world needs another one of our albums. I can so clearly remember the way my adrenaline used to pump when Gavin and I got together to run away with something that inspired us. I don't think I felt that with the last couple of albums. We went into the studio because it was expected of us. We followed that with tours because that's what we do. The albums did well but there were no real breakout hits.

With my father passing, I guess I'm just at a crossroads, trying to sort out how to get more meaning out of this life that is so fleeting. My kids are growing up so quickly and I've already missed substantial periods of seeing that happen by being away on tour. I need to know that being away once more will be worth it, that our efforts as a band aren't just a routine we're stuck repeating.

"This fella bothering you?" Martin asks, not entirely joking as he gestures to Donal who is still sitting in my booth and furiously texting.

"Nah, he's no bother."

"If that's all you're going to do, take it elsewhere," Martin says. Donal ignores him and keeps texting. "I mean it, Donal. This is no way to help a man celebrate his birthday."

That gets Donal's attention and he looks up at his father. Then he looks at me before focusing on his mobile once more as the chirp of an incoming text sounds.

"It's okay," I tell him. "Valentina awaits."

He smiles and gets up, leaving without another word. Martin takes the place he vacated and leans back, stretching his arms along the back of the booth.

"Valentina?" he asks with careful casualness.

"His girl."

"Some girl from one of the clubs, then?"

"No, even better. Someone he met on Instagram."

Martin cringes before closing his eyes for a minute. "If that boy gets some random girl pregnant, there will be hell to pay."

"More likely, there will be *you* to pay," I reply with a smirk.

"Meaning?"

"Nothing. You just take good care of him whenever something goes wrong, you know?"

"What's my alternative, Con? Am I to let him go to jail for spray painting dicks on the side of church walls? He's a kid making harmless mistakes, including posting that shite on his Instagram account, for fuck's sake. But, I *won't* let it ruin his life."

"I'd do the same as you, Marty. I'm just as protective of my kids. I'm just thinking that he's never had to really struggle. None of our kids have, you know? They are loved and protected and given everything they could ever possibly want or need. But is that really benefiting them in the end? How are we going to be sure they can figure shit out for themselves if we keep spoon-feeding them life, you know?"

He's quiet for a moment as he thinks this over. "At his age, we were living in that crap flat in Lambeth, trying to make a go of things in the London music scene." He smiles and shakes his head. "Fuck, the *times* we had."

"The places we saw. The people we met."

We both get lost in a sea of memories. Lambeth, in south London, had a great mix of hotels, pubs, and clubs along the South Bank. With a lively night scene, it was our first exposure to a wide variety of cultures. It was also a rough place, with a fair amount of unsavory characters looking to take advantage of those who shouldn't be in the neighborhood after dark.

"Remember when we woke up to find we had a new flatmate?" I ask with a laugh.

Marty's eyes light up. "Fucking Reginald!"

Reginald was a local hooligan who was often homeless when his parents or girlfriend kicked him out. One night, after we had all gone out to the club and come home pissed drunk, he followed us right into our flat and curled up in a corner to sleep off his own partying. In the morning, we smelled him before we saw him. He had gotten sick in the night but never stirred. Luckily, he was harmless and only needed the shelter for the night. We pushed him into the shower and he was grateful to leave us be after that.

"You're right, those days were incredible," I say, still lost in the memories.

"I'll never forget it. So many ... *firsts*, you know?" he says.

"First time I had Korean food."

"First time I realized food could burn your fucking tongue like it was on fire."

"First and last time I was ever *that* drunk," I say.

"First time I saw people in the club shooting up like it was nothing," he says.

"First time I had a threesome."

"First time I wished I wasn't tied down with Celia," he says with a laugh.

"First time I had a perfect show."

"First time I knew Rogue would make it."

With that, we lock eyes and I feel an unbreakable connection with this man. We grew up together. We struggled together. We made music together. And I know that no matter what happens with Rogue, we'll always have a bond. He'd do anything for me, and I'd do anything for him. I know it as fact.

"Tell me, Marty," I say. "What do you want for Donal? More than just his well-being and happiness, I mean?"

"To have great mates," he says with the slightest nod toward me and I smile. Then his eyes leave mine as he contemplates what more he wants for his son. After a moment, he continues. "To have great experiences. To find his passion and let nothing stop him from pursuing it. To not let a good part of his life go by without being engaged with the world. I mean, I don't want him to play things too safe. I want him to get out of his comfort zone." He pauses. "And, of course, I'd want him to have more than one great love. Though, preferably, not at the same time for the sake of his heart," he says with a laugh.

I'm impressed by the thought he's obviously put into this

question, well before I ever asked it. I've always known he was a good father, but this just confirms it all the more.

"That's all great, man," I say. "You should tell Donal all this."

Shaking his head, he smiles, but it's bittersweet. "I could tell him but he wouldn't hear me. He's got zero respect for anything I have to say right now."

"He'll grow out of it and come back around."

"Fuck, I hope so," he says with a laugh. "At least for now, he's got you as someone he'll listen to."

I nod at that, wondering again at my seemingly outsized influence on the kid.

"What's all this about, anyway?"

"Just contemplating the big questions lately."

"Including the demise of Rogue?"

I raise my eyebrows before taking a sip of whiskey. "Nothing wrong in wanting to think things through, is there?"

"I hope there's more thinking to be done with that, Con. I really do."

"Sweetheart," Felicity says. She's a few feet away and moving closer to our booth. "There's dancing in the other room."

I can feel Martin watching me, still waiting for a response. But my wife has given me an unexpected out and I can't resist it. I stand and take her hand before pulling her into my arms.

When I give Martin a helpless shrug, he mouths "fuck off" for leaving him hanging like that and I laugh.

I know it's not kind to have thrown this bomb and walked away, but I never intended on doing it in the first place, so I'm not prepared to hash it all out. Besides that, it's my fucking birthday and I'm still pretending to enjoy this party. Time to dance with my wife.

As I let her lead me to the other room, the day's various conversations pass through my mind. It's Felicity telling me she was so desperate to see me happy that she planned this surprise evening. It's her telling me we should run away together and me rejecting that in deference to my obligations with the band. It's my mother warning me that I can't linger in this dark mood. It's Sophie giving me permission to do something for myself. It's Donal accusing Rogue of having gone stale. It's Gavin talking about starting a new chapter that I can't even begin to fathom. It's all the things Martin wants for his rudderless son—and him thinking I have an influence on the kid.

But most of all, it's Donal's words that come back to me.

It's Donal saying *I'll go if you go* about my proposed motorbike trip to Spain.

All of that crystalizes to a decision at the exact moment that I see Donal again just before we go into the room set up for dancing. I pull away from Felicity and go to him.

"Hey," I say and he leans closer to me to hear above the noise of the DJ pumping out a Billie Eilish song. "Pack a bag. I'm in. We're doing the motorbike trip. I'll see you in the morning."

"Wait—what?"

"In the morning," I repeat with a sharp nod.

And then I return to Felicity so we can go pretend like we know how to dance.

10

CONOR

I've dozed more than slept in the last few hours. We got home from the party fairly early, at about two in the morning. Felicity fell into bed and was quickly in a deep slumber, but I've only had brief moments of it. Otherwise, my mind has been racing with the implications of the impulsive decision I made last night. It's not that I regret it; it's more that I want to have a sense of how it will all play out. And I hope that Felicity will be okay with it.

At six-thirty, I get up and shower. Dressing in jeans, a flannel under a jumper, and my favorite leather motorbike jacket and boots, I pack a small backpack of other clothes and toiletries. Then, I kneel on the floor next to the bed where Felicity still sleeps.

I watch her for a moment. She's breathing deeply, rhythmically. Her eye makeup from the night before is smudged in a way that makes me smile. She somehow looks both peaceful and sultry, like she went out and had such a good time that she couldn't be bothered with her usual nighttime routine and ended up looking all the better for it. Her shoulder-length brown hair is wavy and I push a tendril of it off her face. Her breath hitches but she doesn't open her eyes until I stroke her freckle-dusted cheek with the back of my hand.

"Hey, you," she says sleepily.

"Hey, you," I repeat.

I don't say anything more and we share a long moment of eye contact. As has long been the case, I feel she can see right through to my inner self. She's always been able to understand me before I do.

Not wanting to drag this out, I say, "I'm going to take a few days, honey. I just need … a little time to sort of reset myself." I hadn't told her of my idea for Donal to motorbike to Spain, nor of my last-minute decision to join him. It seemed too rash, too much evidence of a man embarking on a mid-life crisis misadventure, to say it out loud.

She watches me silently, her eyes scanning over my face. I know her thoughts are racing. I know she must worry that I'm going off the deep end—that she might not be enough for me. Neither is true, and in the end, she must realize that, too.

All she says is, "Come back to me safe. Come back to us when you're ready."

The relief I feel nearly overwhelms me. It makes me want to crawl back into bed with this woman who has always known how to give me what I need, whether it's space or a push in the right direction.

"I'll do that, Fee. You can be sure of it," I say before giving her a long, lingering kiss. "I love you."

She nods. "I know, sweetheart. I love you, too."

Before I leave, I look in on my son and daughter. They had stayed up until almost midnight, hoping to be awake for our return, before succumbing to sleep. The late night must account for why they're both still quietly tucked into their beds in their rooms. Romeo is on his back, an arm slung over his head, a position I very often take in sleep, too. He's recently gotten a haircut to shape his hair into a mohawk and it's made him look older than seven years old, but he's still my boy. We have a grand time together, whether it's wrestling on the floor, playing football in the back garden, or working on logic games.

I don't want to wake him, but I don't want to leave without saying anything either, so I take a few steps into his room and search his desk for paper and pen. The note I leave him reads:

Rome - I'll be back before you know it. We'll have a day for just the two of us then, so think about what you want to do.
Love from your Da

I take an extra sheet of notepaper and the pen with me to Ella's room. She's lying on her side, facing away from me. I dare not get close enough to disturb her sleep, but I wish I could see her beautiful face. With lush, dark hair, deep-blue eyes that take after mine, and the beginnings of high cheekbones, she's already a stunner. She's losing her youthfulness all too quickly, starting to care a whole lot more about being with her friends. But when we're together, she's still her sweet, funny self. She loves to go back and forth telling jokes, the cornier the better. Her laugh is pure magic.

The note I leave her reads:

Ella - I won't be away long. When I'm back, we'll watch all the funny movies you want, and let's do one of your famous joke-offs. I'll leave you with one:
What did the snail riding on the back of a turtle say?
"Wheeeeeee!"

Love from your Da

I CUT the motor to my bike a half a block before getting to Martin's since it's still early yet and I don't want to wake the whole house, only Donal.

Coasting to a stop, I pull off my helmet and dial Donal's mobile. It rings four times before going to voicemail. I disconnect and try again.

"Uncle Conor?" Donal mumbles, his voice thick with sleep.

"I'm outside. Ready to go?"

"Ready to—you've got to be joking me."

"I told you last night this was on. Grab your things and come out. We've got a journey ahead of us."

"There's no way. There's no way you're serious."

"Look out your window if you don't believe me."

After a second, I hear the rustling of bedsheets and then see movement at the corner window on the second floor. Donal appears. He's shirtless, his hair wild, and his forehead scrunched up in disbelief.

"Think about it, Donal," I tell him. "But think fast. This is the chance of a lifetime. Let's go chase an adventure together."

"I, eh, well," he mumbles. Finally, I hear him swallow before saying, "Give me five minutes."

It's more like seven minutes, but I'll give the kid credit for hustling. When he meets me outside, his eyes are wide and he's got a giddy smile on his face.

"This is—this is mad," he says in a rush. "Where are we off to first?"

"Breakfast."

His face falls. "What?"

"I need coffee. Looks like you could use some yourself."

"Oh. I, eh, sure."

I wait another few minutes while he retrieves his helmet and motorbike from the gated side of the house. It's the Triumph Speed Twin I bought and taught him to ride last year. It's a respectable bike but still pales in comparison to my Triumph Thruxton, which was custom built in Spain as coincidence would have it. Still, the pair of us make a striking vision as I lead the way to a little village just past Dún Laoghaire. The commute from Martin's home in Howth back toward my neck of the woods takes almost thirty minutes, making me ready for a full meal to go with the coffee I had promised.

The breakfast place I chose is small, cozy, and off the beaten path. I've been here with the family several times and found that both the staff and loyal patrons are respectful of our privacy. Today, Donal and I take a table outside to enjoy the sunshine emerging from the clouds. We're greeted cheerily by a young woman who has coffee at the ready. After ordering avocado toast with poached eggs for me and a full Irish breakfast for Donal, we're left on our own.

"I have to say, Uncle Conor, I'm not sure what's going on," he tells me as he pours a steady stream of sugar into his coffee.

My teeth hurt just from thinking of how sweet it will be.

"What's going on is what I told you last night about getting outside of your bubble. Only, I'm going to do it with you."

He shakes his head. "But, like, *why?*"

"Maybe I need an adventure, too."

"You? Your whole life has been an adventure, what with, you know—being a world-famous rock star since you were my age?"

I laugh. "I didn't get famous until I was about nineteen, so a little older."

He rolls his eyes. "You know what I mean. You've been to every corner of the world, haven't you? Experienced it all—more than once. So, what is this? Some sort of babysitting thing with me? You and my da conspire to do this to get me out of the house or something?"

Though he laughs with that last comment, I can see he genuinely wants to know my motives.

"It has nothing to do with Marty. In fact, at some point you'll have to tell him you're away."

"What? He doesn't know? You didn't—" He stops and looks even more confused. "Fuck, he'll have my bollocks."

I raise my eyebrows. "Will he? Doesn't seem like the authoritarian type."

He sighs. "No, not by yelling or the like. But in his great bloody attitude of *disappointment* in me. Now, my ma, she'll be the one quick to give me a word or two."

Celia always was the one to run their family, so I can see what he means about her having something to say about this grand plan of mine. That'll have to come later, though. I need to get some forward momentum before we start handing out explanations. Doing so before we've even left Ireland would kill all sense of adventure.

"Well?" he asks, and I realize he still wants me to explain myself.

Our waitress arrives before I can open my mouth in reply. She sets down our food and then lingers, looking from me to Donal and back again. It occurs to me that she's not trying to place me as someone famous, but rather trying to decide whether she can flirt with Donal in front of me, the man she assumes is his father.

Donal is a good-looking kid, though I guess "kid" isn't really the right term anymore. He's a young man who has the kind of innate charisma and confidence that reminds me of Gavin in his youth. I can certainly see that in the way he makes our waitress' decision for her.

"Thanks so much, love," he says with a wink. "You'll be back to check on us, won't you?"

"Yes, of course," she says with a sweet smile, her cheeks gone red. "I'll, em, top off that coffee for you in just a minute."

"Can't wait."

I follow his gaze as he watches her go back into the restaurant. And damn if there isn't an extra pop to her hips as she goes.

"Valentina," I say.

His eyes snap back to mine. "What?"

"This trip. It's about getting to Valentina. But first, we'll take our time to enjoy a few stops along the way."

"Oh, em, yeah. So, you have it all mapped out, then?"

I take a bite of my toast and the soft-cooked egg breaks, dripping yellow yolk onto the blue plate. "In general terms."

"What does that mean?" He digs into his breakfast, piling beans, eggs, a grilled tomato, and a sausage onto a piece of bread before folding it into a makeshift taco and taking a big bite.

"I'm trying to go against my instincts with this trip and not plan it too much. So, that means that I've only gotten as far as sorting out that after breakfast, we will be taking a ferry from here to Holyhead. Then we'll make our way to London and stay for the night."

"London? Fantastic. I suppose you've got a posh hotel lined up for us? We'll be needing it after a long ride, won't we?"

"No posh hotels on this trip."

"What do you mean?"

He doesn't get it. He didn't absorb what I was saying last night about how he should view a motorbike trip to Spain as a way to get out of his comfort zone. Now, I have to make sure he understands that I'm not here to coddle him the way he has been for so long.

"Let me see your wallet," I tell him.

"My wallet?"

"Yeah, let's have it."

His eyes shift back and forth as he tries to sort out whether I'm joking or not. Finally, he decides to do as he's told and hands over a wallet that is made from the finest Italian leather. It's the kind of thing grown men salivate over but which I'm fairly certain Donal has no appreciation for. Why would he? It's just another one of life's little luxuries that he's always enjoyed.

Sifting through it, I see that he has almost two hundred euros and three credit cards. I pull the credit cards out and hand him back the wallet.

"You won't be needing these until we've gotten to Valentina," I tell him. "Until then, I'll keep them and handle all our arrangements."

He's frozen with shock. And then he groans. "Oh Jesus, don't be telling me this is some sort of intervention you have planned? Going to make me do random odd jobs to pay our way or something?"

Laughing, I shake my head. "Nothing so dramatic as all that. Just to be clear, though, this is not a five-star holiday. You've had plenty of those in your young years already. We'll have a good trip, but it'll be more stripped back than you're used to. Just about the basics."

He looks miffed. "I still think you and my da have something in mind to torture me with."

"Eat up, Donal. Our ferry awaits," I tell him with a grin.

I realize that I'm already enjoying this trip and that my decision to act impulsively is just what I needed.

11

DONAL

Donal: *I think I've been kidnapped*
Owen: *For ransom or sex slavery?*
Owen: *Cause, if it's sex slavery, I'd leave well enough alone*
Donal: *Don't be an eejit*
Owen: *What's the story, then?*

What am I to say? That the man I've called uncle since I could speak my first words has pulled me from my bed, insisting I go on a motorbike road trip through Europe—and that he's leaving his family behind to go with me? That I'm not sure he's well in the head after he told his bandmates of twenty years that he was ready to quit it all? And that before that, he spent an hour at his own birthday party making the saddest, most brilliant music I've ever heard on that iconic guitar of his? That ever since we parked our bikes on the lower level of this ferry more than an hour ago, he's been staring blankly out at the sea, ignoring my every attempt to get a sense of what the fuck it is we're doing?

I can't say any of that. Not over text, that's for sure. But also, not to Owen. He's my good mate, but he's very rarely serious about anything. He'd make a joke of it all, tell me to take the experience for all it's worth, and want all the dirty details after I made it to seeing Valentina. That's usually all I need out of our friendship, so I don't know why I texted him about this. He's the good time guy, ready to stay out all night at the clubs with me, the one who'll get drunker than anyone alive and wake up the next day without a care in the world, the one who bashes the drums with the same wild abandon as that mad Muppet, *Animal*. He and I have been playing around at making music together for the last couple years. Him on drums and me on guitar and vocals. We moan about needing a bass player to round us out but neither of us has been motivated to get serious with it. It's all good fun and we figure it'll come together one of these days. We're in no hurry.

At least, that's how it's been until recently. Recently, I've actually started to feel the pressure to figure out my shit. My da's patience is wearing thin, I can tell that much. Even with Lainey urging him to give me time, he's incapable of holding back his frustration with my "lack of ambition."

I scoff just thinking about the self-righteous tone he takes when he says that. As if he didn't hit the bloody jackpot with his band right out of the gates. Oh yes, I've studied my Rogue history. I know far more than I'd like about the beginnings of the band, including how after a pretty successful debut album, they hit mega-stardom with their second effort—all on the back of Gavin's obsession with getting back with his Sophie. I also know all about the drama that came in the years after that, including my own father's nasty public display of fuckery when he was leaving my ma.

So, yeah, my da is incredibly successful, but I don't see how it was ever his *ambition* that got him there. He was practically the invisible one of the band during the first part of their success. It was only after he and Lainey got together that he asserted himself and seemed to find some ambition where making music was concerned. Now, he thinks pushing me to be something he never was at my age is going to help. But it doesn't. In fact, it only inspires me to just keep doing what I'm doing: living the life of leisure, enjoying my semi-fame in the Dublin club scene, and taking my time to figure out what I'll do.

As I said, there's no hurry.

Owen: *Oi. Don't keep me in suspense.*
Owen: *Or have your captors ordered you to perform some sick sex act?*

Owen's text snaps me out of my daze and I quickly reply back, telling him all is good but I'm taking the long way to get to Valentina by my birthday. Of course, he responds just as I'd expected, telling me to enjoy my first taste of the 'V' when I finally get it.

I shake my head and laugh. I can't blame the fella for being exactly who he is. Looking up from my mobile, I see that we're closing in on Holyhead. It's probably less than an hour until we dock. Then what?

When I turn to Conor, I see he's still got his eyes fixed on the green water. True to his usual style, he's wearing clothes that fit him like they were specially tailored for him, even though it's just jeans and an untucked flannel under a cashmere jumper. He's sitting with his arms crossed against his broad chest, his long legs stretched out before him, crossed at the ankles, the epitome, as always, of cool. I wouldn't be surprised to find a photograph of him in the dictionary to go along with the definition for "rock star."

"You're staring at me," he says, still looking out at the sea.

"What?" I say reflexively, looking away.

"I can always tell when someone is watching me, especially when they think I won't notice." He sighs and then turns to me. "It's an exhausting talent of mine. Because I'm stared at a whole fucking lot."

"Eh, I'm just trying to figure out our next move."

"Staring at me isn't the answer."

Well, you're a grumpy bastard, I want to say. But I don't. I have the highest respect for him and wouldn't dare speak to him that way. Doesn't stop me from thinking it, though.

"Okay," I say. "I suppose I should map out the way to London from Holyhead?"

"Is that a question? Or are you going to go ahead and take the initiative?"

Fuck's sake, I moan inwardly.

Out loud, I say, "Yeah, I got it."

Standing, I walk a few feet away, wondering at his sour mood. This trip is going to be no bloody fun with that attitude.

Thinking about it, I realize I haven't seen much of him in the past few months. Not since his father's funeral, that's for sure. Before that, there were the usual opportunities, like with the rotating dinners that have been hosted at one of the band member's houses each Sunday for as long as I can remember. It's one of the few traditions I grew up knowing I could rely on, and even as I've gotten older, I've kept up with it. I like being around the lads and all their kids. But mostly, I like that bit of nostalgia it offers. Every time we're all together like that, I feel a familiar sense that all is right with the world. Could be because I remember being little and noticing the way my da seemed happier, more himself, when he was with the guys. Could be because I couldn't stop watching the way they all fucked with each other, even as Sophie would pretend to mediate a truce, as if she didn't know what they were playing at. Could be because I was mesmerized whenever Conor pulled an acoustic guitar onto his lap and made playing seem like the easiest, most natural thing there was. The talent of that man is astounding and I recognized that even as a kid.

I also remember the way his smile would light up the room. I haven't seen that on him in a long time. It doesn't seem like a good thing that he'll spend the next several hours in that brooding silence of his while we ride to London.

When I look at the map feature on my mobile, I study Holyhead before plugging in the route to London, suddenly desperate to find a way to snap him out of his black mood. It's a bright, clear day, after all. How can an Irishman not be overjoyed to see and feel the sun this way? Before long, I think I've found a detour that might help.

12
CONOR

I'm in a piss-poor mood and it's not fair to Donal. He couldn't hide the hurt on his face when I gave him attitude that he didn't deserve. The poor kid just sucked it up and took it.

The thing about knowing when people are staring at me was true, though I didn't need to hassle him about it. I've spent most of my life living just fine with this particular aspect of fame. The attention is something that has stoked my ego over the years, if I'm being honest. But in the last few months, I've lost that perverse pleasure and instead have felt irrationally annoyed by it. I called Felicity on staring at me, too, at my surprise party because I couldn't take it anymore. She's been staring at me that way for weeks, as if she'll decipher how to pull me from my depression by it.

But neither she nor Donal deserve any hassle from me.

I sigh and shake my head, growing frustrated with waiting to be released to drive off the ferry. We've been sitting on our bikes for over twenty minutes, and the fumes of the cars around us, and of the ferry itself as it docks, is enough to make me want to scream.

It's not like me to be so quick to anger or to snap at the ones I love. I thought getting away on this impromptu trip would help me rejigger myself to an extent. And I was feeling good at breakfast earlier. But once we got started on our way to Holyhead, the darkness I've been so comfortable with lately descended upon me once again and I escaped into it, ignoring Donal. If we can just get off this ship and on the open road, I'll at least have no one to abuse but myself. That's the thing about being on a motorbike trip, we can each of us get lost in our own thoughts without feeling the need to make small talk.

It'll be a relief to have the next several hours of uninterrupted driving and having Donal take the lead with the navigation is even better.

Finally, a horn sounds and then an announcement is made over loudspeakers that we are cleared to depart. We inch our way off of the ferry and into Wales. After making our way through the bottleneck of cars, I follow Donal onward.

Though my mobile is fixed into its usual spot in the hard case between my handlebars, I haven't turned it on or loaded the maps feature. Still, I have the feeling that Donal is taking us in the wrong direction. I wonder how long I should let this go before I tell him to sort it out. If I keep letting him go this way, he'll have to realize his mistake, won't he?

After ten minutes, we find ourselves at a lighthouse along with a slew of tourists who've just come off a bus. I slow to a stop next to Donal, thinking he needs the time and space to reconfigure his directions.

I'm about to call him out on failing his first attempt to lead us to London when he shuts off the engine of his motorbike and pulls off his helmet.

"What's up, then?" I ask, following suit.

"We're doing a diversion," he says simply.

"We're what?"

"Look at this day, man." He waves his arm, drawing my eye to the view.

We've come to the visitor center of the South Stack Lighthouse and are sitting in the car park. I see that it's sunny, but I also see that we're surrounded by cars and tour buses, so I'm not impressed the way he seems to want me to be.

"Come on," Donal says, swinging his leg over his bike. "You said we're taking an adventure, didn't you? Let's go see what it's all about."

This is not what I had been gearing up for. I had wanted a long ride to the city, not a hike with tourists. But before I can argue, Donal has begun walking with the masses toward the trail to get to the lighthouse.

Following him, I pull on a ball cap. Ball caps are not part of my regular style, so it seems like a good way to hide in plain sight. Still, I keep my head down as I walk, not wanting to make eye contact with anyone.

This attempt at subterfuge means that by the time I've gotten to the edge of the path leading down to the lighthouse, I've had no warning of how spectacular the view would be. When I stop by Donal's side and look out at the coastline, I feel something expand in my chest. It's partly a sharp intake of breath and partly the pure wonder at the deep-blue sea surrounding the peninsula where the blindingly white lighthouse is perched. There are dozens, maybe hundreds, of birds gliding over the water before settling into nooks in the walls of the cliffs below us. The sun shines down onto the water, spreading its light brilliantly over the dips and folds of the waves. There's a breeze that carries with it the scent of the sea.

Donal slaps me on the back. "Nice, yeah?"

I struggle for a second to respond. Not because I'm overwhelmed by the beauty spread out before me, though it's certainly capable of stopping me short in that way. But because I can clearly see Donal's intention in diverting us to this spot. He was hoping to shake me out of my bad mood. The poor kid had probably panicked at the idea of spending days on the road with such a sour bastard. And well he should. It wasn't my intention to pull him into my misery. In fact, I had rather selfishly hoped to use the mission of getting him out of his bubble to elevate my own mood. So, it's time to throw myself headlong into that effort, as hard as it is to find the energy. This trip isn't just about me. I need to be a better version of myself—even if it's only for Donal's sake.

I turn to him. "It's fantastic. Just the breath of fresh air I needed after all those fumes getting out of the ferry. Good call."

Relief floods his face, making him look younger for a second. A clear flash of Marty comes across in that unguarded expression, another reminder of the responsibility I have undertaken with insisting on this trip. Donal isn't my son. But I have to care for him as if he were. Thankfully, it's an easy thing to do.

"Let's get down there," I say with a nod to the switchback stone steps leading to the lighthouse.

"I'll race ya," he says with a laugh and starts off.

. . .

NINETY MINUTES LATER, we're back where we started, using the excuse of examining the view once again to catch our breath after having raced back up the nearly two hundred steps to get to the top. Down below, we'd wandered the grounds, explored the visitor center, and climbed the spiral staircase inside the lighthouse for even more impressive views. Donal was filled with wonder at every turn, and it was refreshing to see him engaged in the endeavor.

"On to London now," he says. "Maybe we'll stop off somewhere for a pub lunch?"

I like that idea. But now that we've begun our trip with something unexpected, I have an idea for another diversion.

"Why don't I lead this next leg? I've got an idea where we can eat."

He nods. "Sure, yeah."

At our motorbikes, I plug in Liverpool as our next destination and see it will take us about two hours to get there. That's a perfect time to enjoy the road before taking another break. Once I know that Donal is ready to go, I start off with him close behind.

As we ride, I think about what I want to show him once we get there and it makes me smile. Like a real, unforced smile. That's come about too rarely lately.

13

CONOR

Our first stop is The Phil and it's quickly apparent that Donal has no idea the significance of this place. It's officially known as The Philharmonic Dining Rooms and its late 1800s art-nouveau style with mosaic floors, detailed plastered ceilings, and stained glass and mahogany partitions, makes it a "must see" in Liverpool. But my interest in it is a little more personal.

It isn't until we're each served an ale, along with fish and chips for me and beef pie for him, that Donal questions why we've veered off course.

"Noticed that, did you?" I ask, though this time there's no sarcasm or shortness in my tone.

"I retained a bit of geography from school," he replies with a smirk.

My side trip to Liverpool means our journey to London will take a couple hours longer than if we had gone directly there. But, I think it's worth it.

"I'm guessing we're going to do a Beatles homage tour, then?" Donal asks before I can tell him that John Lennon used to come to this very pub for his regular pint before his fame made it impossible to continue the ritual unmolested.

"Well, a bit, yeah."

I catch him starting to roll his eyes before his attention turns to the buzzing mobile on the table. He grabs it, his face lighting up in response to whatever interrupted us.

The next ten minutes pass with me eating and drinking while his thumbs fly over the mini digital keyboard of his mobile as he trades texts.

I have no room to complain about the rude behavior, not after how I ignored him on the ferry. But I do get a really good taste of the kind of frustration Marty's been dealing with. It's a maddening feeling to be discounted by the person you're sitting with.

Finally, he sets the mobile down again and digs into his lunch, demolishing most of it in just a few big bites.

"Was that your Valentina?" I ask.

His mouth is full, so he nods.

"She knows you're on your way?"

Takes him several chews and a big swallow before he can reply. "Yeah, told her just now. She thinks it's romantic that I'm making my way to her as a sort of pilgrimage. So, you were right about that bit."

"You know what's more romantic?"

"What's that?"

"Writing her a song."

"Yeah, well, whenever I try to write any kind of song, it comes out as corny bullshit. You know, I'm just too *aware* of the process and I can't step outside of it."

"Maybe you haven't had proper inspiration yet."

"Maybe," he says before downing his ale. "Is that something that sort of ... runs dry, then? I mean, like, with you and the band? Is that why you're ready to give it up?"

Back to this again. Rogue ending seems to bother him much more than I would have anticipated. Rather than try to dismiss the possibility of the band breaking up, I decide to get it all out there.

"Listen, we've had a great run," I say. "Truly, an extraordinary career. Like you said, we've traveled the world many times over. We've met and collaborated with incredible talent. Each of us has reaped more riches than we know what to do with. And yes, we have created some really good tunes. I'm proud of the stuff we put out there—even the last two albums you think are shite."

"I don't—"

"It's okay, Donal. I see where you're coming from with your criticism. And honestly, it's your job as the next generation to sort of kick us in the arse. We either have to rise to the challenge or step aside, don't we? That's the very nature of this thing."

"Well, I never meant that you all have to break up. Jesus, if you're saying I'll be to blame for this, I'll go bloody mad from it."

"No, of course not. Sit back and take a breath." I look up and am able to make eye contact with our waitress easily. It's easy because it seems she's been watching us this whole while. Guess my ball cap wasn't all that effective. I gesture to her that we'll take another round of pints and she nods vigorously before springing into action. When I look back at Donal, he doesn't seem to be breathing at all. He's been paralyzed, waiting for me to assure him further that he has no part in Rogue's possible demise.

"Here's the thing," I continue, "we've got this twenty-year

anniversary gig coming up." I stop short, thinking again of how close I'm testing things with this trip. I should be back home, shaking off the rust and getting ready for what will be the biggest performance of our lives. Instead, I'm sitting in a Liverpool pub with my godson, talking about ending the band. I suppose I've run away from home at the most inopportune time.

"Here you are, lads," our waitress says as she sets down two fresh pints of ale.

I look up at her, pleased for the interruption. She's a bottle-dyed blonde in her early thirties, fairly fit, and her big, blue eyes are currently fixed on me. As I suspected, she's recognized me. I take off my hat and ruffle my hair since there's no use in pretending. The gesture brings a flush to her cheeks, and I feel an old dormant thrill rise in me.

Years ago, I made a concerted effort to scale back my natural inclination to flirt out of consideration for Felicity. Not that she ever asked that of me. Rather, I was made aware that it was disrespectful to her by an unlikely source: Danny Boy. He'd pointed it out in relation to a specific instance where I had been playing around with our then nanny. In my mind, it had all been harmless. It was mainly fantasies I'd concocted as an escape during a rough time in my life. But, like his brother, Danny Boy has a talent for reading people and he made it known to me that I wasn't as clever in hiding my ways as I thought I'd been. Since then, I've done my best not to encourage or engage with women who aren't my wife.

But now, that desire for a harmless back and forth with a willing woman asserts itself.

"Lovely," I say, making a point to lock eyes with her. I then take her in, examining not just the surface level but those things that say more about who she is. Though pale, her skin is extraordinarily smooth, and the lines at the corners of her eyes seem less about age and more about a propensity to laugh often. Her lips are a little thin but come together in an attractive bow shape that she's accentuated with just the slightest pink tint, suggesting she knows this is one of her best features but doesn't care to flaunt it. What I say next, I mean, and I think that's part of why my flirting with women has always worked so well. I don't just throw out some line. I choose my words carefully and deliver them honestly. "Lovely as yourself," I say. "Thanks, honey."

"Oh," she says, and the blush on her cheeks creeps down to her neck and upper chest.

Getting that reaction is deeply satisfying.

"Are you, eh, what are you doing in these parts?" she asks, recovering herself a degree.

"Ah, the lad and I are just passing through," I say.

"Is this your son? He's just as gorgeous as you, if you don't mind my saying."

"Eh, no, he's my nephew. In any case, we're very pleased indeed we stopped in at such a welcoming spot."

"Oh, we're pleased to have you. I mean, I'd be pleased to have you."

I can tell by the way her body trembles slightly that she's not used to being this forward. But as is often the case, women take the initiative with me in moments like this where we've met randomly and have little or no chance of ever seeing each other again. I assume they figure, *why the fuck not?* and hope for the best.

I could give her some suggestive reply, like, *Not more pleased than I'll be when I've had my chance with you.* Or *I'd love to have the pleasure in return.*

But this taste of a tease is all I need and I cut it short,

saying, "We appreciate the hospitality. Would you like to get a photo before we leave? Be happy to."

She blinks as it dawns on her that our brief moment is over. "That'd be fantastic. Yes, thank you."

"It's no bother at all."

Nodding, she slowly backs away from the table before turning and making herself busy at the bar.

I'm still watching her and basking in the rush that bit of flirting brought on when Donal brings me back to my senses, asking, "What did you tell Felicity about taking off like this?"

I almost laugh at the way he's brought up my wife at this moment. It's actually quite similar to how I'd brought up Valentina this morning after he'd done his own bit of flirting with our waitress at breakfast. I suppose a declaration of *touché* is warranted. But I'd rather not acknowledge his attempt to call me out with the harmless flirting I just did.

Instead, I say, "I didn't say much, really. Just told her I needed a few days."

He eyes me for a long moment before looking down at his now empty plate. "She's cool with that? I mean, doesn't mind you disappearing?"

I debate what to tell him, how to explain the relationship I have with Felicity and how lucky I am to have ended up with a woman like her. But it occurs to me that my connection with Felicity is nuanced, deep, and complex in ways he likely can't fathom. In ways he really *shouldn't* understand at his age. His experience of love and women is at the complete opposite end of the spectrum from what I currently enjoy and it makes me realize that his youth is such an incredible gift. He's going to experience love, and likely, heartbreak, for the first time. Those are things that leave an indelible impression. Those are the things that make up the best inspiration for songwriting.

Realizing Donal is still waiting for a reply, I tell him, "Thing is, she knows I'm not disappearing. She knows I'll be back to her and to our family. So, me taking a few days away isn't a big deal."

He nods, finishes the last bite of his meat pie, and sits back in the booth. "So, what's next, then, with this diversion of yours?"

"It's less a diversion and more an education."

I get the eye roll from him again. "Am I to hear all about The Beatles being the best band there ever was?"

"Do you know what made them so good?"

He sighs. "You're going to tell me."

"Simplicity. That's it."

"Yeah, they're pretty basic."

"Not like that, Donal. Think about the word choices in their lyrics. They never went flowery or overly symbolic. Think about the progression of their melodies. They didn't try for complexity, at least in the early years. You'd do well to study songs like 'And I Love Her' or 'I Want to Hold Your Hand.'"

"Yeah, I'd say those are simplistic, all right!" he says with a laugh.

"You're not getting it, man. It's the purity. It's the vulnerability of straight out declaring your love. It's telling a girl how she makes you *feel*, that she's got this *power* over you that you're only too happy to surrender to, even if part of you knows you could get destroyed by it. Don't tell me you can't relate to that."

"Eh, well, I suppose if you look at it like that," he says, clearly unconvinced.

"Listen, what I'm getting at is that good songwriting is a lot like love. With both you have to take this leap, this risk of opening your heart to get anything meaningful out of it. If you don't, it's just playing at the effort. So, if you haven't already learnt it, now's the time to understand that when it comes down to it, love is all there is."

He leans forward, his elbows on the table, eyeing me intensely. "I knew it. It's a bloody Beatles homage tour we're going on."

I laugh at him interpreting my proclamation as a twist on Beatles lyrics. But the humor doesn't last because I want him to understand something important. "You can be a cynic and write a good song," I tell him. "But you can't be a cynic and write a good *love* song."

"If you say so, Uncle Conor."

I sink back into the booth and try to suppress my disappointment with his refusal to take this seriously. Looking down, I study the calluses on the fingertips of my left hand. They're not as rough as they usually are, having healed during the time I spent ignoring the guitar. It's a physical reminder of the fact that I just don't know whether I have anything left to say with music.

"Where will we go first, then?"

When I look up, I see that Donal has put cash on the table to pay for our meal and stood. His eyes are wide, expectant. The fact that he's urging me along, despite his own disinterest, makes me smile.

I slide out from the booth and stand, too. Throwing my arm around his shoulders, I say, "Don't worry, there are just a couple of places we'll go to before heading to London."

14

DONAL

AFTER A GRUELING, almost five-hour motorbike ride from Liverpool, I'm ready to relax in one of London's high-end hotels. But Conor has other ideas, steering us instead to Lambeth, Rogue's old stomping grounds.

We end up in a seedy no-star motel, sharing a single room with two beds. The carpet is worn down in random patches, the bedspreads are from an era from before I was even born, and the walls are so thin that we can hear our neighbors having some kind of hate sex.

"This is teaching me something, is it?" I ask.

Conor raises his eyebrows but doesn't say anything.

So, it's not the luxury accommodations I've always known, but I can manage. In fact, a long hot shower to loosen the kinks from being on the bike for so long is just the way to ease into things. But I soon find that our room's tub comes with a ring of fuzzy mildew and I'm put off of that idea. It's going to have to be a quick in and out of that thing.

The next best option is to kick off my boots, gingerly peel back the stiff bedspread, and lean up against the lumpy pillows.

"You'll let your da know you're away?" Conor asks.

He's on his way to the toilet with his bag in hand.

"Yeah, I will." I should warn him about the tub, but I'm knackered. And a little pissy about his millionaire-self putting us up in this dump.

He nods and shuts the door behind him, and I turn to my mobile. Once I've got it plugged in and charging, I check in with Valentina. She's eager to hear all about my first day on this road trip and we exchange a series of texts on the subject.

After I get a sense of her day—she's a uni student in Barcelona, but on summer break and working at her uncle's tour company on the island of Mallorca—I text her an odd question.

Donal: What would you think if I told you I want to hold your hand?
Val: I'm not understanding?
Donal: It's probably stupid. I just wondered. Would that be a good thing? If I told you I want to hold your hand?

I watch as the dots appear, showing she's writing her reply. Then they stop for almost a solid minute before continuing again.

Val: I think it would be sweet.

Huh. Resting my mobile on my thigh, I focus on the water

stain in the ceiling directly above me and think back to Conor's insistence that The Beatles' brilliance lay in their simplicity. I didn't quite see what he was after with that. Not even when we went from the pub after lunch directly to Paul McCartney's childhood home. They offer tours by reservation only, but it took Conor just a few minutes to charm the guide into letting us have our own look around in between groups. He was thrilled to walk through the space of one of his idols, even though it had a weirdly trapped-in-the-past vibe. Or maybe that's why he liked it so much. It was stripped down to the basics. Even so, every nook of the place had a story for the ways in which Paul and John used it to create their earliest collaborations. I could just about see the drool forming when Conor saw the piano they wrote songs on. Though it wasn't allowed, our guide, a woman in her forties who clearly had it bad for Conor, made a show of looking away so that he could toy with the keys for a few minutes.

We went from there to the Penny Lane sign on Mossley Hill for the obligatory selfie. I watched as Conor signed his name on the sign in a tiny corner to mark his presence as so many others had done. He insisted that I do the same, saying my name being found there could thrill fans one day. Then it was a quick trip to the red gate of Strawberry Field. After another photo, that was it for the tourists' stops, but whatever lesson Conor was trying to impart wasn't over because he insisted on taking control of the Bluetooth connection in our bike helmets to play the Beatles for the entire ride to London. I got to hear "I Want to Hold Your Hand" more than once. The main chorus of that song stuck with me, making me wonder if Conor was right about the power of its simplicity.

Valentina would seem to agree, as she texts me: *I want to hold your hand, too.*

Looking at her message, I smile. I wonder if her hand will feel small in mine. I'm 6'2" and she says she's 5'6." Her photographs make her appear petite, though, like I could easily fold her into my chest and hold her protectively.

Donal: I can't wait to hold your hand. Hold you. Hold your everything. I'm dying for you, Val.

There's a long pause while I wait for a reply.

Val: Me too.

I look up at the closed en suite door. I can hear the shower.

Donal: Send me a pic of your gorgeous self?

Val: Let me lock my door.

I like what that suggests. Maybe she's ready to show me some skin. Smiling, I lean back onto the creaky bed and enjoy the anticipation. We've fooled around a little on the phone, but it's mostly been teasing. She's hesitated to fully expose herself or put into text and photos anything too sexy, but I don't mind. It tells me she's smart—and worth waiting for.

Val: I'm back
Donal: What color are your knickers?
Val: Lavender
Donal: Video chat. Let me see.

Instead of our texts turning into a video chat, I get a message with a GIF-style photo. It's her twirling and sending her skirt flying, giving me a brief but tantalizing view of the purple thong she's wearing. I watch it over and over, focusing as hard as I can on the fabric between her luscious ass.

Sweet Jesus.

Staring at the replay, I have to adjust myself. The near-instant swell of my cock pulls at my piercings in a painfully delicious way.

Val: Are you still there?

I straighten up and quickly reply.

Donal: Sorry. I nearly fell off the bed looking at you. You're the most beautiful thing I've ever seen.
Val: [blushing emoji]

"We should get out of here, go find some music."

Now, I really do almost fall off the bed. I hadn't heard Conor turn off the shower or open the door, and the sound of his voice has startled me so much that my heart is thudding in my chest. He's standing by his bed, looking at me expectantly.

"Eh, yeah, sure. I'll just take a quick shower first." And get a quick release, I think, as I unplug my mobile from the charger to take with me to the en suite.

CONOR IS ENERGIZED as we walk the streets of Lambeth, offering a running commentary on where he and the lads had hung out back in their day and noting how much things have changed—and haven't. On impulse, we duck into a club halfway down a graffiti-strewn alley, lured in by the sound of a live band going at it.

Inside, it's dark, the floors are sticky, and the band is playing to an audience of about fifteen people who have left their enthusiasm elsewhere. In other words, it's the complete opposite of the types of places I frequent back in Dublin. The club scene I'm into there isn't so much about Coppers or The

Button Factory, as it is the underground after-hours places. They're the pop-up clubs that move around from location to location and aren't exactly legal. Besides the way they turn an ordinary restaurant or other establishment into a nightclub without proper license, they also tend to be rife with pill poppers—not that I go for all that. I leave that temptation to my pal Owen and instead indulge in a few overpriced cans of beer, content to get lost in the low light, writhing bodies, and pulsing beat of the DJ.

Here in Lambeth, we have no trouble finding a table, taking seats against the wall before realizing that this isn't the kind of place that offers up a cute cocktail waitress.

"What'll you have?" I ask Conor.

He keeps his eyes on the four-piece band even as he reaches into his pocket and offers me a credit card.

"Bottle of whatever their best vodka is," he says.

I should take that as a sign that this evening might go to shit. But no, I simply grab the card and put it to use with the barman, securing a bottle of Absolut and adding into the mix two pints of Newcastle Brown Ale, and four packages of crisps.

Back at the table, Conor is still fixated on the band, so I pour each of us a shot before settling back into my chair. When he reaches out blindly for his glass, downs it, and then refills it without ever taking his eyes off the band, I have to wonder what it is he's enjoying so much. They sound like crap to me. The drummer is clearly off by a beat. The singer seems to forget his own words, mumbling in place of the lost ones. The guitarist is playing his beat-up *Yamaha*, of all things, upside down to accommodate being left-handed—not that that helps him do anything interesting.

I finally lean close to Conor and say, "They're fucking terrible, amn't I right?"

He turns to me with a peculiar smile. "They're wonderfully terrible, is what they are." And then he downs another shot.

"What are you on about?"

"They're in the best phase of their lives right now, is the thing. They're on the cusp of figuring out their sound, of proving themselves by failing, of—hopefully—learning from their mistakes." He shakes his head and sighs with a placid smile. "It's a fantastic time in their career and it'll only ever happen once. I only hope they have some sense of that."

As he helps himself to yet another shot of vodka, I look back to the stage, trying in vain to see what he's seeing. They still look like a bunch of eejits to me.

"Are you feeling some weird nostalgia or something that I'm not getting?" I ask.

"Maybe I am. Maybe I'm just remembering what a special thing it is to start up a band. Those fellas probably don't even know how incredible this time in their lives is." He looks at me, his voice turning insistent. "Have fun with this girl of yours, but don't get too serious. Enjoy your mates. Enjoy the time you have with them before settling down. Because you'll *never* have those days again. Mine with Gav were cut short because of him getting serious with Sophie before he was even twenty-fucking-one. We should have had *years* more to just be kids together, to just party and make music and fuck about. It's one of the biggest regrets of my life that we didn't have longer to do that. I sometimes think of the kind of music we might have made if we'd been able to just continue on as we were in those early days. Just the lads, living the rock 'n' roll dream."

With that, he nods and retreats into silence and returns his focus to the band. I watch him, watch the way his hand taps against his thigh, almost as if willing them to get into a synchronized beat. But they don't. They just relentlessly keep thrashing at their instruments, only occasionally making a sound that is a loose imitation of music.

When I can't take it any longer, I say, "I get what you mean about enjoying time with just your mates, but I still don't understand what you see in these jokers."

"It's the *effort*, man," he says. "It's the effort combined with the passion—that's what you need if you're going to get anywhere. Yes, this band here is pretty fucking shite, but that's no reason for them to give up." He laughs. "At least not yet. I think you could learn something from them because of that."

I take that in for a minute before asking, "Are you telling me I'm lazy?"

This time, when he refills his shot glass, he refills mine too. "Yes, Donal. You're fucking lazy and privileged, but you don't have to be. You could be on the verge of doing something amazing with your life—if you put in the effort."

"Well, don't fucking hold back or anything, Uncle Conor," I say with a stupefied laugh.

"Listen, I'm on my way to being drunk. And I *don't* get drunk. Do you hear me? I don't do that. I *don't* lose control. But I've decided with this trip to just fuck that whole need for control thing and let go. So, I don't mean to hurt your feelings, but I might say some shit that isn't as careful as I'd usually be."

Lucky fucking me to be the one to experience an out of control, drunk-arse Conor Quinn, I want to say. But I don't. Instead, I just nod and watch as he gulps down more vodka.

15

DONAL

WHEN MY UNCLE Conor said he was going on this trip with me because he could do with a little adventure, I never thought that meant him getting so pissed drunk that I'd have to be the one to keep him from getting his arse kicked by the guitarist of one of the worst bands I've ever heard.

And yet, here I am, in a hole in the wall club, trying to break things up. It all escalated quickly once the band finished their set for the night. That's when Conor had approached them with words of encouragement. They nodded skeptically, not even recognizing him.

"No, I'm serious," Conor had slurred. "You've got talent." He stopped, burped, and leaned in toward the singer, looking much more like a random drunk than one of the most highly respected guitarists in the world. "Well, some of you more than others. I mean, let's be honest, lads, yeah?"

"Fuck off and away with you," the singer said dismissively.

"I'm trying to *help* you, man. I'm trying to give you some advice you'd do well to listen to."

"We don't need *advice*. We need you to piss off," the guitarist sneered.

"You," Conor said and pointed an unsteady finger at the guy. "You're left-handed?"

"What?" The guitarist was confused by the question, and I didn't blame him. It took me a minute to remember that I'd seen him playing his guitar upside down, something commonly done by left-handers who can't afford a guitar designed for his preference.

"Thing is, if you're a leftie, you join the ranks of some fucking great guitarists who were left-handed and played the guitar upside down, too. I mean, there's the bluesman Albert King who was so dedicated to open tuning that he *never* used the sixth string. Then there was James Marshall Hendrix. That's *Jimi fucking Hendrix*, to you. And don't forget your man Paul McCartney—"

"What are you going on about? I'm not left-handed, okay? I just like playing that way for the look of it," the guitarist said with a shake of his head.

The expression that came over Conor's face was unlike any I've ever seen on him. He was utterly perplexed, though honestly, for me, this revelation explained a lot about the guitarist's earlier inability to play a decent note.

"Are you fucking kidding me?" Conor asked. "You just *pretend* to be left-handed? As if you're up there playing fancy-dress rock star like it's fucking Halloween and you couldn't come up with anything better?"

"What the fuck do you care, you aged rock fanboy?" the drummer asked and got his bandmates laughing.

"Oh, you bastards haven't the first clue, have you?" Conor said ruefully.

Though I'd only had a single beer and a single shot of vodka, I suddenly felt sick to my stomach. It wasn't the alcohol. It was the fear that Conor was about to utter the most cliched and unforgivable question anyone—especially a celebrity—could ask: *"Don't you know who I am?"*

Before the words could leave his mouth, I said, "Come on, let's go."

But when I pulled on his arm, he yanked it from my grasp so hard that, between the force of the motion and all the vodka in him, he stumbled a few steps, his full weight pushing into the guitarist.

That set all the band off as they went after Conor in an effort to protect their guitarist. Only, I needed to protect *my* guitarist. It was a scramble of arms and legs and shouts as I forced my way into the mix and managed to pull Conor out of it and toward the exit as the lads jeered at us, calling us cowards for running out on a fight.

Jesus, if they had only realized who they were trying to take down. If they had, it might have been the one thing to have earned them some press, since surely their music never will.

"This town looks so much the same and so different," Conor says now as we're walking along the dark streets in what I hope is the direction of our shitty motel. He's making about as much sense as I'd expect of a man who has downed a bottle of vodka.

He's trailing behind me by a few steps and I stop to wait for him. I've had plenty of experience in being the one to manage my pal Owen in this way. That kid goes *off*. He's a blast to be around ... until he crosses into FUBAR territory.

When that happens, I'm left making sure he doesn't do anything irretrievably stupid that might end with us both getting into the kind of trouble my da can't buy us out of.

When Conor reaches me, he says, "Can I tell you something, Donal?"

"Sure, yeah."

He glances down at my crotch, focusing on the way my hand was lingering at the fly of my jeans.

"You play with yourself a little too much."

"Ah, no," I say with more than a hint of defensiveness in my voice. "It's not like that. It's just, it's this piercing I've got. It gets snagged on—"

"Piercing? A piercing on your *cock*?"

He looks horrified. I know he's never had a piercing or a tattoo, that he sees it as messing with perfection. As much as I revere him, I don't agree with that. I think he'd look even cooler with some metal or ink. But I don't get a chance to tell him that.

"Don't tell me you've gotten a Prince Albert?" he asks with a wince.

"No, it's a Dydoe. Just a couple of mini barbells through the glans. Didn't hurt nearly as much as you'd think."

"Why. The. Fuck. Would. You. Do. That."

He says each word as a full stop, his disgust clear.

"I dunno. I thought it was cool, I guess. And the benefits are fantastic."

"What possible benefits could there be to piercing your very manhood?"

I can't help but laugh at that characterization. "Well, for one, it sort of intensifies things, if you know what I mean. And on top of that, it's positioned in just the right spot to hit the girl's G-spot."

His horror turns to exasperation as he rests his hands on his hips and shakes his head.

"Take it out. Get rid of it before you get yourself infected."

"I'm not going to get infected. It's all healed."

"Then take it out and learn to please a woman with your own bits rather than hardware."

"I *can* please a woman without it. That was never the issue. This is just a nice ... enhancement."

"Jesus, will you listen to yourself? You've never even taken the time to really learn what it takes to please a woman, have you?"

"First of all," I say, looking up and down the street. Luckily, we seem to be alone for the moment. "I can't believe we're having this conversation, you and I. And second, yes, of course, I know what it takes."

"Really? So, you know, it's not just about fucking and getting off?"

"Is it not?" I ask with a laugh.

"Well, it's not *all* about that. It's about making a connection before you ever get her clothes off. It's about seeing her. I mean, *really* seeing her for the totality of the woman she is and you letting her know she's been seen. And that is what makes you desperate to know her even more intimately. It's about the soft touches, the anticipation, building the desire until she's so ready she can barely contain herself."

"Oh, listen to him laddie. I'd say he knows what he's talking about, all right."

I jerk my head to locate the raspy voice that just inserted itself into our conversation and find the culprit two flights up at a windowsill in a brick building. An older woman is leaning partly out the open window, a cigarette in her hand and a grin spread wide across her face.

"See?" Conor asks, unfazed by the fact that a random stranger has been listening to us. "Confirmation! Thanks, honey." He blows her a kiss.

"Ah, and he's got a face on him to die for," she says, and her laugh is an unfortunate attempt at flirtation as it's overwhelmed by the sick gurgle of smoker's phlegm.

"Let's be on our way," I say.

"He's right, boy," the lady in the window shouts down. "Take them things out your knob."

This irritates me but so amuses Conor that he's doubled over in laughter and I have to forcibly pull him down the street and away from the earwigging lady.

"Fucking hell," I mutter.

"Well, then?" Conor says. "You'll take it out?"

"I'll take it out when you get yourself a tattoo, how about that?"

He ignores that challenge, saying, "You're joking me with this thing, right? You can't possibly have put bits of metal *into* your dick, have you?"

"Give it a rest, yeah?"

"Can you imagine," Conor says through his continued laughter, "what your Valentina will think when she sees your —your—" He can't get his next words out because he's laughing so hard, amused by whatever he's trying to conjure up. Finally, he says, "When she sees your *robo-cock* coming at her?"

"*Uncle* Conor, can we have some … I dunno? Boundaries, maybe?"

That only sets him off laughing all the more, and soon enough I've given up and joined in, laughing at myself, laughing at the state he's in, and laughing at this weird adventure we've gone on.

16

CONOR

So, here's what I've learned happens when I get absolutely smashed drunk: I make decisions I'd never make while sober. Not terribly shocking, I suppose, since I've seen my fair share of such bad acts in my time. For me, though, the indisputable evidence of how I've fallen prey to the same stupidity is that I am currently sitting bare-chested in a tattoo shop in Soho as a guy named Tito brings a buzzing needle to my skin over and over.

Just another drunk insisting that a tattoo is the greatest idea in the world, right? Well, it started out that way. But it was also a way to get Donal to remove his ridiculous piercings. I'd boldly accepted his challenge and told him to figure out where I could get some ink. He'd laughed me off, but emboldened by alcohol, I insisted that I was absolutely serious and that this thing had to happen *tonight*.

As determined as I was, it still surprised me when Donal announced he knew just the place. It was a shop in Soho that his father had taken him to when he was quite a bit younger. Donal found us a taxi and we were there in no time. It wasn't even that late when we got there, only half-eleven. We were whisked upstairs and greeted by Martin's long-time tattoo artist, Tito, who said he was honored to be the one to give me my first ink.

But he was also smart enough to drag out the process of me deciding what design I'd get so that I could sober up some. That meant that I didn't get something as trite as a guitar tattoo or something as basic as Felicity's name in ornate script —both of which I suggested in my inebriated state. Thankfully, Tito bought me time to think about what I'd really want since even with the drink wearing off, I was still committed to following through on this whole thing.

Unfortunately for Donal, part of the distraction was Tito outing the fact that Donal had a tattoo I hadn't known about.

"Marty told me you got your first ink not long ago," he said. "You should have come to me. I'd have steered you in a different direction, that's for sure."

I turned to look at Donal so fast that I felt dizzy for a second. "What have you done?"

"It's nothing," Donal replied dismissively.

"Don't tell me it's on your arse."

Tito joined me in laughing at that.

"No, it's not," Donal said petulantly.

"Well, let's see it then. Maybe I want to get one to match."

"You do not want to get what he did," Tito said with a laugh. "Definitely not your style."

"Oh, now I'm really intrigued," I said. "Come on, Donal. Drop your trousers and let's see what was so meaningful to you that you had to have it permanently imprinted on your arse."

"For fuck's sake," Donal grumbled over our laughter. And then he sobered me right up by pulling on his bottom lip and leaning down slighting so that we could see the letters F-U-C-K in black ink tattooed on the pink flesh there.

I blinked. Then blinked again. "And you chose this, why?"

"Because, it's a great fucking word."

When I scoffed, he added, "It is a word that is versatile, evocative, transcendent."

"Let me clue you in, Donal. Those last three public-school-learnt words you just used are a hell of a lot more tattoo-worthy than what you actually inked."

He rolled his eyes at that.

"And you chose that spot, because?"

Here he hesitated and his eyes wandered around the shop. Tito had closed it after we arrived so we'd have privacy, so it's just us and the cute front desk/assistant girl. "I just," he said, still struggling for an answer. "It was just for me, I guess."

Something clicked then, as I understood he might have gotten his tattoo and piercings in the least visible areas in deference to me and the way I've always declared that *I'd* never do such things. His father certainly wouldn't have any concerns with it. He's had piercings and tattoos for years. So, this very well could have been yet another way that Donal has shown how much he looks up to me.

"Well, okay, yeah," I said. "Em, there's something to be said about doing something just for yourself. Right, Tito?" I gave the tattoo artist a meaningful look, and luckily, he understood.

"Yeah, for sure. It's all an expression, in some way, of who you are. And that's rad, man."

Donal slowly nodded and the tension in his shoulders released, seemingly satisfied with our approval.

Now, I wince, not because of the pain of the needle against my skin as Tito continues to work, which is fairly mild, but because of the realization that I'm continuing to act out the quintessential mid-life crisis pattern I'm loathe to admit to. First, I ran away from home, then I got drunk and into something of a bar fight, and now I'm getting a tattoo.

But how else to explain why I'm doing something I said I'd never do? I've always thought a tattoo would mar my skin, that I've already got a pretty damn fine thing going on, so why mess with it?

"This is going to be sick, man," Tito says.

He's American, based out of Austin, Texas, but has made regular trips to this shop for years. I've seen his skill all over Marty's arm, neck, and back. He obviously has talent, especially for detail work. Knowing I'm in his good hands has made it easier to go through with this.

This, the tattoo I'm currently getting, is actually something I've had a part in crafting. Tito is damn good at reading people. It didn't take him long to sort out that me showing up at his shop wasn't just based on a deal I'd made with Donal or spurred on by too many drinks. He rather deftly pulled from me confessions of the recent events in my life, including my father's passing and my fortieth birthday.

Like a good therapist, he changed the topic—or *appeared* to change the topic—to what he said was his obsession: Japanese symbols. He asked if I knew what an *ensō* was. When I shook my head, he directed me to a tabletop, put a paintbrush in my hand and directed me to dip it into the jar of black paint.

"The *ensō* is a circle drawn with one brushstroke," he said. "It's done as a meditation with the idea of freeing the mind so that the body can create."

I raised my eyebrows at that, thinking of how I've only rarely freed my mind. I've always kept control over things, preferring that safe way of existing. The chaos I created when

I let my body, my *heart*, rule was too destructive. The last time I did that, I came very close to losing my best friend and my band.

"Whatever you create in this moment," Tito continued, "it doesn't have to be perfect. It's actually meant to symbolize the beauty in imperfection."

"You're suggesting I paint you a circle, is that it?" I asked with a laugh.

"I'm suggesting you take a breath and then use this little act of creation to express yourself at this exact moment. And, however it comes out, just accept that this is what you've got to give right now."

I was slow to follow him in this line of thinking, my head still a little foggy. "A full circle, then?"

"Full or open, whatever is natural as you go."

"I bet you draw a perfect fucking circle," Donal said, once again putting me up on a pedestal.

But perfection was no friend of mine at that moment. I raised the paintbrush, ready to slash out a circle and be done with it but stopped short.

"If it's a meditation, what am I meditating on?" I asked.

"Well, the *ensō* symbolizes both absolute enlightenment, strength, and something called *mu*, which is the absence of something, a void."

I smiled at that, shaking my head. Fuck me. It seemed this was, indeed, the exact right expression of my innermost self, which had lately been dwelling on the shortness of life and how hard it was to hold onto strength as I grappled with the absence of my father and the absence of momentum in my life.

This time, when I raised the paintbrush, I did as Tito suggested earlier. I took a deep breath and, on the exhale, I used one stroke to draw my *ensō*. The brush stroke is about three-quarters of an inch wide, completely filled in at some parts, and lighter in others. It's also open at the bottom.

"Ah, you missed a bit," Donal said with disappointment.

"The open circle is that beauty in imperfection thing," Tito said. "It being incomplete symbolizes room for development."

I took comfort in that idea and immediately agreed that this would make a perfect design for my first tattoo. After talking more, we decided that inside the circle would be a tree, half with green leaves and the other half with bare branches to symbolize the cycle of life. The names of my wife and children would be woven among the leaves and the trunk of the tree would be made of the Celtic trinity knots to bring in both my Irish roots and my faith in God.

Tito marks the last few details onto the rounded upper part of my shoulder where my skin is red beneath a "sick" new tattoo.

I look over at Donal a few chairs over. He's been chatting up the front desk girl the whole night long, Valentina a seemingly distant memory. But now it's his turn to hold up his end of the deal.

"Tito," I say, "will it be you or this lovely young woman who has the pleasure of ridding Donal of his piercings?"

Donal hears that and I swear I don't know which bothers him more—the idea that Tito, a man he's known since he was a boy, will be handling his junk, or that the woman he's been flirting with all night will.

And I almost feel sorry for him.

17

FELICITY

You held my hand
Sheltered me from the rain
Silence was a command
I didn't know how to explain

Conor texted those lines at three-forty-three in the morning but I'm only now seeing them as I wake up at a quarter past seven. It's just those lines, nothing else. No word on where he is or what his plan is. No "I love you." No "I'll phone you later."

Sinking back against the pillows, I throw my forearm over my eyes and sigh. My depressed husband has gone away by himself to places unknown and … I let him.

When he'd woken me to say he needed a few days, it took everything I had not to ask a thousand questions. My thoughts raced as I wondered why he needed to leave, why I couldn't help him, why he couldn't confide in me, where he was going, and when he would be back. But then I saw in his eyes a plea for me to ask none of that, to just trust him. And I also vividly recalled a time when I asked the same of him. It wasn't long after Ella was born and I was having trouble coping. I asked for his patience and took the kids with me to Portugal. It was a very brief time away, but it was exactly what I needed in order to return to him and our marriage in a better headspace. It had nearly broken his heart, but he'd let me go. He'd given me what I said I needed. So, it was time for me to return that favor.

And now he's reached out to me with these lines that must be lyrics. They immediately conjure up the day of his father's burial. It was a rainy day. After the brief graveside words by the priest, everyone had dispersed, eager to find cover. But Conor had lingered, the rain soaking him as he stared at the open grave. I'd gone to him, taken his hand in a firm grasp, and held an umbrella over his head. I didn't say anything, just stood with him until he was ready to turn away. It didn't seem like a big gesture, but it obviously had an impact if he's writing a song about it.

Though I wish he had said more about how he's doing and *what* he's doing, I'm glad that he's reached out in a way that he sees fit. The lyrics are a comfort that I'll hold on to tightly.

After a moment of thought, I text him back.

Lovely to hear from you, sweetheart. Know that I will always hold your hand. Sending you all my love.

Raising the mobile up, I use the camera to take a quick selfie. I'm wearing a white tank top that's sheer enough to reveal the outline of my breasts and nipples. My hair is partially covering one eye, and I definitely look like I need some coffee. But I know this is exactly how he likes me most.

Once the text has been sent, I relax again and think about the day ahead. I have plans to go to Sophie's house for a late lunch and playdate for the kids. If Conor were here, he'd be rehearsing with the lads, but that seems to have been put off.

For how long, I just don't know.

18

CONOR

Felicity's text jolts me from sleep. I'd only drifted off an hour or so ago, but I'm not irritated. Especially not when I see she's added a photo of herself looking sleepy and sultry all at once. I long to be in bed with her, to be back home and not in this shit motel with a softly snoring Donal a few feet away.

But I have only myself to blame. Me and my big idea to get away from everything while also somehow being the one to educate Donal to the fact that there's more to life than his little Dublin bubble. What kind of example am I, anyway? The first thing I do is get so drunk that he has to pull me out of a bar fight. And then we spend the rest of the night in a tattoo joint.

Which reminds me ... I am now officially inked. Laughing quietly at myself, I look down at the clear bandage on my shoulder. Yep, there's the tattoo that I'll have for the rest of my life. As I examine the colors, the brushstroke effect on the *ensō*, the details of the green leaves on one side of the tree, along with the names of the people who are dearest to me, I smile. Though I never thought I'd desecrate my body with something like this, I don't have any regrets.

What I do regret is the pounding in my head. It's been a lot of years since I've felt this kind of a hangover. Turning on my side, I close my eyes and surrender to sleep and the hope that when I wake again, I will be in a better state.

It feels like only minutes have passed when I'm pulled from sleep once more, though my head feels better. It takes me a few seconds to realize why I've woken. But then I focus on Donal looming over my bedside with a large takeaway coffee and a brown bag that's gone greasy from its contents, which, by the smell of it, is fish and chips pre-doused with vinegar. My stomach lurches at the same time that it rumbles with hunger.

"What time is it?" I ask, struggling through my fatigue to sit up.

"Just past noon," he says and takes a sip of the coffee. Apparently, it isn't for me. "Thought we'd better get on the road. I've sorted out the next steps since you said we'll head to Paris after this. We need to get to Dover for the ferry, then it's a bit of a ride from Calais to Paris."

I nod, but I still feel like I'm moving in a daze. "Good lad."

"I already had my lunch. This is for you."

He offers up the bag but I hesitate to take it.

"Trust me, Uncle Conor, that grease will soak up all the vodka and do you good."

I raise my eyebrows at that.

"Plus, I got you a bottle of Guinness. That combo is perfection, you'll see."

I should get up and go for a run. Or find a gym and lift some weights to get the blood flowing. That's what I'd normally do. I'd push through. I'd force myself to reclaim some control. That's what my life has always been about. It's how I've managed to get where I am, out of sheer determination and dedication.

But all of that has nothing to do with where I am now. All of that is the opposite of what I instinctively feel I need. What I need is a taste of the exact opposite. I need to know what it's like to just … let go.

And so, I accept the greasy bag. "I'll take that Guinness, thanks," I say, and Donal smiles the smile of a kid who feels he's done well to please the one he admires.

While I eat, I see that a dozen or so texts have come through, mostly from Gavin. He's asking where I am. And so, too, are Shay and Martin.

I get why Gavin and Shay are asking. I should have met them at our rehearsal space about an hour ago. But Martin should have been able to fill them in. He should have because Donal was supposed to have let his father know he was with me.

"Donal," I say tersely, looking up from my mobile.

He looks up from his own device, not stopping his thumbs from tapping away in some message that is likely to his Valentina.

"You told your father where you were last night when we got in, didn't you?"

His face contorts as if he's trying to remember. "Eh, I don't think so. Got distracted with Valentina, I guess. Then we went out and you know how all that turned out."

"You don't think he's worried about you, then?"

"He probably thinks I'm at Owen's. Happens often enough."

"Get in touch with him before we leave." I finish the last of the chips, crumple up the bag, and lumber to my feet. "I'll shower and then we'll head out."

Donal nods as I pass by.

By the time I've showered in the petri dish of a tub and dressed, I feel remarkably better. Donal's "cure" seems to have done the trick. Still, I'm looking forward to checking out on the ride to Dover.

WE MAKE good time and once on the ferry, I'm in a more social mood. The journey to France will take about ninety minutes, which is long enough for us to find table seating with a view of the sea for the crossing. We both have a cuppa and settle in.

"So, em, last night was—" Donal starts.

"Yeah, sorry about that," I interrupt.

"No, I was going to say it was fantastic."

I raise my eyebrows. "Fantastic?"

He laughs. "Sure, it wasn't the posh hotel I'd have wanted. Or a raging club scene. But it was just … cool to hang with you, you know?"

Examining him, I take a sip of tea. The milky concoction goes down like a medicinal tonic. It's the final piece of the puzzle I need to recover from last night.

"You're good with the whole thing of taking out your piercings?" I ask. In sober retrospect, I realize I shouldn't have insisted on all that. It's his body, his right and decision to do as he pleases. Just because the idea of such piercings appalls me, doesn't mean he can't have his own mind on it.

He shrugs. "We made a deal. And what's done is done."

"Well, I guess you can do it again if you want it back, right?"

"You were probably right about Val's reaction. Maybe I'll just skip it."

I nod and decide to leave it at that. Turning my eyes to the view of the choppy green water, I think of what a kick my father would have gotten out of hearing about last night. He loved living vicariously through me and my exploits, though he had to settle in recent years for embellishing old stories. I've been … tamed, I guess you could say. Not that I ever went off the rails on drugs like Gav. But, I definitely had a lot of years of women, partying, and all-night adventures. That was then. Life now is about my family, and happily so.

"Why do you suppose," Donal says, pulling me from my thoughts, "that there aren't any tabloid stories about you?"

"What do you mean?"

"The waitress at the pub in Liverpool? Tito giving you your first ever tattoo? Shouldn't that stuff have made it to the tabs?"

"Ah, maybe you're not the only one who is disenchanted with Rogue," I say with a wry smile.

"Bloody hell, it really wasn't my intention to make you all think Rogue was … played out, you know?"

I laugh. "It's okay, Donal. Really."

He looks frustrated and takes a second to forcibly shake it off. "Anyway, why no paparazzi on this? It's not normal. You get stories on you going for a fucking haircut."

"I took a page out of your Uncle Gavin's playbook," I

admit, "and sweet-talked that waitress into waiting two days to post anything. Same with Tito, though he didn't need much convincing. He's a good guy. His loyalty to your dad is what really did it."

In what is surely a reflex at this point, he rolls his eyes at the mention of his father. "Why two days?"

"Because there's basically only so long people can keep something a secret. I figured two days was pushing it, but we'll see."

"You don't want people to know where you are?"

"Not if I can help it. Just keeps things simpler."

"Does this mean we'll be spending the night in some shite place in Paris, too? Some sketchy neighborhood where you and the lads stayed when you were trying to break through?"

Laughing, I say, "I hadn't thought that far ahead. But we're still not doing the luxury holiday here. Remember, this is about getting away from all that."

I watch him struggle for a moment with himself. He has something he wants to ask me, but his hesitation tells me he knows he might not like my response.

Finally, he can't help himself and says, "You think I'm a spoilt brat, don't you?"

I squint at him, trying to decide how honest to be. I figure the truth is best. "Yeah, a bit."

"That's grand, thanks."

"It's not your fault. At least not completely. But the thing is, you have the power now to step outside of all that." Resting my forearms on the table, I lean toward him. "Do you really want to be a musician? Like, really want it with everything you are? Or are you just fucking around with it because it's the only thing you know?"

"No, I do. I really do."

I give him a look that says I need more to be convinced and see his eyes bounce around the large space of the ferry dining area, casting about for a way to describe what music means to him. Finally, he huffs out a heavy breath and meets my eyes.

"It's all I've ever wanted, to be honest. I can't imagine doing anything else."

"Jesus, then why haven't you been spending every waking moment learning your craft? Why haven't you a raft of lyrics ready to be turned into songs? Why don't you have more than a drummer for your band? What are you waiting on?"

He opens his mouth to reply but quickly shuts it and shakes his head.

"Oh, I see." I sit back.

"What?"

"You've got nothing to say. Not just now, but in music. So, you just can't get anywhere with it."

"That's not true. I have a point of view that you couldn't even imagine."

I want to laugh, but don't. It's just that he clearly thinks whatever his point of view is, whatever he feels, is something I've never known. As if I've never been his age.

"Okay," I say. "Then, what's stopping you from expressing it?"

"It's just, I mean, like, you don't know what it's like to be the son of a famous person. You don't know the fucking ridicule I've dealt with all my life. For a while it didn't bother me because it was mostly other kids making fun of me and my brothers for Da being the one in Rogue no one could remember. Like, *oh, yeah, his dad is in that band Rogue, only no one really knows if he exists or not.*"

I cringe at that. But if I'm honest, I heard the same sort of things in our early years. Martin was a very solid bass player, but he was content to stick near Shay's drum kit in the back of the stage. He rarely did interviews or made public appearances, always preferring to get home or to whatever hotel we were staying in rather than be any kind of center of attention. He and Shay had that in common, but Shay never had trouble standing out while on stage. His athletic performance on the drums, where he got all his aggression out, has always been spectacular and impossible to ignore.

"Then it all got much darker," Donal continues, "when Da left my ma and made a fucking spectacle out of it." He drops his head into his hands. "It was miserable and relentless after that. *Oh, he's the one whose dad fucks skanks in club toilets. Oh, he's the one whose dad sucks cocks in a San Francisco gay bar. Oh, he's the one whose dad is with that dirty whore homewrecker actress.* There wasn't a fucking day that it didn't go on."

My protective instincts rise up and I want to slap the kids that gave him such a hard go. I swallow down the reaction and try for something more reasonable, something more immediate and helpful to the kid sitting across from me.

"That does suck," I tell him. "But isn't it also something you can use? Something you can funnel into music?"

He laughs and it sounds weary. "What do you think the reaction will be if I try to really have my own band? You think all those bastards out there will give ? Or do you think I'll be shredded to pieces before I can ever get up on a stage?"

"Fuck those bastards. Fuck what other people think."

"That's easy for you to say. Nothing has ever shaken you. Nothing ever bothers you."

"Why would you think that?"

"You think I don't know all about your past? You think I haven't studied everything about Rogue's rise? As soon as I was old enough, I devoured every news story, every gossip post, every YouTube performance, every Tumblr page. I was desperate to know how you all did it. How you became this huge band. Because I wanted a piece of that myself."

"A piece of fame or making music?"

"Both."

"That ambition is good."

He shakes his head. "It's a double-edged sword, is what it is. Because I learnt all about you and Gavin and your thing with Sophie. And then I learnt all about Shay and his mess with his brother and Jessica. And for the fucking cherry on top, I learnt all the shitty ways my da broke my ma's heart."

"So, you believe all the trash tabloids over your own father?"

Waving a dismissive hand, he rolls his eyes again. "I know enough of it is true. I wasn't too young to understand what was happening at the time, anyway. In fact, I remember clear as if it were yesterday when you came round after Da got caught was some rando chick in America. It was *you* who came to check on us. It was *you* who took us out for pizza and a chat. Not my father. Not the person who was supposed to—"

He stops himself and shakes his head angrily.

I see now the things that churn inside of him. I see the anger, the hurt, the disappointment. The reason why he can't cut his father a break. And also why he's transferred his idol worship to me. I could try to rationalize things, to tell him that it's all a whole lot more complicated than he might understand, that he should try to talk through things with his dad. But I know he isn't in a place to hear that. That's not what he needs.

"Here's the thing," I say instead, "yes, you've had to deal

with a whole lot of shit you shouldn't have. There's no sugar-coating it. And there's no changing it. But here's what you can do. You can *use* it. You can turn all that bullshit you had to go through into music. And if you get it right, it'll be something that a lot of other people will relate to. Because believe it or not, kid, you're not the only one who has had a bad hand dealt to them. You say you know our stories. Well, think of what Gavin went through. Think of how he used all that. He turned himself inside out for his music. Not because he wanted to share his innermost pain, but because he *had* to. There was no choice. That kind of artistic expression, the kind borne out of what torments you, is the single most compelling art there is in my mind. I've always been drawn to it, wanted to be a part of it." I take a breath and realize that I need to focus on him and what he should be doing. "You just have to give no fucks and work your own art, Donal."

I can see he's overwhelmed by everything I've just unleashed on him. I don't know if he'll really absorb it all. It's easy to dictate such things to someone, I suppose, and much harder to be the person actually following through on it.

"Anyway, if you want to know the truth," I continue, "I may know how to project the image of looking unbothered, but that's all exterior. On the inside, I'm just as fucked up as anyone else."

He looks disappointed by this admission, and I realize I've been too honest. The kid isn't ready to accept that his hero is just a man. I'll grant him more time to indulge in this comforting fallacy. I give him a wink to mock my "confession" and the gesture works because he rewards me with a relieved smile.

The truth is, I've been shattered many times in my life, but none more so than now when I don't know what meaning my life has or how I'm going to find it.

All I know is that our ship is going to dock soon and we have a four-hour motorbike ride to Paris after that.

The journey continues.

19

FELICITY

As usual, Sophie has arranged a perfect playdate for both the kids and adults. She's designed a scavenger hunt so elaborate that it'll occupy the children for a solid couple of hours, giving us moms the freedom to curl up on the deck sofas to enjoy the sunshine along with a glass of wine and a gourmet cheese and charcuterie platter.

The Mom Squad is here in full force now that Jessica is in town for the special gig. It's rare that she's in person for our get-togethers, but our text chains and video chats have kept our bond tight over the years.

The same goes for Lainey, as she's almost as much of a transient presence with her acting taking her all over the world. But she's made sure her schedule is clear at this time so she can support Martin.

The ladies are chatting about Conor's birthday party, about how much fun it was, as I'm lost in wondering whether the big concert will even happen. As Rogue's media manager, I should be demanding answers from Conor about when he'll be back and getting assurances from him that he'll be ready to perform. But as his wife, I don't want to add that extra pressure to him. I have to trust that he knows what he's doing, that he has a plan. He always has a plan. He's always responsible. He's completely dedicated to the band and ensuring its success, after all.

"That's weird."

I'm slow to look up at the sound of Sophie's voice. There's concern in her tone, but I'm still stuck in my own thoughts.

"What is it?" Amelia asks.

"Gavin texted saying Conor hasn't showed up at rehearsal yet and he's not answering his phone."

When I look up, I find all eyes on me. Clearing my throat, I shake my head a little, at a loss. I don't know where to start because this means that Conor hasn't bothered to tell his best friends that he's taking a few days away. The absence of communication is completely unlike him. He doesn't act rashly. He doesn't disregard his obligations. But more than that, he doesn't leave me to clean up his messes this way.

"Is he," Sophie says and hesitates, "feeling unwell?"

I puff out my cheeks, holding a breath before releasing it. "No, not exactly."

"Well, now my concern has gone to full-blown worry," Sophie says with a nervous laugh.

"Wait," Jessica says, "why would you have been concerned to start with?"

A rare silence falls over this group of women for a moment before Amelia says, "You probably know how hard he's taken the loss of his father."

"Oh yeah, for sure. But I didn't know his grieving was cause for concern, exactly."

"He's been depressed," I admit.

"It's not so much his grieving or depression that concerned me," Sophie says. "It was the fact that he told the guys that he wasn't sure there was a reason to make another Rogue album."

"What?" I ask, unable to hide my shock. Unable to hide the fact that I had no idea my husband had expressed this thought to his bandmates.

"And now he's not showing up for rehearsal or answering phone calls," Lainey says, piecing together why not only Sophie should be worried, but we all should.

"He's fine," I say, wanting to calm any fears that he might be susceptible to self-harm. "I got a text from him this morning."

By the various looks of surprise, confusion, and curiosity I get from the ladies, I realize that my attempt to reassure them hasn't worked and I need to explain further.

"Eh, well, he left on his motorbike yesterday morning. He said he needed to take a few days to sort of recharge."

"Where did he go?" Sophie asks.

I wince. "I don't know. He didn't say and I didn't ask."

Another silence overtakes the group.

"That's a fair bit of trust, I'd say," Amelia offers, and I smile at her gratefully. She, out of all the women here, knows why I'd give him that leeway. She was a part of why I needed to run away to Portugal all those years ago, after all.

"Yeah, I don't think I'd be good with that," Jessica says with a laugh. "If Shay wanted to just leave and not tell me anything about it, I'd … well, I'd probably go a little crazy."

"He just needs a little space to get his head straight, is all," I say.

"So, you just assumed he'd tell Gavin and the guys his plan?" Sophie asks gently.

"Em, well, yeah. I did. I'm not his mother. He's fully capable of getting in touch—"

"But he didn't. And this comes right after saying he's not sure *the world needs another Rogue album.*"

"I don't know what that's all about, okay, Sophie? He hasn't said anything to me about it," I snap. "But I would think that the lads could give him a break, you know? He's struggling and he just needs a minute to himself. Is that so awful?"

"Of course not," Amelia says. "Everyone is entitled to work on themselves."

Sophie takes a breath, followed by a contemplative sip of her Cabernet. I watch as she looks at her mobile. "Do you know when he'll be back?" she asks, trying to sound casual.

I know her worry is not just for Conor, but for Gavin as well. Ever the caretaker, she'll want to manage this situation so that she can lessen the impact on her husband. She's always sought to be the one to navigate his emotions for him.

"No," I admit. "But I know for certain that he wouldn't miss this show. It means a lot to him. He'll be there." Whether he's rehearsed and prepared or not, I almost add but stop myself.

Sophie nods slowly, but I can see that her mind is at work. She's likely thinking through all the things that could go wrong, including what a disaster it would be if Conor didn't actually show up for his own band's twentieth anniversary gig.

Instead of verbalizing that, though, she says with sudden confidence, "I'm sure he will."

I'm grateful for this, especially because within our group,

if Sophie decrees something, everyone else follows along. She's much like her bandleader husband in that way, with a natural ability to engender trust and loyalty.

Now, I just need to convince myself that I believe Conor will return in time.

20

GAVIN

I disconnect my call with Sophie and stand still on the outskirts of our rehearsal space. We've used this old warehouse for so many years that it's practically a second home. But now that I know Conor won't be joining us, the space that is filled with a full-scale stage and all our equipment suddenly feels incomplete.

Closing my eyes, I let the dread I have been suppressing up until now wash over me. I've sensed there was something more than grief happening with Conor, but I hadn't wanted to confront him over it. I would have, though, had I known it wasn't just a general discontent he was grappling with but rather something more life-altering, like calling the band quits.

I'd shut that talk down pretty quickly at his birthday party and hadn't planned on revisiting it. The thought that we'd simply stop making albums is ridiculous. I assumed he would realize as much once he had a quiet moment to think about it. I certainly never thought he'd follow that bombshell by disappearing, especially not right before our big gig.

Opening my eyes, I see Shay and Martin where I'd left them on the stage. Randy, Conor's guitar tech, has been filling in while we've been killing time. At least, that's what we thought we were doing. Just waiting on a friend, as the song goes.

With no other choice, I approach the guys to let them know our Conor won't be making an appearance anytime soon.

Shay is the first to stop fiddling with his instrument. Martin sees Shay's reaction, stills his hands on his bass, and then looks at me. Randy, engrossed in trying his very best to match the effortless way Conor creates his riffs, is the last to trail off.

After a moment of heavy silence, I shrug. "He's not coming."

Standing, Shay makes his way to the edge of the stage. Martin is close behind him. I can feel the eyes of thirty-odd others on me. They're our tour team: sound engineers, our stage manager, lighting techs, roadies, production muscle, and our band manager. It takes a village to get our live act perfect, which is what our aim is for this special gig. But it also takes all four of us to make Rogue a success and we're lacking at the moment.

"What? Is he okay?" Shay asks.

"One of the kids feeling poorly?" Martin asks.

"Em, no." I see James sitting on a folding chair just beyond the beverage catering station, hunched over as he tries to balance his laptop on his knees and type while he holds his mobile to his ear. He's immersed in the details of our upcoming show, no doubt. Still, I find it odd that Felicity didn't reach out to him as soon as she knew Conor had gone. As it is now, he doesn't seem to have the first clue that our guitarist is missing in action.

"What's the craic, then?" Daniel asks, joining me with a slap to my back.

"Your mate won't be making it today," I tell him. "Felicity says he took off on his motorbike yesterday morning. Says he needed a couple days."

"What the fuck does that mean?" Daniel says.

"A couple days?" Shay asks at the same time.

I look to Martin with the expectation that he'll chime in but he's focused on some invisible middle distance, his forehead wrinkled in thought.

"I don't know," I say. "According to Sophie, Felicity couldn't really be arsed about the whole thing. Has no idea where he is or when he'll be back."

"So, the anniversary gig is off, then?" Daniel asks.

"No, Danny Boy," Shay says. "Don't go shooting off your big gob with declarations like that."

"I'm just saying, how do you plan to do this huge show when one of you is missing?"

"He's not missing," I say.

Daniel snorts a laugh. "Sure, right. It's just that no one knows where he is. That's what you're saying? What's the fucking difference, then?"

"You don't think," Martin says slowly and we all look at him, "he's with Donal, do you?"

"Donal?"

"He hasn't been home since yesterday morning either. I heard him getting his motorbike out but didn't think much of it. Same when he didn't come home. Figured he was out with his mate Owen. But now I'm wondering if the two of them—Conor and Donal—have gone off together."

"You're saying he took your kid to do some kind of joy riding thing on bikes?" Daniel asks.

"No, he's not saying that," Shay says. "It is interesting that they're both gone, though."

"Why don't you ring Donal?" I suggest.

"Yeah, sure."

We all watch and Martin retrieves his mobile and tries his son. It's clear almost immediately that the call goes unanswered. I turn away as he leaves a message, catching pieces of him asking about Conor and for a return call.

"Well, if they are together, where do you think they could be going?" Shay asks when Martin ends the call.

I glance at them and see Martin shaking his head.

"Dunno. Con mentioned that Donal has a girlfriend. Someone he met on bloody Instagram. But I don't know anything about her. If he's going to see her, I don't know why Con would go with him, though."

My mind is racing, trying to piece together what could be happening with Conor's mental state. Him leaving at this time, knowing full well that we've got the biggest concert of our lives on the line is so unlike him. He's never bailed on anything having to do with the band.

What if we've run our course? What if we've said all have to say?

Those were Conor's words. I'd dismissed them but now I have to wonder if I've failed my friend in doing so. I chose not to really hear him.

And now he's off god knows where.

Taking out my mobile, I tap out a text:

I've got a question

I wait, expecting Conor to reply quickly just as he's always done when one of us initiates this little ritual. He's supposed to reply back, *I've got an answer.*

But after several minutes without any indication that he's received the message or might respond, I give up waiting.

21

DONAL

The ride from Calais to Paris is a grueling five hours. I'm knackered from lack of sleep and navigating most of the way. At our last piss break before reaching the city, Conor had said he'd lead us from there. I assumed he had a shitty motel lined up for us but instead, we cruise down a one-way street crowded with an assortment of shops, most of which are in the process of closing their metal roll-up façades for the night.

"What's this about?" I ask, pulling my arms behind me to stretch my back. I've never ridden my motorbike this far or for this many hours in a row before, and it's not exactly an easy physical feat.

Conor, of course, appears unbothered by it. He pulls off his helmet and with one swipe of his hand, his hair looks perfect. Though he keeps his sunglasses on, I don't think I'd see an ounce of weariness in his eyes without them. That hangover seems long gone.

"I've heard about this shop. Looks like we've made it

before closing." He nods toward a storefront where dozens of guitars are displayed in the window.

"Seems a bad time to be buying a guitar," I say with a laugh and he looks at me with raised eyebrows. "I mean, can't exactly take it with us on the motorbikes."

"If you really wanted it, you could. If you really have the passion, you'll find a way."

I roll my eyes before I can stop myself. It's a bad habit, one my da has called me on many, many times. But Conor's lecturing me on passion and just wanting something bad enough as being the key to success hasn't exactly inspired me the way he obviously hopes it will. It's like I told him on the ferry earlier, me being Martin Whelan's son has set me up to fail before I can even try. I've got a fucking target on my back, so why should I come out into the clearing to make the shot all that much easier?

"Let's go," he says firmly and, I follow him silently.

Inside, one wall is lined in two rows with all manner of acoustic and electric guitars. An artfully stacked assortment of amps sits in the middle of the hardwood floors. A man with a long gray ponytail greets us in French.

To my surprise, Conor replies in the same language, the words rolling off his tongue smoothly. I studied enough French in school to get the gist of the exchange of pleasantries, but when they keep going back and forth, I lose the thread and step away, drawn toward the guitars.

I have my own guitars at home. They're good quality instruments. Better, in fact, than what I'm seeing here. There's a decent selection, but it seems to be focused on guitars for novices. That, or guitars for people without a budget. They are low-end Les Paul Epiphones, Ibanez, and Squiers. Their cheapness makes me long for my Fender. At the same time, I realize the fact that I learned guitar on my da's acoustic Martin is exactly why Conor says I'm spoilt. It's never really occurred to me before now that other kids would die for what I had handed to me without sacrifice or toil.

Still, I'm not sure what he could be looking for in a store like this. His guitars are of the highest caliber. I can't imagine he'd want anything here.

"Alain's going to bring out a guitar he has hidden in the back," Conor says as he approaches me.

"Oh, good. Because surely you want nothing to do with any of these," I say with a snicker.

He stares me down for a moment before looking at the display of acoustic guitars. Reaching out, he strums the strings of the aptly named Rogue Starter. The sound is tinny, hollow. It has to be the cheapest guitar in the shop.

I wince with exaggeration to show my distaste. This seems to spur him on, as he takes the guitar out of the metal display rack and holds it against his hips to play. But before he attempts a song, he tinkers with the tuning, working the strings until he's satisfied he'll get the best out of them.

And then he puts on a show, playing the driving opening chords of one of Rogue's earliest songs, "Day's Done." I won't say that he's made the cheap guitar suddenly sound expensive, but in his expert hands, the instrument breathes new life. His fingers work the fretboard flawlessly and his mastery is without question.

When he stops, I realize I've been leaning in toward him and have to catch my balance from falling forward.

"Your turn," he says, handing me the guitar.

I don't take it. "I, eh, I don't know that one."

"You just heard it."

"Well, I don't have a fucking photographic memory, do I?" I say with a laugh.

"Take the guitar and I'll walk you through it."

In truth, it's not that I don't know the song well enough to try it out, it's that I don't want to embarrass myself in front of Conor fucking Quinn of all people. I try to convey that in my gaze rather than say anything.

It doesn't seem to work because he tells me firmly, emphatically, "Give. No. Fucks."

There it is again, his suggestion that I can put all of my doubts aside and just … perform. The advice is easy enough to give. Especially coming from a guy like him. There's no way he's ever struggled with self-confidence. He's the epitome of *give no fucks*. And it's worked wonders for him. His cool, somewhat aloof, persona is legendary. There's a whole generation of musicians who want to *be* him. Hell, *I* want to be him.

But I'm not him. And giving no fucks is not going to change that.

Conor ignores my hesitation and pushes the guitar against me. I grab it as a reflex.

"Look at that," he says with a small smile, "you've already got your hands in the right position."

I look down and see that my fingers have aligned to the proper place to begin the song. Happy accident, I'm sure.

"Go ahead and give me the beginning bit," he says.

"Em," I mumble, not wanting to start and get it wrong. Not in front of him.

He leans toward me and says, "Stop fucking thinking and just feel. Feel the guitar in your hands. Feel the tension in the strings. Feel the power you have in making them sing the way you want."

That gets me and I nod. But when I take another second to

try to replay in my head "Day's Done" before starting, he reaches out and grabs the neck of the guitar, pulling it from me as if I've failed his test. Instinctively, I resist, taking control over it once more. Before he makes another attempt to strip me of the instrument, I launch into the song, my fingers flying while my mind checks out.

I don't think.

I just feel.

And in doing so, I manipulate the cheap guitar to my will, creating something to, if not rival my idol, then something that I can hold my head up high over.

"Keep going," Conor says, though I feel like I'm only partly aware of him now. I'm so engrossed in the notes that I don't even know where I am. "Right here, coming up," he continues. "I always hated the hook coming too soon here. Stretch it out. Just give me something that works here."

On pure instinct, I veer off into my own riff, playing off the framework he had originally crafted with this song to create a bridge before that hook. I get lost for a minute, just me and the guitar making a new version of the tune before I segue right back into the hook he had claimed came too soon. Before I know it, I've finished the entire thing, having somehow remembered every bit of how it goes, despite my lack of a photographic memory.

Though I hadn't moved much, I'm left struggling to catch my breath.

It's the thrill.

The unexpected, sweet thrill of having become one with the music in those three and a half minutes of playing. And knowing that I found a way to *give no fucks*.

"*Le garçon a du talent, non?*"

We both turn to see that the shop owner has been watching us from a distance.

"*Oui, exactement*," Conor replies before turning his eyes to me. "The boy has talent."

The smile that spreads across my face is so wide it hurts. It's the best feeling in the world.

I'm barely aware of Conor and the shop owner speaking in French with each other once again, as I'm too preoccupied by what just happened, by the fact that Conor declared that I have *talent*.

"Take a look at this," Conor says, pulling me from my thoughts.

I look up and see he's got a guitar in his hands that bears no resemblance to the cheap models on the floor.

"Alain made it," Conor tells me. "His talent for handcrafted guitars is why we're here. This is a semi-hollow, modeled after a Telecaster but with some of his own deviations."

It's a beautiful guitar, that's for sure. The body is maple and inlaid mother of pearl and has a vintage look about it. Conor runs his fingers over the neck and tells me the fingerboard is made of rosewood and the saddles are titanium.

"Give it a feel," he says.

I return the generic acoustic guitar I'd still been holding to its display and take the handmade guitar. It's surprisingly light. Or I guess not so surprising since it's partly hollow. In any case, it feels like a dream in my hands. The quality is unmistakable, I know that much before I even pluck at the strings.

Alain says something in French that I understand well enough to mean he's giving me permission to plug into an amp so I can try out the guitar. The light hum of electricity once I'm connected is a delicious kind of anticipation that I savor.

"What shall I play?" I ask.

"Whatever comes to you," Conor says. "Whatever this guitar speaks to you."

I smile at that, holding back a laugh. No guitar has ever "spoken" to me. I've only ever had a love-hate relationship with the instrument. I love it for what I *want* to be able to create. And I hate it for rarely being able to actually get the right notes out. As much as I love music and the guitar, I've never felt particularly gifted. It's always felt like a struggle to make what I hear in my head become a reality. That frustration, along with my hesitation to offer myself up for ridicule, has held me back.

With all this swirling in my head, I feel my hands start to move, creating a delicate introduction before opening into the harsher main thrust of the song. Once more, I find that perfect feeling of not overthinking. Of just playing.

Of *giving no fucks*.

When I finish, I've got the same sense of riding a high like no other as I did earlier. No alcohol, no drug has ever made me feel like this. *This* is what unleashing creativity and passion feels like. *This* is working my art.

And fuck, it feels good.

"What a song to pick," Conor says.

I shrug that off. "Eh, just one I like to rage with."

He raises his eyebrows. "'The Pretender' by Foo Fighters. I'd say it's a good fucking anthem for you right about now."

I think about that, about how the lyrics aren't about self-doubt and worrying about being a fake, or pretender, but rather pushing away that idea and insisting those trying to keep you down or box you in are the pretenders. I don't think

I'd consciously considered the lyrics, at least not for this particular moment. But the idea must have been there, pushing me to embrace the possibility that I could do something with music if I flip the script and understand that anyone who might dismiss me just because I'm Martin Whelan's son is the pretender, not me.

Nodding, I can't help but smile.

"You want to give it a go?" I ask, ready to hand over the guitar. "She's a real beauty."

He doesn't take it. Instead, he says, "You just created something special on that guitar."

I shrug. "Yeah, it felt good."

"She's yours, Donal."

"What?"

"I'm going to buy it for you because what you just showed me is too special to walk away from. But it's not completely free. You'll pay me back one day, yeah?"

"Yeah, I can have my da—"

"No," he interrupts. "*You'll* pay me back. With money *you've* earned. I don't care how long it takes. Just don't forget what you owe."

"Oh, yeah. I can do that. Sure."

"That is, if you can be bothered to carry the guitar around with us?"

"Yes, of course," I say quickly. "Sure, I don't mind at all. I'll strap it to my back, it's fine."

I swear that when he smiles then, his blue eyes actually *twinkle* in amusement and satisfaction. If fronting me a handmade guitar that sounds as fantastic as this one does makes him happy, then I'm all for it. The fact that I'm getting a one of a kind instrument to make my own music on is a pretty fucking awesome bonus.

22

CONOR

The two-bedroom flat we have for the night is an improvement from our place in Lambeth. Alain, the guitar shop owner, set us up. It's his friend's place that he lets out as an Airbnb, so it comes well-stocked with all the amenities you'd want, even if it isn't the five-star luxury hotel Donal longs for.

I, of course, take the master bedroom with the en suite. The shower here is immaculate and I stand for far longer than I should under the spray of the hot water, letting it soak me through as I think.

I'd checked my messages before stripping down for the shower.

There were dozens of texts but one stood out. It was from Gavin.

I've got a question

That entreaty is the start to one of the rituals of our friendship, something we've used for over thirty years now.

But the instinct to give him the usual *I've got an answer* reply had deserted me.

Rather than leave him hanging for longer than I already had, though, I replied with brutal honesty.

I have no fucking answers at the moment

It was the first time I'd ever responded that way and I immediately regretted it. But it was just the simple truth. I have no answers. No answers for him and no answers for me.

My voicemail box was also full. Calls from Gavin. Calls from Shay. Calls from Martin. Calls from James. Calls from my guitar tech, Randy.

No calls from Felicity.

If I didn't know better, I'd say her silence was out of spite for me having left this way. But I do know her. I know she trusts me. She trusts me to sort myself.

I've left all those voicemails untouched. I don't need to listen to them to know what they say. They'll all ask some variation of *When are you coming back?*

It's a valid question, one they all have every right to have answered. But I just don't have it in me right now to get into a conversation. Because that's what it would be. It wouldn't stop at *when are you coming back?* There would be an onslaught of other questions demanding to know why I've taken leave of my senses and done something so rash as to disappear at this moment. And more importantly, there would be questions asking if this means I want to leave the band.

I know it was shitty to throw that possibility out there and run, but now that I have, I just need some space to think it through.

Thing is, even though I know I should be thinking it all

through, I don't really want to right now. I need to just empty my mind of everything, that includes what the immediate future of the band looks like. Not fair to the lads, but ... fuck it. This is what I need.

Leaning against the tile wall, I close my eyes and focus on the way the water is beating against my chest. I find myself homing in on the way the water slaps my skin with a staccato rhythm. After another moment, I've conjured up a melody in my head to go with it. It's a bit chaotic, a bit scattered, but there's something about it that works.

The burst of inspiration makes me smile. It's like seeing an old friend after a long period apart and being welcomed with open arms. The kind of friendship where you can pick right up where you left off, no matter how much time has passed.

A flash of Felicity comes into my mind's eye. It's the photo she sent this morning at the same time that I was suffering from the worst hangover I've had in years. Was that only this morning?

I should have told her about the tattoo. Glancing at my shoulder, I'm still surprised at the fact that I've got ink there under a clear, waterproof bandage. What will she think? She'll likely give me one of her amused smiles and shrug it off.

But, what if she has a different reaction? What if she's fascinated by what's behind the markings? What if she traces it with her delicate fingers, leans down to cover the tender skin with soft kisses, maybe even the flicker of her tongue? And then she unbuttons the shirt she's wearing and I see she's got nothing on under it. Her breasts are a perfect handful, but she doesn't let me take them into my grasp. Instead, she grazes the dark pink point of one nipple over the tattoo as I watch.

Yes, I like this version. I fist my cock as I elaborate on this fantasy.

I'M STARVING by the time I've dressed and found Donal on the sofa with his fingers flying over the keys of his mobile.

"Let's get some dinner, yeah?"

At the mention of food, Donal's head snaps up. "Oh, thank God. I could eat my right arm about now, I'm so fucking hungry."

I laugh. "Can't have that." With a nod of my head, I indicate the door and we're soon out on the streets of Paris.

The flat isn't in the most fashionable area. In fact, it's not really near any major hub. The quiet neighborhood was quaint when we arrived after a long day on the bikes, but now I'm up for more action. I'm ready for food followed by another night of checking out with the help of some alcohol.

With that in mind, I summon a taxi to take us to the heart of the city.

"Where we headed, then?" Donal asks when we're underway.

"Not sure. Do you like Moroccan food?"

He groans. "Anything but that. Let's just have a nice juicy steak and potatoes. Something normal."

"Oh, Donal," I say with a sigh. "Remember you're meant to be broadening your horizons?"

He sinks back against the seat in defeat and I quiz our driver on where we might find an authentic Moroccan restaurant. He tells me there are quite a few but we narrow down the options when I tell him I'm not looking for fine dining. We end up at a place that our driver says is as much known for its good food as its boisterous entertainment.

In what I take as a good sign, the place is spilling over with people waiting for a table. I tell the maître d that we're happy to wait in the bar but there's a spark of recognition in his eyes, and we're soon ushered to a booth that is too large for just us. It's just been bussed, and we wait while an older man swiftly resets it for us.

This gives us a moment to look around and take in everything going on around us. It's a feast for the senses, with the scent of aromatic food thick in the air, several large groups talking and laughing, piped-in music sung in Arabic, and a man in a puffy white shirt and a maroon fez hat dancing between tables.

"S'il vous plait, s'il vous plait," the older man says and waves at our table, urging us to sit.

I'm still distracted by everything going on around us when our harried, but smiling, waiter serves us complimentary bowls of olives and pistachios. Both his rapid-fire French and the cacophony of dining room noises has me struggling to follow along with his greeting, however. Thankfully, he senses as much and switches to English.

"I am Emir and am pleased to serve you. We are so happy to have you join us," he says, his English remarkably accentless. "You have chosen a wonderful night to be here, in fact, as we have a special performance coming later tonight that I am positive you gentlemen will appreciate. Now, what may I start you with? Can I offer you some delightful sweet mint tea? Or perhaps a lager beer? Maybe a stronger temptation from our full bar?"

"I can see we are in expert hands with you, my friend," I say, impressed with his flawless introduction.

"I certainly hope so. I have been working at this restaurant for sixteen years."

"Say no more, Emir. The only request I have is for that lager you mentioned. We'll each take a pint of that. Beyond that, we are hoping for as authentic of an experience as possible and trust your recommendations."

Emir smiles and his eyes light up in a new way. He had gone through his speech smoothly, but it was by rote. Now, the glimmer in his eye suggests I've just earned a more personal experience. "It would be my pleasure. But, I have to ask if there are any restrictions? Anything you won't or cannot eat?"

Before Donal can chime in to ask whether they offer hamburgers, I assure Emir that we are open to whatever he will bring us. "All I ask," I say, "is that you make it plentiful. We are very hungry men."

He nods soberly. "*Absolument.*"

"I sincerely hope he's not about to bring something I can't stomach," Donal says once Emir has left us. "I'd hate to disappoint the man."

"You'll be fine. It's a lot about the spices, not really about mystery meat."

He tosses a handful of pistachios into his mouth and chews while looking around at the place. The tables are set close together, and with a full house, the ventilation system is fighting a losing battle. I take off my leather jacket and push up my sleeves.

"What did your da say about you being on this trip?" I ask.

I know something is up when he stops chewing for a second and winces. He does a good job of quickly replacing that reaction with something neutral, but I've already seen the truth. I wait to see if he'll share it or lie to me.

"I haven't actually talked to him," he says.

I can tell that this is the truth, but not the whole truth.

Instead of interrogating him on the subject, I just stare at him until he breaks down and tells me more. Unfortunately, he chooses to lie with this part.

"Well, you, eh, you said you didn't want anyone to know where we were, right? You said it would be easier if the media didn't know, so, I, eh, I thought it better to just go along with that and lay low."

I'm about to call him out on this bullshit rationalization when Emir returns with two pints of Casablanca beer, *harira* soup, and savory chicken *briouats.* Emir explains that our soup is a vegetarian version with a tomato base, chickpeas, lentils, and vegetables. The *briouats* are small triangles of paper-thin pastry sheets filled with minced chicken cooked with saffron, ginger, and cinnamon.

I thank Emir and ask him for refills on our lagers while Donal goes right to the *briouats*, scarfing down three of them in quick succession.

As hungry as I am, I'm more interested in sorting out the truth from Donal than eating.

"I need you to level with me on why you won't talk to your father," I say.

The spoonful of *harira* he was about to slurp up freezes in mid-air, and I can see his mind at work.

"I'm serious. Don't fuck around. You're technically a minor, still. And I just took you out of Ireland on a whim. I could actually get into trouble for that, especially if Martin doesn't know where you are."

He drops the spoon back into his bowl and droplets of the red soup splash up before falling onto the white tablecloth. It strikes me as a petulant move, one that highlights how young he still is.

"I just, I can't talk to him."

I shake my head. "I don't understand. What's the problem? He's your da."

He rolls his eyes at that and I lose my patience. "Did you row? Is there something between you, then?"

"No, it's not that. It's just, I mean, he doesn't get me."

I'm tempted to roll *my* eyes at that. "Who the fuck cares if he doesn't *get* you? He's your da. What more do you need?"

I don't get an answer. Instead, Donal just shakes his head and looks away from me, focusing on one of the large groups sitting in an alcove. They've all donned fez hats and are laughing, taking photos, and generally making a spectacle of themselves. It might seem tacky were it not for the fact that this restaurant seems to have offered up the hats to the group as part of whatever party package they've engaged.

Without some bigger explanation for why Donal won't even tell his father that he's away and safe, I grow frustrated. This kid has had it good all his life. Sure, he dealt with some bullies, but, all in all, he's had it made. His father would do anything for him, but all he gets in return is shunned. I should write it off as a typical moody teenager attempt at rebellion. But my own father comes to mind and I think of all the years I wasted not being around. Yes, I was on tour a lot of that time, but I have to admit that there were far too many times when I was home and let the time slip by without seeing him. That guilt could be why I spent the last six months of his life by his side as he withered away. Regardless, it was time well spent. In those last few months, I got to care for the man I've always respected, the man who always supported me.

It's with this in mind that I tell Donal, "You'd do well to understand your responsibilities. You can't act the kid anymore, not at your age. It's time to grow up." I almost add, *time to appreciate the father you have. Before it's too late.* But I stop, reminding myself that his situation with his father is not the same as mine.

When he levels his eyes on me, I see resentment there. It's the first time I've ever been on the receiving end of that. I've seen that look directed at Martin plenty of times in the last year or two, but never at me.

"Let me ask you a question," he says, leaning over the table toward me, "Why haven't *you* bothered to get in touch with my da?" He doesn't give me time to reply. "Never mind. It's obvious you're avoiding *your* responsibilities, yeah? That was clear enough anyway in the message he left asking me to have you call him, if in fact, we were together." He sits back and shakes his head. "His concern was for where *you* were. Not me."

I find that hard to believe, but I can see that he's not up for an argument about it. He's got triggers when it comes to Martin. They're things that I not only can't solve, but likely have no right to meddle in to begin with.

"This whole thing," he continues, "about you getting me out of my 'Dublin bubble,' that was all bullshit, right? I mean, you were really just looking for some way to run away, weren't you? Using me as an excuse to not even tell your bandmates you want out?"

"Wait a second—"

"Well, it fucking sucks. I thought you were more of a man than that."

I open my mouth to tell him none of that is true. My instinct is to lie to him, to defend myself. But I can't do it. He deserves the truth from me, even if that honesty means I have to confess to something I'm not proud of.

"Listen," I say, "I know you don't want to see me as anything other than this idol you've always built me up as. But

I'm not that. I haven't been … right since my father died." I hesitate to reveal more. Truth is, I don't want to admit all of this out loud. Doing so somehow feels like I'm giving up any last shred of control I've got. But I've got the nagging sense that acknowledging how I've really been feeling is what I finally need to do. So, I take a deep breath and continue. "I've been broken and unmoored by it. It's made me question everything about my life, including the point of continuing with the band. And yes, when you told me about going to Spain for your birthday, I latched onto that and made it into my own escape. Not being up-front about that wasn't fair to you. But I honestly really also wanted all these new experiences for you. I think you're a fantastic kid. I should say fantastic *man*, really. You have so much potential, but I saw you content to just live your privileged party life and it disappointed me. I wanted to find a way to shake you out of it. And if I could do so while also shaking myself out of my own depression, then all the better. I'm sorry, though, that you're disappointed now by the reality of it all. I can arrange to get your bike back to Dublin if you want to go ahead and get a flight to Spain from here."

He had been listening intently, but that last part wasn't what he was expecting. His eyes widen and his mouth drops open a little. The out I gave him doesn't exactly seem to be welcome.

"It's okay," I say. "I won't be offended. But I'll tell you, I've had a hell of a time. You are a great travel partner. But more than anything, you've allowed me to get outside of myself. I've been in my own head for too long, unable to break free. But being on the road with you, well, it's been grand. I appreciate it, Donal."

"And here we are with a lovely lamb tagine," Emir says,

joining us before Donal can reply. He's wielding a tray full of dishes, all in colorful clay crockery. "A nice chickpea stew to go with the braised beef couscous. A shrimp pil-pil. It's a little spicy, yes. Of course, we also have eggplant *zaalouk* and baba ganoush. I also took the liberty of bringing you each another lager, but I am happy to return it to the bar if you have had enough." With that, his tray is empty and he surveys our full table with a pleased smile and a sigh.

"This looks incredible, Emir. Thanks so much." Now I really am famished, having not touched our appetizers earlier.

"You are most welcome," he replies and soon leaves us.

Lifting the lid on the tagine dish, I'm rewarded with the most incredible aroma. I take a huge helping for myself and start to move on to the other dishes when Donal speaks.

"I didn't know you were depressed."

I glance at him, see the concern in his eyes, and then return to focusing on filling my plate.

"I mean, I knew with your da passing, you were a bit off, but I didn't realize—"

"There was no reason for you to be aware of the depths of it," I say, still not looking at him. "It's not your concern. And I shouldn't have dragged you into my problems."

"But you haven't, have you? You haven't shared a word about what you've been dealing with."

"I think you'll understand that means I don't want to talk about it, yeah?"

He's quiet for a minute, and I use the time to dig into my food. It's heavenly. Full of a beautiful blend of cinnamon, cumin, turmeric, ginger, paprika, coriander, saffron, fennel, as well as a list of others I can't quite pinpoint. All I know is that it is the delicious, comforting meal I was hoping for when Moroccan food came to mind in the taxi.

"So, you're saying," Donal continues, "that by being out on the road with me and *not* talking about your troubles, you're feeling better?"

I think about that and then nod. "Pretty much. But I'm also saying you are absolutely under no fucking obligation to stick it out with me for that reason."

"Obligation?"

Now I meet his eyes. "You're a good kid. I know you want to please me, that my approval is something you crave. But it's time to get over that."

"I—"

"Be your own man. Don't look to me. I'm the past. You're the future. This is your time. *I* know you have what it takes. *You* just need to own it."

His eyes dart around the restaurant once more as he seems to struggle to process all of this. I get back to the food, devouring a huge serving of the shrimp.

"No."

The word was said so softly that I almost didn't catch it, but then Donal repeats himself with more force.

"No?" I ask, eyebrows raised.

"No, you don't get to bail. No, you don't get to put an end to this adventure you promised me. No, it's not over."

"You're not just saying that—"

"And *no*, I'm not saying this to keep on with you out of some sort of duty or concern for you. You may have had some troubles, but you're still Conor fucking Quinn, and I know you'll sort yourself. In the meantime, we've got a journey to continue. So, that's exactly what we're going to do."

He nods with a kind of confidence I haven't seen from him

before. The gesture has a familiarity about it, though. After a moment, I realize that it's the same sort of way I tend to nod when I want to emphasize something, when I'm indicating that my say-so on a particular topic is final. Seeing him adopt that makes me smile because I realize I'm watching this kid grow up with my own eyes. He may have taken on one of my mannerisms, but the sentiment behind it isn't plagiarized—it's all him.

And that's exactly the kind of confidence he needs to lead a band.

23

CONOR

With the future of our road trip settled, we're free to indulge in our incredible meal, while washing it down with pint after pint. This is a different kind of drunkenness than last night where I lost control. Sticking to beer is probably a wise strategy as I'm content to just sit back and relax rather than tempted to make irreversible changes to my body.

It helps that I've got my eye on someone else's body. About ten minutes ago, a live performance began. A trio of dancers spread out across the restaurant as a full band of nine musicians set up in an alcove. The leader of the group made an announcement in French briefly explaining that the musicians would play a variation of Moroccan Berber music with instruments that included hand-held drums, guitars, violins, a flute, and *qraqeb*, a type of metallic castanets.

Once they began playing, the already festive atmosphere of the dining room became outright rambunctious. Turns out I wasn't the only one overdoing the alcohol. But it all still feels good-humored.

One of the dancers is a shirtless man in low-slung baggy white trousers with a gold braid belt. He soon works up a sweat with his athletic moves, earning howls of delight from an all-woman table to our left. The other two dancers are belly dancers, both dark-haired, with one wearing a ruby-red bikini top and skirt and the other wearing a matching turquoise ensemble. She's the one I can't take my eyes off.

"She's fit, yeah?" Donal says with a nudge.

Glancing at him, I see that he has his eyes fixed on the other belly dancer. They're both striking, with gorgeous bodies and incredible control of their hips and abdomens. But there's something about my dancer that keeps drawing me back. The fact that she keeps flicking her eyes to meet mine doesn't help to break the spell. Her eyes are dark pools with flecks of gold. Her lips are a crimson Mona Lisa smile. She raises her toned, elegant arms aloft while undulating her torso to devastatingly sexy effect. She's … mesmerizing.

There's no way I can deny the intense attraction I feel for her when she glides in front of our booth and gives me a private show. My eyes lock onto hers. But only briefly, because I can't keep from letting my gaze fall down her body as she moves with incredible fluidity. It's the kind of skill that would translate fantastically into bed. She's the kind of woman who can spark a thousand fantasies.

Before I can get too lost in this thought, she gives me a barely imperceptible wink and moves on.

"Fuck me," I murmur.

"Yeah, I think I like this whole Moroccan thing," Donal says with a grin.

I laugh and shake my head. "Another drink and then we'll go?"

"Eh, yeah, if that's what you want."

The reluctance in his voice makes me raise my eyebrows. "Neither of us are in a position to be looking for anything more than what we've already gotten here. That is, if this thing of yours with Valentina is real."

"It is," he insists quickly.

"Okay, then. We'll be on our way soon enough."

He considers that. "Well, no harm in enjoying the view in the meantime, yeah?"

"No, no harm in that," I agree as I get up from the table. "Be back in a minute. Off to the jacks."

He nods, but he's already set his eyes back on the dancer he fancies.

I catch Emir as he's on his way to deliver a heavy tray of food to another table and he directs me to the toilets. They're at the back of the restaurant, down a quiet, dimly lit hallway. It takes a moment for my senses to adjust to the lack of discordant sound and colorful decor, but when I do, I realize that there is a couple rowing halfway down the corridor.

It's my dancer. But it doesn't look like a lovers' quarrel. It looks much more like a drunk restaurant patron has her cornered and is pawing at her hips, imploring her in French to give them a shake just for him. He's not much taller than her, with a protruding gut and balding hair pulled back into a tiny ponytail. My dancer looks repulsed and frustrated. Her eyes find mine just as I close in, grabbing the guy by his pathetic hair so that he stumbles backward and away from her.

I get a stream of curses from him before he looks up to see me looming over him.

"The lady does not want your company," I tell him in French.

He speaks so rapidly in return, his voice full of venom, that

I can't quite keep up. It doesn't matter. All I need to do to scare him off is a fake lunge with a slightly raised fist. I have no intention of hitting him, but I know that's not what it looks like, especially when he reacts by scampering away with his hands up in surrender.

"*Comment ça sava?*" I ask her.

"Fine," she replies.

"You speak English?"

"Not well, but enough, I think."

"That happen often?" I nod toward the opposite end of the hallway where the ponytail guy ran off.

She shrugs. "Sometimes."

We lock eyes and there's no doubt that the attraction I feel for her is mutual. It's like there's an invisible electric current connecting us and we each lean in, unable to resist the pull.

"Thank you for, eh, coming to my rescue," she says.

"It was nothing."

"It was something, for certain." She smiles and then laughs. "Did you see his face when you moved to strike him? He looked like a frightened little mouse."

"Funny how bullies can be easily intimidated. Just have to stand up to them in a way they understand."

She bites the corner of her lower lip before taking a moment to adjust, first, her bikini top, and then her skirt, though neither of them was out of place. We both know her effort was designed to draw my attention to her luscious figure. It worked like a charm.

"You're a fantastic dancer," I say, even as I know I should say goodnight and walk away.

"You're a fantastic guitarist," she replies.

I raise my eyebrows and give her a small smile. "So, you must know my name?"

"*Oui.* Conor Quinn."

"And you are?"

"Fatima."

"Fatima," I repeat, trying it out and liking the way it feels on my tongue. "What does your name mean?"

She blushes and turns her eyes down. It gives me another chance to take her in. To devour her with my gaze. Her eyelashes are dark and thick. Her olive skin is smooth, especially at the swell of her bikini enhanced breasts. Her belly is slightly, pleasantly, rounded. Her skirt hugs shapely hips. Her reticence is at odds with the way she had just flirted with me. I'm not ready to be done with our back and forth.

"Tell me."

Something in my voice brings her eyes back to mine. Maybe it's the way I dropped it an octave without even thinking about it, the instinct to seduce coming naturally.

"*Captivante,*" she says softly.

I smile. "Perfectly suits you. I thought you were captivating the moment I saw you out there."

"I saw you watching me with such … what is the word? Longing?"

I cringe at that. I'm usually good at keeping control over my emotions but must have lost it earlier. That loss of control bothers me as much as the fact that she probably sees me as just another restaurant diner coming on to her.

"Sorry about that. There's no doubt you're beautiful, but I don't want to be another one of the men bothering you."

Smiling apologetically, I start to move away, but she puts her hand on my forearm, and I freeze. "I get off work at eleven if you want to get a drink?"

When I hesitate, she adds, "I would like to be bothered by you, I think."

All the ways I could *bother* this sexy young woman flash in my head. It would be one of those nights when there's no sleep, just overwhelming lust satisfied and renewed over and over again. I haven't had one of those nights in a very long time. I can imagine lying shirtless on her bed, watching her dance just for me. I can imagine her turning her moves into a striptease as she releases the catch on her bra and wiggles her way out of her skirt, revealing smooth, taut skin. I can imagine her on top, her hips gyrating against mine.

And yet, the imagining of it is enough. I don't have any desire to make it a reality, proving, at last, that there appears to be a limit to what I'll do as a part of this mid-life crisis I seem to be indulging. What I've known for years has just been reaffirmed in this brief little encounter: the only woman I want with my body and soul is Felicity.

Fatima must sense my impending rejection of her offer because she looks away. "My mistake. *Je suis désolée.*"

Now it's she who starts to turn away. I stop her by taking her hand into both of mine. "There was no mistake, Fatima. No need to be sorry. Thing is, I'm just not available." I look down at the wedding band on my left hand and she follows suit, understanding that I'm married, but she'll never understand the depths of my commitment to my wife. It goes far beyond a wedding band. It goes to the ends of the earth and to my dying breath.

"In another life, *oui?*" she says with that Mona Lisa smile.

"*Oui.*" I kiss the back of her hand, intending to leave it at that.

But she leans forward and goes up on her toes to kiss me on either cheek. Her lips linger with each kiss and I could swear she's inhaling my scent before she pulls away.

I watch her hips appreciatively as she goes down the hall.

Just then, my mobile buzzes, and I grab it automatically, guiltily, thinking it must be Felicity. That she must have sensed I was playing too close to the line.

But when I see that it's a text from Gavin, I relax. Until I realize I have no way out from answering him this time, that is, because he's come back at me, saying: *I still have a question.*

I grimace, but know I need to text back with the usual expected reply, *I have an answer.*

Gavin's next words don't take long to pop up, which indicates his sense of urgency with the question, *Where the fuck are you?*

It's an easy enough question to answer. I could reply "Paris" and feel I've fulfilled my obligation to be forthcoming. But I hesitate to type that because the true answer of where I am, of where my head is, is still evolving. I'd taken on this adventure with Donal to get away, to escape the relentless sadness I couldn't seem to shake. But there has become a bigger purpose to it, something that's about more than just me and my problems. This trip has become something I'm still sorting out, but I think it now has a lot to do with helping Donal not just get out of his Dublin bubble, but really become the man—and the musician—he's meant to be.

With that in mind, I text back: *On a journey*

Just as I'm about to return my mobile back to my pocket, it buzzes again.

Do I need to be worried about you?

I don't hesitate to reply: *No*

I wait a minute to see what the three lightly pulsing dots indicating Gavin is writing back will turn into.

Journey your arse home soon, yeah?

I laugh and type, *Yeah*

24

FELICITY

I'd fall at your feet if I was there
Caress your alabaster thighs
Stroke your hips, breasts, and hair
Take your lips with mine, make you sigh

IT'S ALMOST two in the morning when those words appear in a text from Conor. Just like last time, they seem to be lyrics of a song. Nothing about where he is. No inquiries about the kids. No sending his love.

Still, he's making it clear he's thinking of me, and this time it's not about how I'd taken care of him when his father passed, but rather how he'd like to take care of me—at least in an intimate way.

I should go back to sleep. The kids will be up early and I'll have my hands full with them before I need to get to work. The preparations for the anniversary gig have gone ahead unabated. When James learned that Conor wouldn't be showing up for rehearsals, his face turned the same shade of red as his hair. He was furious at being the last to know and I don't blame him. I was in an awkward position with wanting Conor to have the chance to get away for his own sake while also knowing how much he was needed here. I chose my loyalty to my husband over my loyalty to my job. I did my best to convince James that the reason I'd done that was because I *know* my husband. I *know* he will be back in time for the gig.

He wasn't truly convinced until just a few hours ago when I called him with word that Gavin had gotten a response from Conor. Sophie, of course, relayed the information to me. It seems all Conor would tell his good friend is that he is on a "journey" and that there was no need to worry. That was enough for Gavin, and so it was enough for James. Or, at least, it lessened his anxiety a notch. James doesn't know how to exist without being in a constant state of stress. It fuels him and is likely what makes him a damn good manager.

Though I'd wished to have some communication with Conor myself, I went to bed feeling better knowing he'd responded to Gavin. That desire to hear from him must have put me on alert for his text. There was no way I'd sleep through whatever message he might send this time.

But now I'm not sure what to make of the sexually suggestive lyrics. I suppose there is the chance that, wherever he is, he's meeting women and finding opportunities to flirt ... or more. He's always been an outrageous flirt. It's a trait he got from his father, this ability to charm the wool off a sheep.

That, combined with his drop-dead good looks, and most women don't stand a chance. I surely never did.

If that's the case, anyway, and his response is to text me this, then I'm okay with it. His flirting with other women never really bothered me. Well, I did worry a tad back at the beginning of our relationship when he almost immediately left on tour after we'd gotten together. But I soon learned who he is, that his commitment to me runs deep. Along the way, I also came to understand that the way he flirts with other women is really about playing a game to him. He loves getting a response, loves the thrill of knowing he *could* have that woman in his bed if he wanted.

It occurs to me in thinking about this now that his legendary flirting hasn't been nearly at the same level as it once was for quite some time. At least, not so that I can see it. I can't pinpoint when it changed, but it makes me wonder what caused it. I never said a word about it. In fact, it's always sort of amused me to see him work his charms on women I know he'll never be with. That need he has to flirt is just a harmless way to boost his own ego.

I don't know that he'd admit to that, though, since he takes pride in his ability to woo. With that in mind, I text him back and keep it light: *I miss you too, loverboy.*

Before I can put my mobile down and settle back into bed, he texts a reply. It seems he isn't bothered by my flippant tone. In fact, it seems to have been the exact right response, because he tells me: *I love you so fucking much*

I can almost hear the tone of his voice as I read his words, the sexy, insistent, commanding way he has that still thrills me.

Even by text.

25

DANNY BOY

It's just past ten when Roscoe and I return to the house from our walk. Though, "walk" is putting it generously, I'd say. My old Roscoe isn't the pup he once was. He's getting on in years and it just about kills me anytime I give over to thinking his time is waning. So, mostly I don't allow myself to think about it.

The kids are at their summer day camp and Amelia is at work getting ready for the school year to start up, so it's quiet. I always get antsy when it's quiet like this. I'd much rather have them here with me, but Amelia is convinced that the artsy-fartsy camp where Gavin and Conor's kids also go is the best thing for them, even if I'd rather have the boys running me ragged and making trouble here at home. That's the compromise of a relationship, I suppose.

It's been almost six years that I've been with Amelia and just about every day still feels like I'm figuring it out as I go. I may be older, but the wiser part that is supposed to go along with that hasn't caught up. Not that my Amelia minds. She's my saving grace and has been since the day I sat my arse down in her hideously green-walled office.

I'm due at Rogue's rehearsal space in an hour, giving me enough time to sit at the kitchen table with a cuppa and a toasted cheese sandwich with Roscoe at my feet. I have the morning's paper in front of me but none of the news stories grabs my attention.

Thank God for Google alerts to ease the boredom because I get a notification on my mobile that gives me something quite entertaining indeed. Seems our wayward Conor Quinn has been spotted in multiple locations over the last little while: Liverpool, Lambeth, SoHo, and Paris. In each stop, he picked up a souvenir: a Beatles nostalgia tour and selfies with a starry-eyed waitress in Liverpool; a fight with a young no-name band in Lambeth while smashed out of his mind on vodka; a beauty of a tattoo on his shoulder in SoHo; and a candid photo of him standing very close to a gorgeous belly dancer in a dark hallway in Paris.

Shaking my head, I laugh out loud. It's been quite some time since one of the lads caused a media stir like this. Sure, they still get tabloids reporting on the most banal aspects of their day-to-day, but the scandal has long since drained out of their lives. Now, Mr. Perfect is back at it with generating headlines.

I don't know what I'm most impressed with—the fight or the tattoo. Both are out of character, so it's hard to decide.

Opening up my text option, I type: *Still some of the rogue in ya, innit there?*

Not that I expect Conor to answer because he hasn't replied to any of my other messages. Still, I get a kick out of sticking it to him, just as I always have.

. . .

Gavin, Shay, and Marty are huddled together when I get to the warehouse rehearsal space, no doubt talking about Conor's exploits.

"Well," I say as I join them, "now we know where he is. At least where he was for a time."

"It would seem so, Danny Boy," Shay says.

"Who would have thought that fella'd get a tattoo?"

"Had to ring Tito when I saw that," Marty says. "Mind, he wasn't the one who shared the photo and was upset that his assistant did, but still. He says Con came in reeking of booze, demanding a tattoo so that he could fulfill an agreement he made with my Donal."

"What sort of agreement was that?" I ask.

Marty shakes his head in dismay. "The kid promised to have his piercings removed if Con got a tattoo."

"What piercings? I don't remember him having any."

"You wouldn't, would you? He had his dick pierced, of all things."

With that revelation, I burst out laughing and can't stop for the life of me. The others laugh with me, but I really can't handle the absurdity of it. My eyes water as I double over, laughing harder than I have in a long time.

At length, Gavin says, "Anyway, I had a text with him last night. He's fine."

"I bet he is," I reply, wiping the tears from my eyes. "By the looks of it, he's got some fine company with that belly dancer."

"He's not fucking around, and don't be suggesting otherwise," Gavin says quick, looking ready to murder me over the mere suggestion that Conor could be cheating. As if it's somehow out of bounds. These guys like to pretend the past never happened.

Before I can say as much, Shay levels his hard stare at me and says, "Enough gossip. Let's get to work."

"Work," I scoff. "Yeah, I'll get to work on lighting an empty spot where Conor would be."

"He's not fucking gone for good," Shay says. "Now, shut your gob and get on with it."

"Lighten up, lads. You all need a sense of humor about yourselves. You're always so serious and quick to close ranks when it's to do with one of you."

"Yeah, well," Gavin says, "you can count yourself lucky that you're included in that scenario, too. In fact, you can thank Conor for it. If he hadn't given you a second and third *and* fourth chance back in the day, you wouldn't be here to be making a joke out of it all."

I consider that for a moment. "Can't argue, I suppose."

Gavin slaps me on the back a couple times. It's his way of moving on from the sharpness of his last comment. I have no room to do anything but accept the gesture. These guys are my mates. They've let me off the hook more times than I care to admit, so me letting this one go is a no-brainer.

"Aye, I've got an idea," I say as everyone starts to break up. They stop and look at me. "How about if I put Roscoe on stage to mark Mr. Perfect's spot? Swap one old dog for another, yeah?"

Martin is the first to laugh, but Gavin and Shay soon join him. Finally, I've gotten them to see the lighter fucking side of things. It makes me smile. After all, it's better to be the comic relief than the punching bag. I learned that lesson a long time ago.

26

DONAL

We make it to Lyon in the late afternoon. I was well into the five-hour ride from Paris before I managed to find just the right way to angle the guitar strapped to my back in a soft case so that the wind didn't throw off my balance. With my backpack cradled against my chest, I was fully loaded and relieved when we rolled into town.

Conor must have learned his lesson in Lambeth with the shitty motel because he steers us to another Airbnb. It's a two-bedroom loft in the heart of the city and a step up from our Paris accommodations. One more city, and I may be able to lure him into a five-star hotel, after all.

My mobile had been blowing up while we were on the road. I assumed it was Valentina but now as I collapse on the sofa, I see from the notifications that it was Owen.

D, your man is in a heap of shit.

I have no idea what that means, so I scroll on through the succession of texts.

What, has he gone off the deep end?
Pub fight?
Tattoo?
Ah, jesus, but that belly dancer is feek.
Ok, don't get me wrong. I'm not after breaking up a family, but I'm sort of hoping he got the ride with that one.
Why aren't you answering?
You're not up to your bollocks in that V-alentina already, are you?
Fuck, I'm dying to know the behind the scenes with this Conor thing. What's he all about with this? See what your da says, yeah?
Answer me ya tool.
Gummy spanner.
Alright. I'm not angry anymore. Just let me know you're well, yeah?

Reading all those messages back to back is a roller coaster, but it's clear enough the highlights of our trip have made it to the tabloids. At least, Conor's starring role in it, since Owen would have gone mad over thinking I was with Conor for all of this. The bit about the belly dancer is a mystery, though. We both had our eye on the dancers last night, but nothing came of it. Not that I know of, that is.

Conor's not around to ask. He called using the shower first, so I'm free to search the web. Doesn't take much to find the photo Owen must have been talking about. In it, Conor is in the hallway that leads to the toilets at the Moroccan restaurant. It's not brightly lit, but it's clear enough that he and the belly dancer have some intense attraction going on. She's looking up at him with a faint smile. His eyes are directed lower, to her chest. They're both leaning into each other. Though they're not touching, they still give off a sexual energy that is hard to deny.

Anger and betrayal washes over me before I can understand the emotions. It's a feeling I recognize, but one I don't want to revisit. I toss my mobile down and throw my arms over my head in a huff. This reaction is childish. I know that. Still, I can't help feeling like another man I look up to has disappointed me.

I had a delayed reaction to my dad fucking around on my ma. At the time, I was just desperate for them to stay together. Then, I saw how destroyed my ma was by him leaving. And finally, I learned all the dirty details of who he fucked in the most public way. It was then that I understood the absolute humiliation my ma suffered. She was heartbroken, of course, but it was the shame of it all that I think bothered her most. She took us away to Burgundy for our usual summer holiday but being there without my da and with her in such a state was a terrible time. I'd escaped as much as I could, chasing after a local girl in a clueless attempt to distract myself from the misery of that house.

The lasting impression of that time is that the father I'd always worshipped as a hero was exposed as a fake. He was nothing more than human and a flawed one at that. I never doubted that he loved me, but I doubted that he was a good man. I doubted that he was someone I wanted to be like. Because if he could treat the mother of his children as if she were disposable, then what kind of person was he at all?

That anger and disillusionment eventually faded. But it never disappeared. It's why he still rubs me the wrong way so often. Every time he tries to tell me how I should be behaving or giving off this impression that I've disappointed him, I want to spit back at him: *You have no idea what disappointment is.*

And now Conor is lining up to be just another one of these Rogue fellas who fucks around. Closing my eyes, I laugh and shake my head. What a load of examples I've had. It's probably why I've jumped so deep into this thing with Valentina. Calling her my girlfriend, wanting so much for this to be some romantic love story—it's got to be some perverse rebellion against the way I've seen relationships around me treated so callously. It's as if I'm out to prove that I won't be that way. That *I'll* be the one to do it right.

Even as I admit this, I can't deny the feeling that Valentina really is something special. That she and I do have the kind of connection I've never had with anyone else. I won't talk myself out of thinking this is real. We at least deserve a shot at it, if nothing else.

With this in mind, I reach for my mobile, wanting to let her know that we've made it safely to the next leg in our journey. But before I can text her, I dutifully respond to Owen, telling him the tabs have blown things up in their typical fashion, that I'll give him the dirt on everything as soon as I can.

I'm not sure why I haven't told him I'm with Conor. Maybe because Owen would focus on all the wrong shite like he has done with the belly dancer. Maybe it's that I know I'd find myself leaping to Conor's defense because despite my negative reaction to the suggestive photo I just saw, I really don't believe he did anything with that woman at the restaurant. Not only didn't he have enough time when I think back on it, but he's just not that guy. In truth, there'd have to be a whole lot to truly change my opinion of him. He's still the man I aspire most to be like.

That settled, I breathe easier, letting go the burst of tension and anger I'd felt.

Though I know she's probably working, I phone Val. I want to hear her voice, if only on the message saying she can't answer. After a few rings, that's exactly what I get. I love her throaty voice. It's insanely sexy. I'd been surprised by it the first time we spoke. She's two years older than me but she looks younger. That may be partly because she's the type of girl who goes for the natural look and is all the more gorgeous for it. She doesn't do makeup. Her hair is a wild mane of dark loose curls that make her green eyes pop. A total stunner. Though, it took me a minute to realize it. She didn't come on heavy to me. The first time I ever interacted with her through my Instagram messages was totally innocent. She had come across some photo I posted. It was a selfie I'd taken randomly in my bedroom and put up with #boredtotears. She wrote me to ask where I'd gotten the Doctor Who figurine. It'd taken me a second to realize she'd recognized the Funko Pop toy sitting on my desk since it was only a quarter visible in the photo. I replied back, asking if she was a fan of the show.

I didn't even look at her profile or scroll through her posts. It was such a curiosity that she'd approach me about Doctor Who when most girls either ask me about my da and Rogue or just straight-up proposition me. I did consider the possibility that this was her clever way of distinguishing herself, but after some back and forth I believed it when she said she'd searched my exact hashtag because she felt the same.

We spent the next three hours messaging each other about Doctor Who. It wasn't flirty. It was ... nerdy. She confessed she'd binged the show—an impressive feat given that the modern iteration has been going non-stop since 2005—to help her learn English. We debated over who was the best Doctor (my favorite is David Tennet, but she's partial to Matt Smith) and which was the best episode (mine is Blink, hers is The Day of the Doctor), and then went down the rabbit hole on other random trivia.

As much fun as it was connecting with her like that, I didn't think to reach out to her again until a week later. I was in one of the after-hours pop-up clubs, zoning out to the music while still trying to keep an eye on an increasingly drunk Owen. A girl slipped into my line of sight, giving me *the look* I've come to know so well. I've had girls falling all over me ever since I got over the worst of the bullying stage in school. That happened to coincide with a good growth spurt that saw me rise to 6'2" and fill out my frame. So, this girl giving me the eye wasn't a surprise, nor was the fact that it only took a few minutes of chatting her up before we were snogging with the promise of a quick shag.

But before it could come to that, I had a fleeting thought. I almost didn't even register it. But then it stuck: *I wonder if Valentina would be up for watching Doctor Who together?*

The girl's confusion when I abruptly stopped kissing her turned to anger when I walked away. She cursed me out, but I didn't care. I'd not only grown bored with her but with the whole club scene. It had been building for a while, hence the #boredtotears Instagram post that connected me with Valentina in the first place. But me losing interest in the girl I was actually kissing and thinking of someone else was new.

That was the start of it with me and Valentina. I went home and searched through her page, learning that she was beautiful, with a sun-splashed life in Barcelona where she went to university. When I messaged her, she didn't play any coy games. She responded quickly, saying she was out with friends but she'd get back to me within an hour. And when she did, we stayed up all night watching Doctor Who "together." It was effortless. It was satisfying. It was exactly what I needed.

It's been near constant contact since then. And in just a

few more days, I'll get to be with her in person. As much as I can't wait to go to bed with her, I'm also craving the intimacy of her company. And even before that, the anticipation of that very first moment when we'll be face to face. That realization reminds me of the song "I Want to Hold Your Hand" and Conor's insistence that the simplicity of it is what elevates it to such a great song.

Sitting up on the sofa, I reach for my guitar, the one Conor gifted me. There's a spark of something playing in my head, and I rush to replicate it.

27

CONOR

I'd purposely avoided looking at my mobile until after showering. The sheer number of notifications as we rode in from Paris could only mean one thing and I wanted to avoid the ramifications a little longer. I'd assumed the story generating all that action on my mobile would be from our fawning Liverpool waitress finally posting about meeting me. But when I check the news, still dripping water down my back and onto the white towel slung low around my hips, I see that everything has been exposed. Not just the trip to Liverpool, but the fight with the band in Lambeth, the tattoo in SoHo, and the belly dancer in Paris.

Closing my eyes, I grimace before forcing it off and examining the photo of me and the dancer. It doesn't look good. In fact, it's quite ... suggestive of impending infidelity.

As if reading my mind, a text from Felicity appears on the screen.

Felicity: *You have made my job harder than it needs to be.*

Irritated at the aggressive way she's coming at me, I reply, *Are you speaking as my wife or as my band's media manager?*

It was a smartass remark, so I'm not surprised when she puts me in my place in response.

Felicity: *It's rare that I think of being your wife as a job, but you're onto something at the moment.*

A smile tugs at the corner of my mouth. I've always adored it when she called me out and forced me to examine myself. She's made me a better man many times over by doing so.

Me: *What can I do?*
Felicity: *I could have used a heads up about your escapades. Especially your time with the belly dancer.*
Me: *There was nothing there to warn you about. I went back to our place, wrote those lyrics, and wanked to imaginings of you.*

I leave out the part of the fantasy where she'd been dressed in a belly dancer's outfit. In any case, she's not amused.

Felicity: *For fuck's sake.*
Me: *Exactly.*

The screen indicate she's typing. It takes a long minute before her message comes up.

Felicity: *Dear boy, I love you to pieces. Just let me know if there's anything else I can prepare for with the media, okay?*

Her use of "dear boy" makes me smile. I haven't heard that

in a long, long time. My wife, she's an old soul with an ability to strategically snap me out of my childish ways.

Me: *I love you, Fee. I'll try to stay out of trouble, but honestly, I'm in a give no fucks mood. I don't mean to make your job harder. I just need to live without calculation for a bit.*

There's another lengthy pause and I suspect that she's had enough of my rebellion. But then she texts back and what she says makes my dick jump.

Felicity: *That tattoo is incredibly sexy. Can't wait to get my hands on it—and on you.*
Me: *Thank god for that because you're the only one I want, honey.*

With that, I count myself lucky that the missus let me off the hook. She's been exceptionally patient with me over this whole disappearing act, which only makes me love her all the more.

DONAL IS quiet as we walk the streets of Lyon. I didn't have a plan as we set out from the Airbnb other than to get some air. We'll eventually find a place for a drink and dinner but it's still early. I've been keeping my own company as we walk along the Rhône river. I wouldn't ordinarily mind the silence between us, but I sense some undercurrent of discontent in it.

"Everything all right?" I ask.
"Yeah."
"Valentina okay?"
"Yeah."
The monosyllabic replies irritate me, in large part because

it's a vision into my future for when my own kids become moody teenagers.

Shrugging it off, I look up once again at the basilica towering over the city. It's impossible to ignore and now I'm thinking going to it so we can view the town from up on high will break whatever dark spell Donal's under. The helpful street signs for tourists point us in the right direction for the Basilique Notre Dame de Fourvière and we begin ascending a series of stairs and ramps.

"Bloody hell," Donal groans when we've been climbing steadily for fifteen minutes. "Where are we going and when will we get there?"

We stop on a landing, halfway to our destination. The exertion has left us both with a light layer of sweat on our foreheads. But whereas it seems to irritate him, it makes me feel good. I've always gotten a lot of satisfaction out of exercising and pushing my body. The last couple of days have been a break from my normally strict routine and so this bit of effort is welcome. Donal is fit in that way guys his age tend to be—that is, blessed with a fast metabolism and a tendency to gain muscle that fills out his frame in such a way that he appears to be more man than boy.

Slapping him on the back, I tell him, "It's not about the destination, it's about the journey."

Predictably, he rolls his eyes. "Okay, buddha."

"Seriously, though. Look around. This is a gorgeous city." I scan our view, taking in a quaint community garden overlooking the Saône river, magnificent spires of centuries-old churches, and the pleasing uniformity of the red-tiled buildings. But when I turn my eyes back to Donal, his eyes have remained fixed on me.

"What is it?" I ask.

"Can I—like, I mean, you didn't actually do anything with that belly dancer last night, did you?"

I squint at him. "What are you on about?"

"I just, I saw the photo. And it looks, well, it looks bad. I told myself there was nothing to it and I tried to just forget about it. But the thing is, your kids are gonna see that, man. They're gonna see it and think that you're stepping out on their ma."

"Really? That's what my *seven*-year-olds will think?"

He opens his mouth to speak but forces it closed. His eyes dart around as he struggles with himself and it dawns on me that he wasn't much older when his parents separated and Martin got into a whole lot of very public drama. While I sympathize with the fact that all that traumatized him, I'm not in the same situation as Martin was. I'm not willfully destroying my marriage. But I also don't feel any obligation to convince Donal of this.

Instead, I try a different tact. "Listen, people fuck up. They make bad choices. They hurt the ones they love. But the sooner you realize that those things are not actually fatal flaws, the better off you'll be."

He scoffs. "Lower my expectations, is that it?"

"*No.* Understand that every single person you know struggles to get it right. Everyone. There are no perfect people. That certainly fucking includes me. And that also includes your da."

He looks surprised, as if he hadn't even connected his "concern" for my fuckups with the fact that he's still holding a grudge against his father. Or maybe it's that he wouldn't have thought *I'd* connect the two things.

In any case, I continue undaunted. "The thing you need to look for in people isn't some purity test, it's whether they are *trying* to get it right. That's what matters. Because, whether you like to admit it or not, we all fuck up. The key is understanding whether someone's fuckups are a pattern or an exception. I mean, Jesus, you know what it's like to be unfairly judged. Don't rush to do it to others." With that, I take a deep breath and survey the view once more.

Chastened, Donal nods.

"And for the record," I continue, "I did nothing with that belly dancer. My wife knows it. And if my kids have questions, I'll speak with *them* about it."

"Okay, sure. I meant no harm."

When I look at him once again, I can see in his face the way he's straddling the line between childhood and adulthood. He still has notions of heroes and villains. He still wants to view the world through black and white when in reality, it's all muted shades of gray. The remarkable thing is just how hard kids cling to these ideals, despite all evidence to the contrary. But then again, we parents are to blame. We raise our children to believe in all that, setting them up for disillusionment and disappointment in the end. I pity the kids who have no outlet for these feelings. Luckily, Donal isn't in that position. He's got music, the same thing that has saved me over and again.

"Let's carry on, shall we?" I say with a nod toward the stairs.

"The view better be worth it," he says with a grin, back to his lighter self.

"Only one way to find out."

28

DONAL

By the time we reach the top of the climb to the basilica, almost a thousand steps in total, I've managed to shrug off the regret I felt over calling out Conor for the photo of him and the belly dancer. I had put aside my disappointment back at the Airbnb, but once he emerged from the shower and suggested we head out to explore with no acknowledgment of what was all over the tabloids, it all came flooding back. I fixated on the image that his kids would see. I worried over how their impressionable minds would view it. I couldn't push it aside like I had before and it all came out in a messy rush. Conor's pushback on me was fair. It's not my business. But his philosophizing on the fact that people are fallible and I should get over it was harder to accept. I suppose I should get over the fact that so many people end up being a disappointment, but I'm stubborn.

Conor lets out a slow whistle in what I expect is appreciation for the church before us. But then I see that his eyes are instead focused on the panoramic view of Lyon that seems to go on forever.

"It is nice," I agree.

"Yeah, but not just that," he says. He raises his hand and points at the peak of a mountain in the distance. "That's Mont Blanc."

It's an exceptionally clear afternoon, with a pale blue sky dotted with only a handful of clouds. Seeing the highest mountain in western Europe so unexpectedly is enough to make me draw in a sharp breath. I've been to some beautiful spots, traveling mostly with my parents when I was young and then with my father and Lainey when I was a bit older, but this is something else. This is truly that taste of *adventure* Conor promised me. That's the only word for it when you've happened upon something so grand without planning it. It's a gorgeous sight and I reach for my mobile to get a photo to share with Val.

Conor snatches it from my hand and I look at him in surprise.

"I'll get one of you in it," he says.

I do my best pose for the photo.

"How about one of us together? You can post it to your Instagram if you want," he says.

"Really?"

"At least that way your da will know you're alive, yeah?" He smiles, amused with himself.

"Like, post it in a few days?"

"Nah, you can post it now."

I shrug, though I'm surprised he's given up trying to hide the steps of our journey after how he got burned with the tabloids today. Then he throws one arm around my neck and snaps off a few pics. I take the mobile back and sort through the options to post.

"Why don't you have an account?" I ask absently.

"Too vain."

"What?" I laugh and glance at him.

"I'd probably post too many photos of myself. It'd get tiresome for my followers."

"Ah, man. That's just the point. The girls would go fucking nuts for a selfie account of yours."

"The other thing is, I'm too old for that shite."

"Well, that may be true."

He punches me in the bicep hard enough for the impact to radiate down my arm.

"Do you want to take a walk through the basilica?" he asks with a nod to the tourist-laden church behind us.

Rubbing the now tender spot, I say, "We'd better. Shame to come all the way up here and skip that."

THE BASILICA WAS IMPRESSIVE INSIDE, with an abundance of gilt, carved and slab marble, stained glass windows, and colorful mosaics amongst the sea of wooden pews. I was left to wander and gawk while Conor went off to light a candle, then kneel at the altar for a prayer, no doubt with his father in mind.

After our exploration, we found that there was a funicular, offering an easy and quick ride to and from the basilica, making our earlier efforts to climb all those stairs a fool's errand. Conor laughed, saying he vaguely remembered there was such an option and dismissed my groaning over it.

We were both ready for a drink and a meal after that. When Conor pointed out that Lyon is known as the gastronomical capital of France, with many Michelin star restaurants, I began to salivate over the gourmet food we might be treated to. But he quickly insisted that since this still wasn't a five-star holiday, any random bistro would do—especially because the food was bound to be nearly as delicious as any of its award-winning competitors due to the town's universally high standards.

On a whim, we popped into a little low-lit cafe that seemed all the dimmer for its wood-paneled walls, wood floors, ancient wood-beam ceilings, and wood tables. It was nearly full, though, and the good-spirited chattering made for a warm welcome. We were seated without delay and I let Conor take charge of ordering both food and drink.

The place didn't disappoint as we started off with black-truffle soup, followed by sea bass in pastry crust with tomato purée béarnaise, along with roasted mini potatoes and a spray of delicately steamed haricots verts.

We were both so busy eating and tucking into a bottle of red wine, that there wasn't much conversation until our plates were cleared.

"That was fantastic," I announce, sitting back in my unforgiving wooden chair and patting my stomach.

"Shall we go all in and have Cognac?"

I smile. "Won't say no to that."

Once we have our tumblers, I check my mobile. Val has texted in reply to both my earlier voicemail and the selfie I'd sent. She says that if she cannot be with me on this adventure as she would want to be, then at least she takes solace in knowing I'll be with her soon for our first meeting. It's always jarring to realize we're about to meet in person for the first time because it feels like we know each other so well.

"That smile would be for Valentina, yes?" Conor asks.

I realize I have looked like a lovesick dope and I clear my throat to brush off the evidence. Checking my Instagram next, I see that I've somehow accumulated over four hundred thousand likes for the post of Conor and me. No doubt the hashtags helped. It seems that #Rogue and #ConorQuinn are popular.

"Check this out," I say and hold up the post so he can see the many comments swooning over him. He does not look like a forty-year-old. He's still got the tight, sculpted jawline and high cheekbones he's always had. There's no gray hair on his head or in the stubble of a beard he's let grow. His smile appears relaxed but at the same time he comes off like the coolest motherfucker alive. It's no wonder he has women of all ages still falling all over themselves with comments like *Conor Quinn is God* and *I'd suck you so good* and *Can I have your babies, pleeeeeeze?*

I watch him scan the comments, see the corner of his mouth turn up in what must be the satisfaction to his ego.

"Proves my case," he says and sits back in his chair. "It'd be a terrible thing for me to have my own account."

"What would you say to me posting photos of the rest of our trip?"

"You mean with me in them?"

"Eh, yeah."

"How many more followers have you gotten since you posted that?"

"Oh, it's not about that—"

"But it doesn't hurt, does it? How many more have you gotten?"

Checking my account, I see that I've increased my followers by thirty thousand. And it's climbing by the second. I tell him as much.

He watches me for a long moment. "You can post all the photos you want if you do something in return."

"Shit," I say with a nervous laugh. "What is it?"

"Call your father."

I let out the breath I'd been holding. It's a simple ask. As much as I don't want to do it, I know it's the right thing. And I'll get a hell of a reward by being able to feature Conor Quinn on my Instagram. There's a not quite formed sense in the back of my mind that this could help legitimize my future music efforts. It seems Conor saw that a mile off and is still willing to play along. At least, if I do my part and call my da.

"Sure, yeah. No problem."

"Now."

"Oh, em." I glance at my mobile. "It's half ten. Maybe in the morning?"

"*Now.*"

The steel in his voice has me nodding. "I'll just step outside, then?"

"Have Marty text me when you're done."

"Well, I'm not going to lie about it, if that's what you're thinking."

"Just have him text me."

My eye roll is very deliberate this time. As is the sigh I unleash as I stand. "Don't let them clear my drink," I say, pointing to the mostly untouched Cognac snifter at my place.

"Got it."

As soon as I'm outside, I dial my da and pray he doesn't answer.

But, of course he does.

"Donal, you all right?"

"Yeah, fine."

"Happy to hear it. Though, it would have been good if you'd let me know you were leaving the country."

"I—"

"All for some girl you met on bloody Instagram, is it?"

"Jesus, Da, can we *not*?"

"I'm just saying you should have spared a word of your plan to leave my house and traipse all over Europe, yeah?"

"Maybe I didn't want the lecture," I reply.

"Is this a lecture?" he snaps back.

There's a long silence when neither of us speaks.

"What'd you make of Lambeth, then?" he finally asks in an obvious effort to de-escalate the tension.

"We stayed in the shittiest hotel I've ever seen, so I guess I got the taste of what you all lived through back in the day."

To my surprise, he laughs. "One of the best times of my life, it was."

"Yeah, so much better than your current life of luxury."

"I didn't say that. But those early years with the lads, I wouldn't trade them for anything."

"Uh huh." Looking down, I kick at the ground and watch as loose pebbles skitter away.

Another long silence passes between us. Then I hear my da sigh.

"Well, I have to say, motorbiking all the way to see a girl is a pretty cool thing. I don't know how you got Conor to go off with you on this journey of yours, but I'm happy he's with you."

I don't correct him about this whole thing not being my idea, partly because he seems impressed by it and partly because there's a sadness in his voice that makes me think he would have liked to be the one with me.

"Do us a favor?" he continues, and I tense in anticipation of hearing something from him I don't want to hear. "Call or text your brothers. Maybe send word to your ma, too. They miss you."

I swallow hard at that and nod. "I will."

"Keep safe and enjoy. I love—"

"Wait." I spoke just as he was telling me he loved me. I hadn't meant to cut him off, it's just that I remembered that I needed to tell him something.

"Yes?"

"Em, Uncle Conor says he wants a text from you. To prove that I called you. He's, em, been telling me to call you since the day we left."

"I see. Will do. Take care now."

He ends the call before I can reply. Before trying to tell me again that he loves me. Which wouldn't be that big of a deal except for the fact that he's always been *that* da. Even before he and my ma split, he was very deliberate in telling me and my brothers that he loved us.

I have the sudden urge to call him back, to tell him all about the horrible bar band, the nosey woman in the street listening to Conor's horror over my piercings, how I watched Conor design his own tattoo, how in a random music shop in the suburbs of Paris, I found some confidence and inspiration in playing guitar, that I'm traveling with my own custom guitar strapped to my back, that this has been the best trip I've ever been on.

That last bit might land a little sourly, though. He's gone to great lengths over the years to show me beautiful parts of the world. And while I appreciate those trips, they haven't left the kind of impression this one has.

So, I don't call him back. I leave it. Because I suddenly feel a kind of tenderness toward him that I haven't in a very long time, and it seems that not telling him I'm having the time of my life right now is actually the kinder thing to do.

Instead, I take a few minutes before heading inside to text my little brothers. Ever since I moved in with my da, I've been too distant with them, only seeing them when it's our da's custody time. We used to be a hell of a trio when we were little. I suddenly have the desire to get back into closer touch with them. Luckily, they're not the type to hold a grudge as both text me back right away.

In between their texts, I send a quick note to my ma, telling her all is well, that I'm on a bit of a holiday but will come see her as soon as I get back. She replies quickly, too, telling me to be safe and she can't wait to see me.

Satisfied, I head back inside the restaurant.

29

CONOR

Donal is still lingering out front of the restaurant when I get a text from Martin.

Martin: *Heard from Donal. Thanks for watching over him.*
Me: *He's watching over me more than anything.*
Martin: *Unlikely.*
Martin: *Anyway, we'll be seeing you soon?*
Me: *That's the plan.*

I put away my mobile and watch as Donal approaches the table. He sits down heavily in his chair, takes his snifter of Cognac into both hands and stares at the rich copper liquid.

"It went that well?" I ask with a small smile.

"What?" Though he glances at me he doesn't really see me. His mind is elsewhere.

Sitting back, I let the silence wash over us and use the time to finish off my drink. I feel warm and relaxed, though I'm curious what happened in that phone call to turn Donal moody once more.

I try to recall whether I ever had this sort of contentious relationship with my father but come up empty. I'm sure I pulled an attitude with him on occasion, but in general, all I can remember is that he was the most open-minded, supportive parent I could ask for. In fact, Gavin used to tell me when we were kids that I had no idea how good I really had it. He was always rowing with his father. I guess I took my good relationship with Da for granted. And not just in those early years, but for all of our time together. That regret over not appreciating every moment has been heavy with me since he passed. It's not just the loss of the man who meant so much, but the realization that I wasted so much time. It's the understanding that time is finite. Time is something you can never get back.

"Do you think my da is ... bothered that I'm doing this trip with you?"

Now I'm the one to glance at Donal and not really see him, my mind still on my dark thoughts.

"I mean," Donal continues, "I think he might be."

Forcing myself to focus on the kid across from me, I say, "What makes you say that?"

He shrugs. "I dunno. I just got thinking, I suppose."

"If he'd been the one to suggest this trip instead of me, would you have gone?"

The very idea forces a laugh out of him.

"What's funny?"

"For one, he'd *never* have thought of something as cool as this. And for another, he'd have spent the whole time being bloody disappointed in me for one thing or another."

"Is that how you really feel? That he's disappointed in you?"

"Pretty much."

Shaking my head, I sigh. "You're just wasting time, Donal. You're wasting precious time by presuming he sees the worst in you."

"I–"

"Especially when just the opposite is true. He thinks the world of you. He only wants your happiness." I see him still struggling to accept this and continue. "I know that because it's exactly what he told me at my party the other night. He wants your happiness. He wants you to find your passion in life. He wants you to find love. He wants you to take risks. He wants everything for you. Because he loves you. Because you're his child, and there's no fiercer love in this world than a parent's love for his child."

Donal finishes his Cognac and keeps his eyes on the table for a long moment. Finally, he looks up and meets my gaze. "So, you're saying I should invite him along on the next road trip?"

The notion that Donal would be up for another trip like this pleases me. And the suggestion that it be with his father makes me smile.

"Absolutely."

When he then goes off on saying we should teach his father how to ride a motorbike so they can explore parts unknown, I order us another drink. I just want to sit and enjoy this moment of a son finding a new appreciation for his father.

LATER, we wander along the Rhône, making lazy progress toward our flat. The night is still warm and the Cognac has left us both comfortably numb, so we're in no hurry. The moon is bright, reflecting off the river and it's quiet, the streets fairly empty.

But then there's a burst of applause in the near distance. I meet Donal's eyes and see he's mirroring my curiosity. I tilt my head as a suggestion that we track down the noise, and he nods, following my lead.

Before long, we find ourselves in the enormous La Place Bellecour, a square in the middle of the city bordered by both the Saône and the Rhône rivers. The square is surrounded by stores and restaurants, some open but most closed. There's a statue in the center of a man on horseback and at the far end there's a Ferris wheel. That's where the action seems to be as a crowd of about fifty or so is gathered there. We follow our ears, picking up the sound of street musicians.

Once on the outskirts of the crowd, we can see there is a trio busking. They're wild. Untamed but not without talent. The singer plays bass guitar, leading a guitarist and a drummer in a surprising rockabilly style, complete with jeans rolled up at the cuffs, western-style shirts and pompadours. They've got the crowd whistling, hollering, and clapping. But the most impressive thing is their energy. They're not just performing; they're having a fantastic time with each other.

I watch as they catch each other's eyes, see a sly grin pass between them, the way they lift each other up as they go.

God, it takes me back. Back to those early days with Gav and the lads when all we had was music and each other. It was so pure, so perfect.

"We've come across a band."

I turn to see Donal filming with his mobile.

"What do you make of them, Uncle Conor?" he asks and turns the focus on me.

"I think they're fantastic," I reply. "They've got the kind of synergy that'll take 'em places."

Donal turns the camera to himself. "There it is. Conor Quinn, esteemed music critic, has spoken." Turning back to the band, he adds, "You can find these fellas here on the streets of Lyon."

While he uploads the video to Instagram, no doubt tagging me, I watch the group wrap up their song. The crowd shouts and claps like they've just witnessed their favorite band, not some unknown trio trying to make enough in donations to buy a drink later.

As people start to break up, I go to the front and empty my pocket to throw Euros into an open guitar case.

"*Merci!*" the singer says with a wide grin.

I wave off the thanks and retreat back to where Donal is still fiddling with his phone. Turning my attention to the Ferris wheel sitting idle in front of us, memories from a time in London years ago when I rode on the same kind of contraption rush forth. It was a time when I was similarly struggling with how to move forward in my life. It took me longer than it should have to figure out my path. Felicity, of course, was the one to guide me to where I should be. She's always been the one I gravitate toward, the one who sets me right.

"Synergy, aye?" Donal asks, eyes still on his screen.

It takes me a second to pull myself away from my thoughts and absorb what he's asking. But then it clicks and I reply, "Synergy. It's that intangible thing you gotta have with your bandmates. The thing that when you're together makes each of you better than when you're on your own."

"Like you have with Rogue then?"

"Exactly. And like what you'll need to have with whoever is in your band."

He looks away from his mobile and at me. "Owen's the only one I trust to make music with."

"I get that, but does he make you *better*? Or are you just comfortable with him?"

"Maybe it's both."

"Maybe. But there aren't too many two-piece bands out there, Donal. You're going to have to expand your horizons."

"Let me guess your advice on how I do that."

I raise my eyebrows and wait him out.

"Give no fucks?"

"Exactly. Who else is going to believe in you if you don't do it first? Be your own fucking leader and I swear to God you'll see others follow."

When he nods, I'm gratified to notice there was no hesitation.

"Now, it's all well and good of you to give these fellas," I say, gesturing to the musicians breaking down their equipment in front of us, "some media attention, but I say it's time for you to put yourself out there."

"What do you mean?"

"Let's fucking debut Donal Whelan on your Instagram. I'll record you playing that gorgeous guitar I got you, yeah?"

The confidence he showed a moment ago when agreeing with me about being a leader vanishes at this suggestion.

"Eh, no, I'm not ready for that."

"Listen, I'm not saying this because you're family. I'm saying this because it's true. You've got talent. And more than that, you've got that kind of thing that draws others in. It's a rare fucking commodity. It's time to put it out there. Proudly. Unapologetically."

He shakes his head. "I may be able to play Rogue or Foo Fighters, but I don't have anything original to share."

"Bullshit. What were you playing back at the flat earlier?"

"That? That was just messing."

"It was good, Donal. It's worth putting out there."

He considers it for a moment. Just when I think he's going to agree, he says, "Nah. Can't do it."

"Bribe me."

"What?" He laughs.

"Bribe me, then. Tell me you'll do it if … I dunno, we leave our ordinary flat and go to the finest hotel in town instead. I'll get you your own suite."

"Really? I can *bribe* you?"

"We've been making deals this whole time. I'm good for it. I know you're good for it. Let me have it."

His eyes leave mine and dart around. And then a wicked smile transforms his face. That's when I realize that I've completely misjudged how big his ask might be. This kid isn't going to settle for a night in a fancy hotel. He's got something far grander in mind.

30

FELICITY

Remember when I said you are the light?
It's been that way since before we spun the Eye
I promise you everything will be all right
I promise you this love won't ever die

I've just settled onto the sofa with a glass of wine when Conor's latest lyrics come through by text. The message has come earlier tonight than the past couple times, but it's still late. After dinner with the kids, we played a board game, then they bathed, and finally we went through the bedtime routine. Once it was quiet, I did a couple hours of work before finally closing my laptop and giving myself permission to unwind.

Tonight's text has veered away from last night's sexually charged theme to a proclamation of deep love. Reading the lines over for the fourth time, I take in a breath and exhale with satisfaction. Conor never hesitates to let me know how much he loves me but seeing it like this is something special. He and Gavin have always collaborated on lyrics, but his part has mostly been as the one to tinker with a word or phrase to get it just right. As far as I know, he's never written a song for or about me. Being the center of one now is incredibly flattering. Thrilling, even, to think that I'm not only song-worthy but that this could one day be shared with the world.

I laugh to myself as I think, *no wonder Sophie could never get enough of Gavin. He's written a dozen songs about her.*

The reference to the "Eye" made sense right away. It's the London Eye Ferris wheel. The spot years ago where I knew I'd fallen for him. He'd managed to pull strings to get us our own pod for an after-hours ride, along with a bottle of champagne. He'd noticed my feet were aching from the heels I was unaccustomed to and insisted on giving me a massage as the city went by beneath us. All that was enough to make a girl fall for Conor Quinn, but there was more to it for me. That night wasn't about the grand gesture of whisking me off on a romantic adventure, it was about the way he listened to me, the way he leapt to my defense, the way he held me as if he couldn't bear to ever let me go.

That night wasn't our fairy-tale ending, of course. We never did have a picture-perfect "moment" to declare our feelings. Instead, it came out in fits and starts and in its own time. I've never begrudged that fact. I'm a realist, have been even before my first marriage ended abruptly. But in his own way Conor has broken through that self-protection mode and made my every dream come true.

And now, there's a song to add to that list.

Reading the lyrics again, I smile and try to conjure up a reply. We'd had a brief but heated moment of texting earlier when I'd felt blindsided by the tabloid stories. It was impossible to deny feeling jealous over the photograph of him with the sexy belly dancer. That morphed into calling him out on needing to be warned about such "news." But he had apparently been in no mood to spar over it all, immediately pushing back at me. I decided not to push the issue, not by text, and not when knowing he's not in the best state. Pivoting to complimenting his tattoo was the easy out. Besides, I do think it's sexy. There's not much he could do that I wouldn't find sexy, including the fact that no matter what, I trust him. I use my text reply to express why that is the case.

Me: *One of the many things I love about you is that you always keep your promises.*
Conor: *To my dying day, honey.*

His text comes back so quickly that I imagine he was watching his mobile the whole while, waiting for my response. It makes me long for a real connection. I know why he's leaving it at texting rather than phoning or video chat. He wants some distance. It's important to him that he feels he's got some separation from everything at home so he can sort himself out. I respect that because I know exactly how that feels. I've been there.

Still, it doesn't stop me from missing him.

Opening Instagram, I find Donal's account to once more view the photo he posted of himself and my husband. Conor hasn't shaved since he left, meaning he's even more devastatingly handsome than usual. I love a little scruff on him, but he's almost always clean-shaven. The other thing that stands out is that his eyes don't seem to be nearly as weighed down under the burden of his depression as they had been when he was here.

When I watch the short video clip again, I can't help but think there's something to the way he says the street musicians have "synergy." The reverence in his tone bodes well for Rogue. If he's appreciating that invisible force which binds band members together so that their totality is better than the individual, then he must be thinking of his own situation, too.

It's almost one in the morning. I shouldn't text Sophie and risk waking her. But I also know she's the kind of friend who won't mind. Anyway, it's just one word:

Synergy.

I take a sip of wine and close my eyes to savor the rich, dry Burgundy. That's all the time Sophie needed, apparently, because my mobile buzzes.

YES!!

I can practically feel her excitement through the device, and I smile. If she has this positive of a reaction about the word, it means Gavin reacted well to it first. And if it meant something to him, then I'm right in thinking that Conor is coming back around to being more engaged in the world, and, very likely, wanting to rediscover the *synergy* of his own band once more.

I'm relieved not just because I'm the band's media manager, but because no one—including Conor—is prepared to live in a world without Rogue.

31

CONOR

Conor: *I have a question.*
Gavin: *I have an answer.*
Conor: *Who do you know in Monte Carlo?*
Conor: *I'm going to need help pulling a few strings.*

32

DONAL

I'll admit that going out of our way to Monte Carlo means a delay in getting to my Valentina, but this is a once in a lifetime opportunity.

I mean, when might I ever again get the chance to bribe Conor this way?

When he first suggested it, I came up blank. I couldn't think of anything that would be big enough to counteract the fierce desire I have to *not* put out a video of me playing guitar. The idea of staying in some posh hotel didn't sway me. But it did spark thoughts of how I could maximize that idea.

What better way to do that than make a deal to go full-on high roller in the so-called "Billionaire's Playground"?

It took five hours to get from Lyon to Nice, but I've been grinning inside my motorbike helmet almost the whole way. The final push from Nice to Monte Carlo is stunning, setting the tone for our impending arrival at the French Riviera. The single-lane meandering road is bordered alternately by quaint towns, bougainvillea-adorned gated estates, palm trees, and the dazzling deep-blue Mediterranean Sea. Along the way, we motor through mountains blasted open to create tunnels, pass hordes of tourists, and weave past slower-moving cars. I don't think I've seen so many other motorbikes on a stretch of road but with the sun shining brilliantly overhead and the August weather so warm, it's the perfect day to be out.

Conor leads us all the way through to the very center of town, to the iconic Casino Square. It's bustling with both pedestrian and auto traffic making their way around what is really more of a loop than a square, with people both gawking and wanting to be seen. Slowing to a stop at the side of the road halfway around, Conor takes off his helmet and waits for me to do the same.

"There's the casino you're so keen on visiting," he tells me. "We'll come back later tonight for some gambling."

I survey the architecture of the casino. It's impressive but more classy than over the top. The palm tree-lined fountain in the middle of the square is teeming with people, some with evidence of their recent purchases as they seem to flaunt bags from Hermès, Zegg & Cerlati, Prada, Cartier, and Louis Vuitton. There are more Ferraris, Lambos, and McLarens driving slowly past us than I've ever seen in person in my life. And I've never seen this many perfectly put-together women in one spot either. It's the epitome of glamor and wealth.

"Jesus," I say in awe. "Even the air smells like money."

Conor shakes his head. "Remember, money can buy you toys. Money can buy you a measure of convenience. But money can never buy you authenticity."

I roll my eyes. "Let me enjoy the moment, at least."

He laughs. "You do that. Then we'll get to the hotel. It's just over there." He nods to his left, indicating the ocean-facing side of Monte Carlo and I smile at the prospect.

This excursion keeps getting better.

. . .

I'M FLOORED by the grandeur of the Hotel de Paris where we'll be staying. And that's based off the lobby. With a high, arched white ceiling decorated with detailed plasterwork and crowned by a delicate stained glass dome, it's stunning. There's a statue of a man on horseback, and the marble floors are covered by an enormous, gorgeous Oriental rug.

"That fella looks familiar," I tell Conor, gesturing to the statue.

"Louis XIV, France's longest ruler," he replies nonchalantly, as if everyone should recognize the former king.

"How do you know this shite?"

He shrugs. "I can be clever."

"Fuck off," I say with a laugh.

"You must have recognized it from last night, Donal. This one is a much smaller version of the statue in La Place Bellecour."

It clicks now. The same horseman, same curious lack of stirrups. I have the feeling that if I asked him about this absence, he'd have the answer. But I don't ask because if he really did know, I'd be too freaked out by his smarts. No man should have his good looks, talent, and intelligence. It's just too much.

"Monsieur Quinn, welcome!"

We turn away from King Louis to find an impeccably dressed silver-haired man greeting us.

"I am Paul Pouille with Guest Relations. We were anxiously awaiting your arrival. I am so sorry our doorman did not give me better notice," he continues in a tone both reverent and apologetic, though there's no need in my mind. We weren't waiting or put out in any way. "Please, I am happy to escort you to your Diamond Suite."

"Diamond Suite," I murmur, loving the sound of it.

Two bellmen sidle up to us and relieve us of our things before we can protest. We're led to the lifts and step into a waiting carriage.

"Monsieur McManus let us know all of your requirements, and I think you will be pleased," Paul Pouille says.

"We appreciate the assistance," Conor says.

Pouille nods. "We have you in a lovely two-bedroom suite with a sea view. Of course, there is champagne awaiting you, but would you perhaps like some food brought up to the room? Or can I arrange a table for you at our restaurant?"

The deference from this man is amazing. It's like having a personal valet. I bet Conor could snap his fingers and Pouille would answer the call, day or night.

"Yes, I think something at the restaurant would work. Say, in an hour or so?"

"*Oui.*"

The lift lets us out and our little gang walks to the end of the hallway to a room with double-doors.

"Monsieur McManus offered to cover your stay, but it is our pleasure to host you for the evening," Pouille says as he opens the doors and reveals a large entryway that opens up to a larger living space with a terrace and view of the water beyond. "Shall I give you a tour?"

"I think we can find our way, thanks very much, Monsieur Pouille."

I watch with distraction as Conor deftly shakes the man's hand while also slipping him several high mark euros. My attention is being pulled to the view beyond the terrace where yachts, one bigger than the other, compete for space along the coastline below. The sun bounces brilliantly off both the sparkling blue water and the shiny white fiberglass and chrome of the boats. I focus on the deck of one large vessel where a party of sorts seems to be going on. Faint music floats up to my ears, but what draws me in is the topless women lounging there.

"Good view?" Conor joins me, clapping me on the back.

"Fantastic."

We stand there for a few moments, taking it all in, before I say, "What was that bit about them *hosting* us for the evening?"

"Eh, they're comping us the suite."

"What?" I glance back inside at the large and luxurious suite. It's got a formal living area with a brown suede seating area, a separate dining table, and apparently, two bedrooms from what the man said earlier. It's beyond even my imaginings of the kind of five-star hotel I'd wanted to stay in with this trip. "Why would they give this to you for free?"

Conor raises his eyebrows and then lets out a breath. "It's the great paradox of wealth: once you have it, people trip over themselves to give you things for free."

"*Why?*"

"To curry favor? Because they think it's expected? Some unwritten rule? Who knows." A small smile tugs at his mouth. "In our particular case, though, I'd say your Uncle Gavin had a whole lot to do with it. That guy knows someone in every corner of the world and somehow manages to engender their loyalty. I asked him for his help getting us sorted for this side trip of ours. As usual, he delivered."

I try to absorb that while also trying to take in our surroundings. "How much do you think this room goes for? I mean, for people who actually pay?"

"Well, I bet this room is reserved for V.I.P. guests. But, if someone were to actually pay the rate, it'd probably go for something like fifteen."

I burst out laughing at that. "Fifteen? As in *fifteen thousand per night?"*

His straight face tells me this estimate is clearly not a joke. "You wanted one night as a high roller. You got it."

"I'll drink to that!" I say with a laugh. "Let's get the champagne they left."

There's a bottle of Dom Pérignon on the coffee table by the seating area and I grab it out of its ice bath.

"You know how to open that?" Conor asks.

He's eyeing me with an amused smile.

"Eh, sure. Just give her a shake and let the cork pop."

"For fuck's sake. That's *definitely* what you *don't* do. Especially not with a bottle of champagne that expensive."

"Show me how it's done then," I say with a laugh.

"You do it. I'll tell you how."

I roll my eyes but, as with most things, I'm ready to take direction from him.

"Wipe it down with the napkin they left there. Then wrap it around the bottle to get a good grip."

When I do as he says, he positions my hands so I'm holding the bottle at about a forty-five-degree angle.

"Now, twist the cage counterclockwise six times, but keep the pressure on the cork."

"I'll pull at the cork now?" I ask when I have the cage off.

"No, you'll twist *the bottle*. You'll feel the pressure against the cork. That's when you pull the cork—gently. You'll get your 'pop' but won't waste any of the good stuff."

The pop I get isn't explosive, but it's still satisfying, especially because I had a sense of control over it. And, I wasted none of the delicious golden bubbly. I fill two flutes and hand one over to him.

"Cheers, mate," he says, holding his glass aloft.

Grinning in response, I tap his glass with mine before

taking a big sip. It goes down easy.

"We should clean up and get over to the restaurant for something to eat," he says.

I agree and we separate to our own rooms. I'm grubby from the road and as I finish off my glass of champagne, the idea of a hot shower sounds good. I see that the bellman has left my backpack and guitar on luggage racks at the foot of my king-sized bed. The bedroom is spacious, with its own en suite and a walk-in closet. The light is on in the closet and I notice that the racks aren't empty. Instead, there are several suits hanging there. The shelves have a variety of other men's clothing, too. The shoe racks have leather dress shoes and trainers.

"Uncle Conor?" I call out.

"Yeah?"

"Some fella's clothes are in my closet. Are you sure we're meant to be in this suite?"

Conor comes into my room and joins me in the closet. Seems he'd been on his way to the shower because he's shirtless, his feet are bare, and his jeans are half unbuttoned.

"Those are for you," he tells me.

"Get the fuck out. What do you mean they're for me?"

"Listen, we've been wearing the same couple of shirts and jeans this whole time. It's all well and good for a road trip but you're in Monte Carlo now. You need to clean up and dress the part. So, Gav passed along a couple extra requests to help us sort ourselves. This includes some clothes. Some of those nicer jeans and a button up will do for lunch. A suit for gambling tonight. Okay?"

"Well ... wait, how do I know any of this fits?"

"You'll find there are a few sizes of everything so you can wear what works best."

With that, he nods and then turns and walks out, as if this is all perfectly normal. As if being catered to like this, no expense spared, is just a part of his daily routine.

And all I can think is, *I want to be Conor Quinn when I grow up.*

33

CONOR

The view from the eighth-floor restaurant is spectacular, so I can't fault Donal for filming it. We're seated on the narrow terrace, lingering after having been lavished over with wonderful service that included two glasses of wine each and a meal of pesto and wild mushroom risotto, duck breast with roasted peaches, and the restaurant's signature soufflé. The gentle breeze, warm afternoon sun, and picturesque coastline has made us hesitate to give up our table.

"Check out the size of those yachts," Donal murmurs as he records. "Squint a bit and you'll make out Corsica in the distance there."

After another few seconds of pointing out all the extravagant features of our view, he turns the focus on me.

"Tell the kids where we are, Conor Quinn."

I raise my eyebrows and force a smile. "We are at Le Grill."

"And does this restaurant have a Michelin star?"

"Yes, it does."

"The portions are tiny but fucking delicious." With that, he turns the mobile on himself and gives a wicked grin. "More later."

"Is that going to Instagram or to Valentina?" I ask when he bows his head and starts keying furiously.

"Both, I suppose. I mean, it'll go on Insta and then Val will end up seeing it. She'd love to be here, I can tell you that."

"Is she into this sort of thing?"

He looks up at me. "What do you mean?"

"Wealth for wealth's sake? Is that her thing?"

"You still think she must be some sort of gold digger if she's into me, is that it?"

"I didn't say that."

"It was implied."

"It was inferred. There's a difference."

He rolls his eyes. "Anyway, no, she's not particularly into this sort of thing."

"Tell me about her."

His expression changes. His eyes grow unfocused, a reflexive smile transforming his face as he thinks of the girl he'll soon meet in person for the first time.

"At a loss for words?" I ask with a smirk.

"Eh, what can I say? She's beautiful, smart, sweet."

"No offense, but plenty of girls fit that description. What makes her worth traveling all this way?"

"I told you. We have a connection."

"Tell me about that."

"Ah, you wouldn't understand."

"Wouldn't I?"

Focusing on me, he considers that. "I don't think you would."

"Because? Give me something here, Donal. I mean, I'm a pretty understanding fella, wouldn't you say?"

"It's just—how we connected in the first place was, I dunno, I just think you'd laugh at it."

His discomfort makes me sit forward in my chair. I drop the smirk and try my best to adopt an open expression. "I wouldn't, I swear."

He struggles for a moment before finally shrugging. "It was Doctor Who."

Thankfully, I'm more confused than amused, so laughter doesn't come to me. But I'm still at a loss, and he can tell that.

"She messaged me on Instagram because of a Doctor Who Funko doll I had in the background of one of my posts. So, the way we connected is because we're both basically nerds for Doctor Who."

Leaning back, I train my eyes on the sun-dappled blue water.

Donal laughs. "Didn't expect that, did ya? Yeah, didn't think Mr. Cool Conor Quinn would appreciate that sort of thing."

"It's not that. It just takes me back to when your da and I were in school. He was really into that show, too."

"He's the reason I'm into it."

I meet his eyes and can tell there's more to the story. "Is that right?"

Another shrug, this one more forced. "When my parents first split, my da had this big empty house not far from ours. We'd spend time there and it always felt so … hollow. But then we got into watching the show together and it was those times that really just helped carry me through. As silly as it sounds, it was something I could rely on. Me and Da sitting together binging on one episode after another. Colm and Sean didn't really take to it, so they'd usually be off in their room playing video games or in the back garden daring each other to eat worms or some shite. That left me and Da to have this … thing that was ours."

I nod. "I can imagine that left an impression."

He clears his throat. "Yeah, so when Valentina contacted me, it wasn't some come on. She wasn't looking for some 'in' with the son of Rogue's bassist. She was truly only into the Doctor Who thing."

He's right. It is nerdy. And sweet. The last vestige, perhaps, of his childhood carrying over into adulthood. But there's no harm in that.

"Tell me something," I say, mock-serious.

"Yeah?" He looks wary.

"You brought the Doctor Who Funko thing to give her, right?"

Relief floods his face. "I did indeed. Almost forgot it as I was half-bloody-asleep when you came round but I ran back to grab it."

I give him a wink. "Good lad."

THERE'S a noticeable addition to our suite when we finally return in the early evening, having walked off our lunch with an exploration of the Monte Carlo Harbor, where the yachts are even more impressive up close.

It's the Marshall amp I had requested.

Donal eyes it suspiciously. "Is that—"

"It is, Cinderella. When you get turned back into your pumpkin self after tonight, it'll be time to make good on your promise."

I get the eye roll once more, but there's a hint of a smile, too.

"I'd say I'm less Cinderella and more a well-kept mistress

at this rate," he says with a laugh. "Fancy hotel, closet full of clothes, Michelin star meal? Can't do much better than that."

I raise my eyebrows. "Count yourself lucky I'm asking for so little in return."

He laughs again and shakes his head. "I'm going to give Val a call before we head back out."

"Sounds good."

We separate to our rooms and I collapse on the king-sized bed, weary from this trip. Weary from missing my kids and my wife. Weary from having avoided confronting myself over the last few days. This whole thing of going against my instincts and giving up control has been good in the sense that it snapped me out of the worst of my depression. But it's also taken me away from those I love most. At the point where I'm feeling time is the most precious thing there is, have I just fucked myself by pissing more of it away?

Rubbing my face hard, I force myself to discard that regret. It does me no good now. I have to remember that I was at a breaking point. I *needed* something to jolt me out of my despair. I *needed* to break away from the comfortable cocoon of my depression.

In the last few days, I have found some joy again. I've gotten a lot of satisfaction out of knowing I'm capable of guiding Donal in the right direction. I've found some musical inspiration with the lyrics I've sent to Felicity and the vague melody that's been in the back of my mind. I've come to realize that while I may not be in that same stage of possibility that Donal is in now, I'm not done with my journey. I've got more life to experience, more love to give and receive, more music to make with my band. And my father, I know, would be proud of me for having found these answers.

I'd avoided calling Felicity and the kids until now because

I thought it would interfere with my mission in getting away. I thought if I heard their voices or saw them on video, I'd lose any momentum I'd had in trying to sort myself. But I've discarded that notion now. Because I know they are the very ones to fuel me for the rest of this trip until I can get home to them. That's all that I want and need now: to get home to them.

It's half-seven when I call my wife. She answers on the first ring and quickly turns the call into a video chat, setting her mobile up at the dining room table so that I can join my family for dinner. She's a dream, light and yet careful to make this impromptu call into something almost normal. The kids follow her lead and act as if I'm actually there and it's just another meal together where we go around to discuss the best part of our day. Romeo's is having blocked three goals during his football club's practice. Ella's is a new joke she learned: *What's the best thing about Switzerland? I don't know, but the flag is a BIG plus*. Felicity's is that the kids have eaten all of their vegetables without her having to ask. She gives both kids a wink and a tickle as she says this, making them laugh.

"What's yours, Daddy?" Ella asks.

"Mine? Mine is this. Being with you all right now."

"When will you be home?" Romeo asks.

"Soon, Son. Just as soon as possible."

And then, just like the distractible kids they are, Romeo asks permission to watch Arsenal playing Manchester City on television and Ella says she wants to go write down the joke she just told. Felicity releases them only after they've blown kisses to me and sent their love. She then takes her mobile upstairs to our bedroom.

"Sweetheart," she says once she's closed the door. "How are you really?"

"God, I'm a thousand times better for having just done dinner with you. I miss you all."

"We miss you."

"Are you all right? I'm sorry I left you on your own with the kids. It was shitty to do that, especially now. I know you're crazy busy."

"It's okay. Really. As long as you're ... feeling better?"

There's a question in her voice that I don't think she meant to reveal, but I don't blame her. "I am, honey. I'm getting there. Thanks for your patience."

"Always."

We share a moment of just looking at each other. I long to reach out and stroke her pale cheek, to trace the freckles there.

"So," she says with an amused smile, "Monte Carlo, is it?"

"I made a deal with Donal. My part is to show him the high roller life here in the 'Billionaire's Playground.'"

When she laughs, I realize how much I've missed the sound of that. Not just being away the last few days, but before then, when I was in such a dark place that I brought her down with me as well. She mustn't have felt she could enjoy life if I didn't.

"And what is his part of the deal?"

"You'll see later tonight. That is, if you're following his Instagram?"

"I am now. All in the hope of seeing your handsome, scruffy, face."

I laugh and run my hand over the light beard that's grown in. "Get a good look. It's going away tonight."

"Why tonight?"

"We're going to the casino. Best to do the clean-cut thing there."

"Ah. Place a bet for me?"

"I already won big when I made you my wife, Fee."

"Aww," she half-coos, half-groans. "So corny. But I love it."

"I love you."

"I love you, sweetheart. Come home to me safe, won't you?"

"It's a promise."

She blows me a kiss, blinks away the tears that suddenly cloud her eyes with our goodbyes, and disconnects.

34

DONAL

I've only worn a suit once, when my ma remarried. It was itchy and stiff, which matched the occasion, as I think of it. My stepfather is just as dull and formal as that brown suit. But he somehow pleases my ma, so it's all well and good.

The suit I have on now is an entirely different story. It's navy blue and the fine material flows over my frame as if it had been tailored to my exact measurements. It was the second suit I tried, the first being a bit too snug. Paired with a crisp, white dress shirt and brown leather belt and shoes, it makes me look older. If I could get the blue tie patterned with tiny triangles of yellow and red knotted correctly, I'd be all set.

I finally give up and leave it hanging around my neck as I go out to the living area. Conor is standing by the wet bar, though he's not drinking. He's got on a black suit that absolutely has to have been made for him because he looks like a walking advertisement out of *GQ* or one of those male models on the catwalk. He's shaved and his short hair is styled perfectly.

"Well, you certainly *look* of age," he says. "Still, it's a good thing I have a way for you to get into the casino since they're sticklers for being eighteen."

"Sneak in the back, will we?"

He looks at me with elaborate patience. "Not at all. We'll have a private escort through the *front* entrance."

"Of course."

"Now, what's with the tie?"

I stroke the fabric. "I couldn't make heads nor tails of it, honestly."

"Every man should know how to tie a tie. Knowing when and how to dress up is essential—even for a rock star."

I laugh at that because it seems he's including me in the category of rock star and I'm nowhere near being that. Still, I let him show me how to flip the strip of material this way and that until I've got the tie properly knotted.

"Good enough for a selfie, I'd say," Conor says with a wry smile.

Pulling out my mobile, I then throw my arm around his neck and snap a couple pics where we're both doing our best to look serious before we both fall into laughter. I get some of those, too, thinking to add one of each version for the next Instagram post. I've started using #QuinnAndWhelan on my posts with the two of us and the reaction is wild. I've gained thousands of followers and while I know it's all due to Conor's rabid fanbase, I'm enjoying the extra attention as it has extended my "fame" beyond the Dublin club scene. Because despite the dread I feel about presenting myself as a musician, I'm also thrilled at the prospect. Thrilled at the idea of just putting myself out there and *giving no fucks*. The freedom in that attitude is priceless.

But that's for later. First, we do the high roller thing.

Leaving the hotel, we have a short walk to the casino. The square is even busier tonight than it was earlier, with people gaping at the endless stream of sports cars.

Conor lets out a low whistle as we watch a Mercedes Benz Maybach Exelero, a Bugatti Divo, and a McLaren P1 LM purr past us.

"Hang on," he says and retrieves his mobile. He takes a video of the parade of cars that now also includes an Aston Martin Valkyrie. "Shay is going to orgasm for days when he sees this."

I laugh in agreement. My Uncle Shay's love of expensive sports cars is legendary, though he's had an obsession with high speed sailing for quite a while now, too.

We linger outside in the still-warm night air, taking in the spectacle. It's a fascinating display. Beautiful cars and beautiful people. But there's something underneath it that gives me pause.

Before I can figure it out, I hear Conor laugh. He holds out his mobile to show me Shay's response.

Shay: *That little display is worth over 20 million. And I bet not one of those fuckers owns it for more than show.*

I laugh, too, but it strikes at what was bothering me just before about the scene we're witnessing here. It's relentlessly surface-level. Everything in this town comes off as a *display*, as if the wealth wouldn't quite be as worthwhile if there weren't others to see it and admire it.

"Let's go in, yeah?"

I shake off the thought and agree that we should go into the casino. Conor drops some name at the door and we wait only a few minutes before a man arrives and greets us as if we're old pals. He's short and bald with a silver mustache and an ingratiating smile. After introducing himself as René, he escorts us through without an ID check.

The main hall has rose-colored marble columns supporting what is the first floor of an open atrium-style interior decorated with ornate frescoes and gold leaf accents. The skylight is a soft glow against the night sky. Heads turn as we walk by, and I straighten my spine, even if they're probably all focused on Conor. As usual, he doesn't betray any reaction to the attention, just keeps his cool.

We're led past an open area with slot machines to the roulette room, an appropriately round room with a gorgeous stained glass dome and dripping with crystal chandeliers. René asks what we'll drink and then leaves us to produce both our order and the chips we'll need to play. How this is being paid for, I have no idea, but it's hard to argue with being this well taken care of.

There are people mingling or congregating all around and the vibe is definitely *on*. Not in the wild way I imagine Las Vegas to be with gangs of guys falling over themselves, laughing and shouting. But in a more reserved, serious way. I'd guess that the amount of money being gambled here lends a different atmosphere.

It's a little disappointing, actually.

But then I take notice of the plentiful array of beautiful women throughout the room. Though there are blondes, brunettes, and redheads in the mix, they all have a similar sort of uniform that consists of a short dark dress and a delicious display of cleavage.

"Don't get too excited," Conor says, leaning into me. "They're hookers."

"What?" They can't be. They're so perfectly put-together,

wearing dresses and heels that reek of money. And they're not obviously giving anyone a come on, but rather easily moving through the crowds, stopping to smile and chat with ... men as they go.

"They'd make you believe otherwise, but you'd still be paying at the end of the night."

I nod slowly, pulling my eyes away from the blonde I'd been fixated on just as René returns with a young man in tow who is holding a tray of our drinks—I'd insisted on martinis in homage to all the James Bond movies filmed here. René is holding a stack of chips.

"I will check in with you gentlemen often during the evening," he says. "Until then, I wish you good luck." With a little bow and our thanks, he and his pal depart.

With a martini in one hand and a thick stack of chips in the other, I feel like a baller as I survey our options.

The only problem is that feeling is short-lived. Within a couple hours, I've downed three martinis and depleted three-quarters of my chips on roulette and craps. As much fun as it is to play with the big boys, luck is not on my side.

"Don't feel bad about it," Conor tells me. "There's a reason they say the house always wins."

"I'm not savvy enough at poker, but a bit of blackjack might be just the thing to turn it all around?"

He raises his eyebrows. "Hope springs eternal."

I have a brief winning streak at the blackjack table, betting 100 euros per hand while Conor watches over me. He won by a slight margin at the other tables and has decided to quit while he's ahead, so won't be gambling anymore.

My table-mates are all middle-age men of differing nationalities. They are very serious about their gambling, ignoring my attempts at chatting. That's when I realize what had bothered me outside when we were watching the sports cars go by: there's no joy in this show of excessive wealth, only spectacle.

As much as I've always enjoyed the finer things in life and craved upgrading our trip, this side of it all just feels so … shallow. Especially in comparison to the experiences we've had before this, including visiting the modest house of Paul McCartney, getting drunk lectures from Conor on how a terrible band still has all the possibility in the world, happening upon a magnificent view of Mont Blanc, and having a conversation with my father that opened the door to seeing him with a little more kindness. All of that because Conor took me up on the dare I hadn't even meant—that I'd do a motorbike road trip if he'd come with me.

Looking around now, I see the elegant casino, the well-dressed people, the staid atmosphere, and I'm … ready to leave. I've gotten a taste and it's like biting into a puff pastry: too much air, not enough substance.

With that in mind, I put all my remaining chips on the next hand. I get a king and a two. I make the "hit" gesture and get a ten. The closeness of that bust makes me laugh. The house always wins.

Turning to let Conor know we can go, I see he's moved a few feet back and is speaking with one of those high-class hookers, his head bowed so he can speak into her ear. I can't hear what he says, but after a moment she smiles at him dreamily and slowly sashays away.

I stand and join him. "What was that?"

"I told her I regretfully have to pass up the chance for her company," he says.

"*That* was enough to make her look at you like that?"

"Well, I also said that I sincerely hope she has a man who

worships *her* at least as well as I'm sure she treats the friends she makes in this place. Because surely, *her* needs deserve to be attended to."

Laughing, I say, "Only Conor fucking Quinn would worry whether a hooker is sexually satisfied."

"Hey, everyone has needs."

"True," I concede. Though, I have the feeling not every man would consider such things when it comes to a sex worker. The guy is always giving me a new way to look at things. "Anyway, I'm officially out of chips."

"You need a cash infusion?"

"Nah, I'm good. Let's get out of here."

He raises his eyebrows but doesn't say anything. Instead, we walk side by side out of the casino. This time, when the heads turn to stare as we go, I realize the attention is for both of us. While I don't think I've quite leveled-up to match Conor in the natural confidence he projects, I have come a long way from where I started. And it shows. I nod to myself.

It's time for me to make good on my promise.

35

DONAL

"Okay, Cinderella," Conor says, "play for me what you were playing yesterday in Lyon."

We have my guitar connected to the amp and I've tested a few chords while Conor made adjustments to get the sound just right. Now I've got no excuse to keep from playing.

Still, I hesitate, running my hand up and down the fretboard uselessly.

"What were you thinking about when you were playing?" Conor asks.

"Eh, Val. I was thinking about her and what it'll feel like to be with her for the first time."

"In bed, you mean?"

I groan in embarrassment but reply honestly. "Yeah, but also, just that very first moment when we'll actually be face to face."

"Tell me more. What exactly are you thinking of?"

"I dunno." I strum the guitar gently but the amp makes the notes hum deeply. "Just, I can't wait to really look into her eyes. She's got gorgeous green eyes but I want to see how the light changes them in person. I want to know her scent, feel the smoothness of her cheek under my touch, bury my face into her wavy hair."

"That's a song, right here."

I look up at him, feeling oddly surprised that he's just heard me. I almost thought for a moment that I'd only said those things in my head.

"But focus on that first bit. The part of how you can't wait to just take her in. Imagine you're standing together. Looking at each other. Not touching. Just *appreciating* what you see. That's the kind of connection that elevates desire to passion."

"What's the difference?"

"Desire is commonplace and fleeting. Passion is all-consuming and where next-level satisfaction is found. Always strive for passion. Whether it's with a woman or with music or with life."

I nod. And though I understand what he means and how it relates to my impending meeting with Valentina, I can also see why he's earned a relationship as a playboy. His reverence for women and treating them with such deliberate care is not exactly the way most guys I know operate.

And then the last bit about striving for passion in life strikes me. Because it's coming from a man who not just a few days ago admitted that he was depressed and didn't know if his band should continue to exist.

"What about you?" I ask, unable to stop myself.

He raises his eyebrows. "What do you mean?"

"Has your passion for life been ... restored?"

Sitting back against the sofa, he considers that. The silence stretches out and I force myself to keep quiet.

"Let's just say I've turned the corner in my way of thinking," he finally says.

"For fuck's sake," I reply with a frustrated laugh. "You have to give me more than that. Are you still depressed? Are you breaking up Rogue?"

"Donal, I can't make any declarations. I can't say I've totally shaken my dark thoughts and doubts."

"Oh." I look down in disappointment. There was a part of me that wished this trip helped him somehow. That *I'd* helped him.

"But when I say I've turned a corner," he continues, "that means I'm headed in the right direction. I've got movement. And it feels good. For the first time in a long time, I can appreciate how lucky I am and that I've got more good ahead of me than I realized for a time. That includes my family. Families, I should say. Felicity and the kids, of course. My mother, too. But also, Gav, Marty, and Shay. And all of us together, meaning the wives and kids. It's a rare privilege to have so many good people in your life. I don't take that for granted." He takes a deep breath. "I don't take Rogue for granted, either. What we've created together is exceptional. It's something only the four of us can do. It's something I'm looking forward to continuing."

I let out a heavy sigh of relief.

"Now, let's get to your end of the bargain. No more fucking around. Let me hear you play."

He's got his signature small smile, showing me his directive is a gentle one, that I can trust him with this thing I'm about to do. That my putting myself out there will be handled with care. I know that he will listen to me play, nudge me to get better, and only allow the very best version to be posted.

And so, that's what happens. With Val in mind, I craft a few minutes of guitar playing that evokes the wonder and passion I know I'll have when I finally meet her in person. I get lost in the music. I give no fucks about what any detractor might think or say. I put it all out there.

And damn it feels good.

Once the video is posted, I sit back on the sofa and can't help the smile of satisfaction that spreads across my face.

Then Conor says, "This wasn't some grand way of me handing you the baton, you know?"

There's a hint of jest in his expression, but mostly he's serious. "No?" I ask to goad him.

"No. It's more like this: you'd better up your game because you've got some tough competition. Rogue ain't done. Not by a long shot."

It's the best thing I could have heard. "Challenge accepted," I reply.

"Challenge yourself to write some lyrics, kid. You've got the bones of a good one from what we were talking about earlier."

"I will."

He stands and stretches. "On to Barcelona tomorrow. It's a long ride. Get some sleep while you can."

"Will do."

He's halfway to his room when I call after him.

Turning back, he waits for me to speak.

"I just wanted to thank you."

He starts to wave me off as if there's nothing to thank him for.

"No, I mean it," I say, standing. "I have so much to thank you for. This trip. These experiences. The guitar. The way you've pushed me to believe in myself. Even for … getting me to think differently about my da."

"It's been my pleasure, Donal." He starts to turn back toward his room but stops and looks at me once more.

"Thank you for letting me tag along. Thank you for being a big part of me realizing I've got a lot more to enjoy in this world before I'm done. Marty has an amazing kid in you."

With that, he turns and disappears for the night.

And I'm left with a lump in my throat that I have to force down.

I distract myself by scrolling through my mobile. After a time, I get up and search the suite for one of those complimentary notepads hotels seem to have. This place is too fancy to have something so basic. Instead, I find fine letterhead and a hefty ballpoint pen.

It'll do.

I spend the next four hours writing the lyrics for what will be my first song.

I fall asleep on the sofa, never even sleeping in that plush bed of the five-star hotel I'd been longing for.

And I don't even care.

36

MARTIN

Lainey slipped from bed and away from me only a minute ago, but I'm still lost in a post-sex delirium. With Donal away and my other boys with their mother, we've had the run of the house in the last few days, taking advantage of our privacy to freely reacquaint ourselves with each other's bodies. She'd been filming her latest movie in New York City for the past eight weeks before getting home in time for Conor's birthday party. The plan upon her return was to celebrate both Conor's fortieth and the band's twentieth.

Or so I thought.

The festivities took a turn when, first, Conor cast doubt on Rogue's future, and, second, when Conor and Donal both disappeared.

It wasn't until I knew they were together and well, that I was able to relax and take advantage of the sudden free time I had with Lainey.

We enjoyed ourselves, as I said, all over the house, including the kitchen island, on the bench press in the gym, the steam shower afterward, and now in bed.

Our jobs mean we are often apart for long stretches of time but this has become something we've accepted. Lainey has always enjoyed her independence and times of solitude, and I've always enjoyed giving her what she needs. That is especially easy for me to do knowing that our reunions are filled with the kind of hot sex people our age might not expect to still enjoy.

Tonight was no exception. I'd pressed the length of my body to hers from behind, holding her delicate wrists together in one of my hands and using the other to balance as I grinded myself deep inside her. The total control, combined with her unfettered moans, made me rock hard. And when she pushed her ass back against me, I rose to my knees and leaned back on my heels, bringing her with me so I could squeeze her tits as she took charge in reverse riding me.

We've always had incredible sexual chemistry, and it's a sort of point of pride that it continues even after all the years we've been together. Part of what makes it so good is how confident she is in bed.

Like when after I'd pulled her up with me and she rode my cock until I was ready to burst, she grabbed my hand and sucked hard on two fingers. The friction of her tongue mirrored the tightness of her pussy as she slid up and down on me until all I wanted was to time her orgasm with mine. Taking my hand from her mouth, I used it instead to tease her clit. I held off giving her sustained pressure until I could gauge how close she was to coming.

"Yes," she moaned. "More. Please."

That's all I needed. That's all she needed.

Between my hand on her clit and her ass bouncing up and down against my hips as she took the thick length of me deep inside her, we were soon both releasing satisfied groans.

Sweaty and sated, I'd collapsed onto my belly, eyes closed. "It's good to be home."

I cracked an eye and saw her wry smile. Reaching out, I pulled her to me. She's slight of frame and I love that I can feel like I'm protecting her when I hold her. Though, truth be told, she does not need the likes of me to make her feel safe. She's her own woman and even though she calls our place in Howth "home," she also has a place in Santa Barbara where she spends a good amount of time. I learned long ago that she never wants to feel tied down. It's why I won't ever ask her to marry me. She made it clear that marriage wasn't something she believed in. But she's also made it clear in ways big and small that she's in this thing with me for the long haul. She's helped me raise my boys in the most non-intrusive way possible. We've become each other's sounding board for work. We've traveled the world together and made plans for what life will be like when we're old and gray. It might not be the most traditional relationship, but it works. And I've never been happier.

"Good to have you home," I tell her. "Always."

She kisses me quickly before getting up and half-closing the en suite door behind her. The sound of the shower lulls me into a light doze, a smile still on my face.

A notification sounds from my mobile. It's on the nightstand, just out of reach, and I almost ignore it, preferring to succumb to sleep.

But the thought that it could be a message from Donal stirs me into action. Our call last night had been bittersweet. He'd been his usual moody self until he mentioned his stay in Lambeth. Sure, he'd complained about the shit motel they'd stayed in, but there was a lightness to his voice that belied his words. It was a tell that revealed he was having a good time out on the road with Conor. That was the bitter part—knowing that another man was guiding my boy in the kind of journey I'd love to have with him.

The other negative part was hearing that he was only calling because Conor insisted on it. I still don't know where we went wrong in our relationship. He has to know I only want the best for him ... doesn't he?

With a groan, I reach for my mobile and then return to my stomach to read the notification.

It's an alert that Donal Whelan has posted something new to Instagram.

Great. Another photo of my kid with Conor Quinn, I think, as I open the app. What I find both thrills and perplexes me.

It's Donal playing the guitar. Not just any guitar, but a gorgeous Telecaster. And doing so in an effortless way, his fingers gliding over the strings as he creates a unique riff that drips with longing and anticipation.

I watch the video three times, awestruck by his natural talent. He's rarely shared his guitar playing with me, and when he did, it was only bits and pieces of Rogue songs. The song he's playing in the video is original. It's also compelling, with enough of a hook to stick in your head. Sure, I'm biased in the whole thing, but the performance really is ... magnetic. I can't look away. Not even when Lainey returns from her shower, naked and still damp, and climbs on top of me, molding her body to mine.

"What are you watching?"

"Eh, it's Donal."

"Really?"

She rests her chin on my shoulder and we watch the video together.

"He's incredible," she says at the end.

"He really is. Seems Conor's turned my son into a rock star."

I feel her fingers in the hair at the nape of my neck, followed by her lips as she presses a kiss in the same spot.

"Conor may have pushed him, but he got his good looks and talent from you, babe."

While I appreciate her effort to take the sting out of the realization that my kid has found his confidence through the guidance of another man, it still leaves a lasting impression. I can't help but wish I had been able to connect with him in this way.

With a sigh, I comfort myself with the thought that if any other person was to take this role in his life, I'm at least glad that it was Conor.

Lainey slides off of my body but doesn't go far, settling next to me with her head on my pillow. I turn to face her.

"What will you tell him?" she asks.

"What do you mean?"

"You should text him. Tell him what you think about his post."

"Oh, yeah. I should."

"I'm sure whatever you say will mean a lot to him."

I don't exactly agree that Donal wants to hear anything from me, but I don't argue the point. Because it doesn't matter what I believe. The thing with parenting is that you very often have to act as if your kid *will* hear you, even if that means it won't actually sink in for years to come.

With that in mind, I start my text.

37

FELICITY

So, this is happiness, my felicity
This is passion, my purpose
This is what's meant to be
All I need is the four of us

Four is the number of my life
Four brothers, family is four
Four decades and many more
Forever yours, forever yours

I blink back tears in reading the latest lyrics from Conor. The affirmation that his happiness is with his family isn't a surprise, but it's still comforting. The reference to four brothers has to mean Gavin, Shay, Martin, *and* Danny Boy. There's no doubt that for Danny Boy to be named as a brother to Conor in a song would be the honor of a lifetime for him. It seems Conor is assessing what matters most to him and putting it into beautiful perspective.

All of this makes me realize I did the right thing in letting him go unquestioned on this journey. It wasn't easy. I wanted more than anything to jump out of bed that morning he left, wrap myself around him, and plead for him to stay. I wanted him to know that *I* could help him through his troubles. *I* wanted to be his salvation, even as my own experience told me there are some things that one has to do for oneself.

I had restrained myself from imposing on what he needed to do for himself, though I second-guessed that decision for the first couple of days. But he's taken me with him on his journey in a way. The lyrics he's been sending have told me so much. I don't know if he'll ever really turn it into a song, but it feels like a good start to this next chapter of Rogue. It's raw, it's personal, it's honest. That's the way forward—for Conor, for Rogue, for all of us.

I text him back: *Yours right back, forever and always*

38

DONAL

When I wake, I'm face down between the sofa cushions. Apparently, I leaned over at some point to rest my eyes and ended up deeply, awkwardly asleep.

Even though my neck already feels tweaked, I don't move. Instead, I keep my eyes closed and relive last night. Not the dressing to the nines and gambling in one of the world's most famous casinos part, but after all that. The part when I crafted an original tune on the guitar and posted it to Instagram, thereby announcing my musical aspirations.

I did the thing I feared most: I put myself out to be judged. But only because I was able to get to a place where I worried less about what people might say and more about what my guitar could say. I gave no fucks and worked my art.

I won't lie. I did check the comments on the post after Conor went to his room. At first, they were a rush of disappointed girls wondering where Conor was. They'd gotten accustomed to seeing his face on my account. But the video I posted was just me. Me on this same sofa in the low light of the suite's living room, wearing the ratty black T-shirt and black jeans I've worn repeatedly on this trip, and holding a gorgeous guitar. Just me pouring all my energy and heart out into those two minutes of playing.

As I kept scrolling through the comments, I started to see a new pattern. It was a stream of girls mostly saying how hot I am, how I make the guitar bend to my will, how they'd like for me to strum them the same way I do the strings. And then there were some comments that didn't come from horny Rogue fans ready to settle for me. Those comments were actually thoughtful and complimentary, often asking the name of my band and where they can stream the song. Those messages gave me a thrill and boosted both my confidence and my ego.

But that feeling came crashing down when a text notification from my father popped up. All at once, I realized that this would be the first time he's seen me really play and I braced for his reaction. Turned out I needn't have worried about anything negative.

Da: *What an amazing gift you have, son. So glad you're ready to share it with the world. Can't wait to see what you do next.*

I found myself smiling at that and responding right away.

Me: *Thanks, Da. Maybe we can jam together when I get back?*
Da: *I'd love it. Truly.*

And that was how we left it. I spent the rest of the night working on my lyrics and crashed at some point. It can't have been long ago, though, because I'm exhausted. Happily exhausted and ready to drift off to sleep some more. But then I hear a rustling of paper and startle fully awake.

Groaning, I turn my aching neck to follow the sound and see Conor standing by the coffee table, reading my lyrics.

In a flash, I'm up and lunging at him, grabbing the sheets.

"Calm down," he says mildly.

"You should've asked." I fold the papers in half, then once more, and tuck them into my jeans pocket.

"I like the chorus bit. *These senses of mine, they've just been born/'cause, honey, all I want is to be yours.*"

The compliment takes me by surprise. "Oh." I clear my throat and try not to sound too eager. "Yeah?"

He nods in that sage, cool way of his. "But seems you're missing an ending?"

"Eh, yeah. I'm sort of waiting until after I meet her. I mean, this whole thing could go one of two ways, couldn't it?"

"Meaning?"

"What if we just don't click in person? What if it's strictly an online romance?"

He considers me for a moment before laughing. "Either way, it'll make for a great resolution to the song."

I smile and shake my head at that. "All about them life experiences, yeah? As long as it makes a great song?"

"All I can say is it's always worked for me."

That answer brings to mind what I know of his and Gavin's songwriting partnership. How all the tabloids and online Rogue fandoms I'd explored had pointed out that his rumored affair with Sophie was responsible for some of the greatest love songs ever written.

"Anyway," he continues, "we should grab some breakfast and hit the road."

"Yeah, I definitely need coffee."

"Grab whichever of those new clothes you can fit in your bag. The rest will be shipped back to your da's house."

"You think of everything, don't you?"

"Not always. But I make an effort these days."

I laugh and shake my head. He's the most put-together, talented, and decent person I know. And he's humble, too. Seems I chose well to have him as a role model.

39

DONAL

We make it to Barcelona by eight in the evening and I follow Conor to an upscale hotel in the center of the city. The wide, cosmopolitan streets are busy with the sense that the evening is just getting started, but I'm knackered and tell Conor as much when we're in the lift on the way to our rooms.

"You'd better shake it off, man. This is our last night. We're going out at eleven," he tells me.

"Really?"

"You turn eighteen at midnight. We have to ring it in properly. Tomorrow you'll be on your way to Mallorca, and I'll be back to Dublin. This is our last night. Can't let it get away from us."

I feel an unwelcome pang at the thought that our trip is almost over. As excited as I am to see Valentina, this time with Conor has been more than I ever could have asked for. He's not just an uncle or godfather to me. He's a true friend.

The lift doors open and we step out. Our rooms are next to each other.

"Order room service if you want. Something to tide you over, yeah?" Conor says with a nod before disappearing into his room.

My room isn't extravagant like the one we had in Monte Carlo, but it's more than comfortable. I drop my gear and head straight for the shower. The thing with being on a motorbike all day is that you pick up a million bits of the road, including dirt and bugs and petrol. It has been both an exhilarating and exhausting way to travel, and one that I'd repeat in a heartbeat. Another thing I'm feeling bittersweet about is the fact that today was our last day on the bikes. Conor is arranging for them to be picked up from the hotel and shipped back to Dublin. But man, it's been a thrill I won't soon forget.

In the shower, I let the hot water rain down over my body while thinking of Val and our meeting tomorrow. I have a flight to Palma at one o'clock in the afternoon. It's a quick hop to get there, less than an hour. Conor's offered to take my guitar with him back to Dublin, but I want to hang on to it. I have a vision of finding my way to Val at her uncle's place, the guitar slung over my back, showing up as the man I've become in these last few days. The musician that I've become. The rock star on the verge of doing something big with his life.

What will she make of this new me?

When I first planned to celebrate my birthday with her, I was a kid with no real ambition. I just wanted to enjoy the Dublin club scene, screw around with silly things like graffiti, joy riding, messing with the idea of music with Owen, and giving over to the notion that Val was my girlfriend even though we'd never met in person. It was something to latch onto. It was something that gave me a hint of a direction rather than the continuation of my stagnant life.

I laugh at the whole idea now and rub my face, smiling into my hands. It was almost comically naive, I admit to myself. Yes, she and I have a connection through Doctor Who and an attraction, but I can't honestly say it's more than that.

Conor would tell me that's nothing to worry about. That the experience of having given into the idea itself, that she could be something special, makes all this worth it. If only for the potential song that might come out of it.

With this in mind, I shut off the water and vow to go to her tomorrow with no expectations. All I can do is see where things lead once we meet. And the anticipation is something to savor.

OUR NIGHT out to celebrate my birthday is at a club right on the beach and is a blur of too many drinks, a DJ spinning so loud that conversation is impossible, and girls with short skirts and low-cut tops rubbing up against both me and Conor.

We drink and dance until we closed the place down. Then we wander drunkenly along the sand as the sun comes up, thinking we're heading in the right direction toward our hotel. But as we stagger on, we find ourselves further from signs of life rather than closer to the main drag.

"Fuck, I'm drunk," Conor says, somehow smiling and frowning at the same time.

"So. Am. I," I reply.

"You don't understand. I don't get drunk."

I sputter out a laugh. "Could have fooled me. What about the first night of our trip? What was that?"

"That? That was me going recklessly, ridiculously against type."

"Why?"

"To ... see if I could escape it since I couldn't control it."

I'm not sure if it's me or him who isn't making sense. "Escape what?"

He hangs his head. "The black pit of sadness I'd been stuck in."

That sobers me up. And though I know the answer, I still ask, "And did it?"

He's quiet for a long moment, and then he laughs. Like, *really* laughs. Though, what he says doesn't seem particularly funny.

"No, it fucking didn't."

"Then why'd you get drunk again tonight?"

"Completely different reason," he says. "This time, I just wanted one more taste of that freedom. Not to escape but to just let loose and enjoy a good time with you. To celebrate your birthday and our trip and all the amazing possibilities we both have in our lives from here on out."

I love that sentiment, but there's something more I have to ask. "And that black pit of sadness?"

He shrugs. "Not entirely gone, but no longer overwhelming my every thought."

I nod, relieved once more that he's admitting that his mental state is moving in the right direction.

"Okay, then," I say, "I've got one last way you can taste a bit of that freedom. And it just might help sober us both up."

"What's that?"

Turning my gaze to the Mediterranean Sea on our left, I start to kick off my shoes.

"You're joking?" he asks, amused.

I pull my shirt off over my head. "When will you ever have this chance again, Uncle Conor? A lovely dip at sunrise?"

It takes him only a second before he says, "Fuck it."

Soon, we each leave a pile of clothes on the sand as we run bare-arse naked into the water, diving under the small waves and swimming to a calm spot. It's cold enough to be a shock to the system. But also refreshing and exactly what we need.

We don't stay in the water long, just enough to feel a sense of renewal. Or at least, I know that's what I feel. It solidifies the sentiment Conor had mentioned before we went in, about celebrating the *possibilities* still to come in our lives. We may be in different stages of our lives, but there is no doubt we both have a lot more ahead of us.

Afterward, we struggle to get our clothes on over our still-wet bodies and end up laughing all the way back to the hotel. Conor gives me back the credit cards he'd confiscated from me on the first day of the trip. And then, we say our goodbyes in the hallway, clapping each other hard on the back as we embrace. No more thanks or other conversation are needed. The depth of what we've experienced together doesn't need to be addressed. It just is.

With only a couple of hours of sleep before my flight, I'll be running on fumes, but I don't care. Not when I've just had the best time of my life and have so much more to look forward to.

40

CONOR

I sleep most of the nearly three-hour flight home to Dublin, which does a world of good for my aching head. Even with the hangover, I'm still smiling at the memory of last night and early this morning as I catch a taxi.

It won't take long to get to Croke Park where I know Gavin and the lads have a rehearsal and sound check scheduled. I use the time to text Felicity the last bit of the song I've written.

Remember when I said you are the light?
I promise you everything will be all right
I'm coming home, honey
I'm coming home to you
I'll always come home to you

When I get to the stadium, I luckily come across one of our longtime techs who is only too happy to guide me through the maze of gates, doors, and corridors until I'm at the side of the large stage.

Everyone is in place, with Randy, my guitar tech, filling in for me as they rehearse "You're My One." It's a song that needs no practicing for any of us. In one of the longest streaks on record in the music industry, we've played it at every single gig we've ever had. It's a song that once held a lot of meaning for me, but I've long since let that go. Gavin, however, has never done so. Not only does it still hit home for him to this very day, but he feels a sense of responsibility to give the fans what they want with playing it so regularly. It was the song that sent us over the top, after all, giving us this incredibly fortunate life.

As if sensing my presence, Gavin glances my way. I give him a nod, and he returns it without missing a word.

But my attention is soon fixed elsewhere as I spot Felicity on the opposite end of the stage. She's got a raft of papers balanced in one arm and is staring at her mobile in her other hand. Maybe at something to do with her job of getting our anniversary gig ready to showcase to the world tomorrow. Or maybe at the lyrics I've sent her.

In any case, I need to get to her. I take the shortest route, striding across the stage with the same sort of confidence I have when we play that I know borders on a cocky strut. The boys play on, no doubt urged by Gavin to continue as he'd likely intuit my purpose. He and I have that kind of understanding after all these years.

I'm just a few steps away when she looks up and sees me. I wrap one arm around her waist, pull her body to mine, and slip a hand into the hair at the nape of her neck.

"Told you I was coming home," I say and see her smile before I lean down and kiss her in a way that sends her up on tiptoes to get more.

I hear that stack of papers she'd been holding fall to the

floor as she wraps her arms around my neck and presses her body to mine. Her soft lips and insistent tongue have the same mixture of passion and relief as mine do.

I don't want to stop, but she pulls away and buries her face into my chest. "I knew you'd be back in time," she whispers.

"Only just."

When she looks up at me, her eyes search mine. "I *missed* you, sweetheart."

"I know. I missed me, too, if you know what I mean. But, I'm here now. I'm here now."

That sinks in and she nods. It's a blessing that this woman understands me so well, that she knows I'm saying a part of me was lost for a time, but now I've found my way. And I'm right where I want to be.

"I think this belongs to you."

We both look up to find Randy, my guitar tech, holding out my Telecaster. Smiling, I take it from him.

"Thanks for filling in, mate," I say.

"Yeah, well, don't let my attempt to emulate you fool you. I was petrified you wouldn't be back and I'd have to go on tomorrow. Thank Christ that won't be necessary!" he says with a phlegmy laugh that takes me back to Lambeth and the woman in curlers who listened in on me arguing with Donal over his horrific piercings.

I laugh and shake my head. "No worries."

Gavin, Martin, Shay, and even Danny Boy join us and we do a bit of hugging and asking after each other. There are no recriminations for my disappearance, no questioning where I'd been. Just the same unwavering support I've always gotten from these brothers of mine.

When there's a break in the conversation, I see the hungry

look in Martin's eyes and know he's eager for more information about Donal.

I give him a nod and say, "He's well. Got a really good head on his shoulders, Marty. I don't think you have much to worry about."

The tension leaves his body and he smiles. "Good to hear. Thanks for looking after him."

"I'm not joking when I say he looked after me."

He nods before reluctantly giving into the idea. "That's grand."

"Okay, time is slipping by," Gavin says. "Con, let's get you up to speed on the setlist and get rehearsing it so the fellas can check their sound and lights."

"I'm ready. Let's do this."

And just like that, we're a foursome again, launching into the songs that made us a band to reckon with. We play for more than an hour and I get lost in the groove that only we can create. It's a homecoming, for sure, and it feels fucking good.

"Aye, Gav," I say when it seems we've done enough with the old hits. "Mind if we toy around with something I've got in mind?"

"Something new?" he asks with a hopeful smile. It's a smile that tells me he's only delighted to think I'm ready to push past this twenty-year anniversary nostalgia and into the next phase of our careers.

"It is," I affirm.

"Got a title for it yet?"

That's a question I usually ask Gavin since it's a common practice of his to use a title as a jumping-off point for song writing. I hadn't thought to give my lyrics a title but now that he's asked, one comes instantly to mind.

"Yeah," I say. "It's called 'Coming Home.'"

A grin spreads across Gavin's face. His obvious excitement sparks the tingle in me that happens whenever the creative juices get flowing.

I'm ready for whatever comes next.

41

DONAL

My vision for how I'd make my way to see Valentina was spot on. I tried to clean myself up for the occasion, though, of course. I'm wearing the new jeans supplied in Monte Carlo, a fresh white T-shirt, and my motorcycle boots and black leather jacket. In addition to my bag, I've also got the guitar slung over my back. Her uncle lives in Old Town Palma where the streets are medieval, the churches are gothic, and the charm is plentiful. After a taxi has taken me as far as it can go, I follow my map app along several narrow streets until I'm walking on a pedestrian-only uneven path bordered by buildings covered in foliage that has started to turn copper-gold with the changing of the seasons.

Finally, I find the right door and use the heavy iron knocker. At first, I hear nothing and I worry I've bothered the wrong address—or that Val has changed her mind about seeing me. But then the sound of laughing and steps coming closer is clear.

This is it. I remind myself to take my time, to soak up the sight of her, to breathe her in. This is the only moment that we will be this unfamiliar to each other. We'll never again have this opportunity to wonder what it's like to touch, taste, inhale, and hear each other.

The door swings open and there she is, eyes wide and expectant, but a smile turning up the corners of her generous mouth. She's wearing a yellow blouse with fluttery short sleeves and cut-off jean shorts with flat leather sandals. Her dark-brown hair is down, the loose curls shifting slightly with the breeze. Those green eyes of hers look darker in the shadow of the doorway, the gold flecks less visible.

I don't know how long we stand there, just taking each other in, but the whole time, I'm trying to imprint this moment in my mind. To remember how lovely and nervous she looked. How she smelled not of perfume but of some kind of tropical lotion. And how she gazed up at me with her own anticipation.

"Hola, Donal," she says and laughs once more.

I've never seen her so uncomfortable. What a difference being in person makes. There was a kind of ease when we were behind our screens that is gone now.

"Oh, and happy birthday!" she adds, leaning in to kiss me on the cheek.

But I was setting down my bag at the same time and awkwardly miss her kiss. To cover, I start digging inside.

"Hang on," I say. "I just want to find, em, I wanted to give this to you."

Locating the Doctor Who figurine amongst my stuff, I pull it free and present it to her.

Her reaction is not what I expected. She looks surprised—and not in a good way.

"But, you remember my favorite Doctor is Matt Smith?"

"Oh, I, eh." That stumps me. Our whole connection began

because she admired my David Tennet Funko doll. "Yeah, I remember. I just thought you'd like this, too?"

"It is sweet, Donal," she says and takes it from me.

I watch as she smiles down at it before placing it on a side table just inside the door, her appreciation for it obviously fleeting.

Maybe I'd overestimated the importance Doctor Who. I go back to what we'd texted about when Conor got those Beatles lyrics stuck in my head. Reaching out, I take her hand into both of mine. She's petite, with fine-boned, delicate hands.

"Remember I said I wanted to hold your hand?" I ask, and I could swear I see her forehead crease as she struggles to recall what I'm talking about before she clears it away.

Jesus, what am I doing? I keep trying to create these moments instead of just letting this all happen. I thought she was nervous. But I'm even worse. I roll my eyes. This time, at myself.

"Do you want to come in?" she asks. "My cousins are here but they won't bother us."

"Eh, could we maybe go for a walk? Would the cousins be okay on their own?"

Turning to look back inside the house, she fires off a few words in Spanish and gets a disinterested reply. "Okay, yes," she then tells me. "Leave your things here inside."

I do as she says and it feels good to be unburdened. But as we start to walk, I can't help but feel disappointed in our meeting so far. All the anticipation, all the conversations I had with Conor, led me to create this romantic vision in my mind of how this would be. But so far, it's been decidedly ... ordinary.

"Are you hungry? We can get something to eat?" she asks and pushes her hands into her pockets.

"I'm fine. But—if you want something, we can eat."

She shakes her head and we walk on in silence for a minute. "Your video, it went virus."

I smile and say gently, "Viral." Taking a deep breath, I shake my head. "Yeah, seems to have gone over. My mate Owen is probably responsible. Says he watched it one million times exactly to get the numbers up."

Glancing at me, she raises an eyebrow.

"Joking. He's joking. I think."

She forces a laugh. "Okay."

We turn right and onto a larger street that includes auto traffic, so it's louder, less intimate. I feel our chance to connect slipping away.

"Val, maybe we can go somewhere quieter?"

She thinks for a moment before nodding to a street lined with restaurants and shops. I follow her lead and we soon end up in a gelato shop.

"This place has the world's best gelato," she tells me, and I don't know if she's being deliberately obtuse or not because the neon sign out front literally says "World's Best Gelato." But then she cracks a smile and I laugh. "Sit. I'll get us something."

There are three round tables in the small shop, two of which are taken. I grab the free one and watch as Val chats with the young man behind the counter. The stilted way she's been with me is gone as they enjoy an easy back and forth while he scoops out the gelato. The contrast is another blow to my expectations of how we'd be with each other.

Joining me, she has a large, chocolate-covered cone filled with what looks like chocolate gelato sprinkled with nuts.

"I hope you like the candy Ferrero Rocher?" she asks. "We can share."

"Love it, thanks."

I welcome the distraction of the gelato, anything to shake off our odd disconnect.

I watch her take a lick, focusing on the way her lips part and her tongue darts out to claim a taste. She glances at me as she pulls away and I curse myself for not kissing her as soon as I saw her.

"So—"

"Do—"

We'd both started speaking and stopped at the same time. She laughs again and shakes her head, her curls swaying with the motion.

Since conversation isn't getting any better, I lean in to try the gelato in her hand. But she's done the same and we end up bumping foreheads.

Jesus. I groan inwardly, feeling like an eejit.

"Wait a minute?" she asks and jumps up from the table.

For a second, I think she might skip out the back door and wouldn't blame her. This isn't exactly the way I'd envisioned things. We were so effortless on the phone, whether it was chatting, texting, or video calling. But this has been excruciating.

When she turns around from the counter, though, I see she hasn't made an escape. Instead, she's coming back to our table with a lit candle carefully cupped in her hand. In a voice barely above a whisper, she sings happy birthday to me.

It's a sweet gesture, making me smile. Besides the voicemail my ma left me early this morning, she's the only person to sing to me today.

"Make a wish," she says.

I wish ... that I can start over with her. That, I can think with less calculation and act more on impulse. Because I realize that when I showed up at her door and stared at her, saying nothing, I freaked her out. I was *taking her in* as a way to remember the moment and trying to elevate it into something song-worthy when I should have simply remembered that we *already* have a connection from the last few months of talking non-stop. That no matter what happens, just as Conor said, I can craft a great ending to my song. So, what's more important is just enjoying this beautiful girl in front of me.

I blow out the candle. And then I lean over, slide my hand along her jaw to cup her cheek, and kiss her.

And she kisses me back.

The connection I've been wanting is there. It's in the way our lips touch, of course. But it's also in the way her hand naturally finds the nape of my neck, her nails trailing through my hair. And most of all, it's in the way that when we pull apart our eyes are both filled with a mixture of relief and desire.

I know Conor says to seek passion, not desire. But, for fuck's sake, I'm eighteen. I'll indulge in anything and everything I can right now.

Not that I'm discounting all the good advice and life lessons I got from Conor, but I've got to find my own way, make my own mistakes, go on my own adventures. I've got my whole life ahead of me, after all.

"Val," I say.

"Yes?"

"What's the best hotel in this town?"

"Why do you ask?"

"I want to celebrate my birthday in style—with you."

She smiles and her green eyes shine brightly. "Let's go get your things first. I want to hear you play that guitar—for me."

Now, I smile. There's no need to tell her the guitar won't

sounds the same as my Instagram video without an amp. I can still play for her, still give her an idea of what I'm capable of.

What matters now is that the vibe between us has changed completely. Now it's easy and sexy and perfect. All I needed to do was relax and be me.

"Let's go," I say, pulling her to stand with me before kissing her once more.

She fists my shirt, leaning into me. And when she moans softly into my mouth, my dick twitches.

"We have to go," I say.

"We really do," she replies with an exaggerated nod, making me laugh.

Wrapping my arm around her neck, I lead her out of the World's Best Gelato shop and back toward her house. We talk the whole way this time, all awkwardness gone.

And we make quick work of picking up my things.

We've got some celebrating to do.

I'm ready for whatever comes next.

EPILOGUE
DONAL

Nine months later - Santiago, Estadio Nacional de Chile

I'm standing on stage, trying to absorb the enormity of the stadium spread out in front of me. It's still early afternoon and the seats and general admission floor are empty. In a matter of hours, though, the venue will be packed with just over 60,000 rabid fans.

But first, the setup and testing of light and sound equipment continues all around me. It's the opening night of the tour and you might think there'd be a frantic vibe to get things done in time for the gig, but this crew knows what they're doing. There's no panic. Rather, it is relentless efficiency as dozens of techs go about their business.

I try to imagine the energy generated by a crowd this large. The thought of commanding the attention of tens of thousands of people is daunting.

Closing my eyes, I use a technique my father's girlfriend

taught me. First, two deep breaths. Then, imagine the version of myself fans have come to adore. The one that is a larger than life performer. The one they idolize, at least in part, because I embody their hopes and dreams in one way or another. I'm either their perfect boyfriend or greatest mate, delivering either the release of a sing-along chorus or the catharsis of sharing in the emotion of heartfelt lyrics, all of which draws them in a little closer. Envisioning *that* person is how you *become* that person. If only for a night. If only for a gig.

A smile tugs at the corner of my lips as I feel a sense of confidence overwhelm me with this little exercise. I can hear the crowd clapping, singing along, and shouting out my name. Without conscious thought, I raise my arms out from my sides and up in a moment of victory that feels so real I can taste it.

And then, with my eyes still closed, I feel the heat of a spotlight trained on my face. Rather than fueling this fantasy, it jolts me back to reality.

Opening my eyes, I immediately use my hand as a shield from the glare.

The light is coming from twenty feet up above me where one of the lighting crew guys has harnessed himself into safety gear and climbed up a long, untethered, retractable ladder.

"If you're done jerking off down there, you can go ahead and make way for the real rock stars, yeah?"

It's Danny Boy, of course.

He's taken perverse pleasure in giving me hassle ever since the Instagram video of me playing guitar went viral. My Uncle Shay tells me it's Danny Boy's way of initiating me into the music scene. Sometimes I believe that and laugh it off. And sometimes I just think he likes being an arsehole.

"Mind your own, Danny Boy!"

It's my da coming to my defense as he makes his way to me across the vast stage. I've broken the bad habit of rolling my eyes, but I still cringe a bit inside. He means well, but I need to fight my own battles, even the relatively harmless ones like with Danny Boy.

The light shifts away from me, falling onto my da. He keeps moving and so does the light.

"Just having a laugh!" Danny Boy shouts down.

"We get it," I reply before my da can jump in again. "You're fucking hilarious. If only to yourself."

Danny Boy cackles, amused. "Be sure you watch and learn how it's done, Donal. Rogue is still the biggest band in the world, after all!"

The instinct to reply, "Not for long!" surprises me, even as I know it's truly what I believe.

I've spent the last nine months working my ass off, and I'll soon put all my efforts on display with a series of club gigs in Dublin, Cork, Belfast, London, Manchester, and Birmingham.

After I got back from Spain, I finally got serious about working with Owen on music, including finding ourselves a bass player, a girl named Sadie. She's the perfect complement to Owen. Where he's wild and undisciplined, she's methodical and practical. And besides having a great music sense and desire to push the boundaries of our sound, she's also tough as nails, ready with a quick retort to shut Owen down when he thinks he's being suave with his attempts to flirt. They bicker all the time, but I think the tension between them helps their musical rhythm. I just pray they never give in and sleep together. Our band would be fucked if that happened, no doubt about it.

In the meantime, though, we've gelled into a trio that I think has the kind of *synergy* that will one day (sooner rather than later) rival the likes of Green Day, Nirvana, and The Police. Yeah, big ambitions, but what's the point if you don't aim high?

Conor said he wasn't handing over the baton to me and it's true. That's not why I'm here in Santiago. I'm along for the ride for the first five dates of Rogue's South American tour to learn, just like Danny Boy said. I want to soak up every aspect of how a band this size operates. I'd planned to sit on the sidelines and observe.

That is, until I got ahead of myself just now while standing on stage and fantasizing about being the one 60,000 people have come to see. I've got a ways before that's my reality. Still, I took to heart when Conor said that if I be my own leader, others will follow. I'm on a path now that is entirely focused on getting somewhere with my band.

Where does that leave Valentina? Well, we are definitely on good terms, seeing each other when we can, but we're realistic enough to understand that our lives are going in different directions.

That won't ever change the fact that I had the very best time of my life with her when we spent four days together on Mallorca.

After that first awkward meeting, we fell into the easy way we'd had with each other on the phone. I took her to a flash hotel overlooking the crystal-clear water of the Mediterranean and we tore each other's clothes off before the door to our suite closed. The chemistry we found in that kiss at the gelato shop was there and then some. I might not have taken the care to really listen and watch the way she reacted to my touch before that epic road trip with Conor. But he got me thinking about so many things, including how I connect with the woman I take to bed. It elevated fucking into something else. I guess it was the pursuit of passion rather than trying to satisfy simple desire. Whatever it was, it meant that Val and I shared hours of the hottest sex I've ever had.

Late that afternoon, she arranged to borrow her uncle's motorbike so we could explore the island. My fantasy of having her on the back of my bike, her chest pressed to me as she held tight to my waist, was deliciously realized. We wandered all over, enjoying the views of the coastline until we came to a secluded spot high above the water so we could watch the sunset. We stayed there until the moon was high in the sky, just talking and kissing and holding each other.

The next day, we went inland to Randa Valley to the horseback riding operation her uncle runs. We had a private trail ride on gorgeous Andalusian horses, enjoying the lush greenery, vineyards, almond and olive fields, and the panoramic vistas.

We got back to the hotel in time to shower together, go for a bite to eat, and then find our way to the pub Val heard was planning on hosting a watch party for Rogue's twentieth-anniversary gig. We got a table and a steady stream of drinks and enjoyed a world-class performance by the best band I know.

I may have ignored Val a bit during that viewing, as I was intensely focused on watching the lads in a new way. I zoned in on how each man commanded the stage and their instrument. Gavin, of course, was the most eye-catching. He's the type you can't keep from watching his every move. There's something magnetic about him. That showmanship was what

I wanted to study, to absorb and internalize. Then, there's Shay, steady and forceful on the drums. And so explosive when he comes off his stool to loom over his kit and crash down on it in dramatic fashion when he takes charge. Conor was as I always saw him: cool, controlled, somehow both effortlessly and staggeringly talented. He can manipulate the guitar in ways that are astounding—a real-life guitar hero. Finally, there's my da, the guy who spent years hiding at the back of the stage, doing his part well enough but not daring to strive for more. Those days are long gone now. Now, he makes himself seen and heard, dominating the side of the stage to Gavin's left with his own bit of swagger as he conjures up one incredible rhythm after another.

They had the huge audience at Croke Park bouncing and singing along en masse just the same as they had the audience of forty crammed into our pub doing so.

I was proud watching them that night. Proud of all that they've accomplished and proud of the enormous audience they still have to this day.

But more than anything, I was enthralled by the way they interacted. I probably took it for granted before, but watching them closely that night, I could see the subtle ways they communicated throughout the gig. It was a glance, a grin, a nod, a nudge—even a hug from behind as Gavin threw his arm around each of his bandmate's neck in a sweaty embrace at one point or another. It all suggested that they had a deep connection. Or as Conor might call it, *synergy*. Together, they are ... a force to be reckoned with.

And something to aspire to.

The following day, Val's uncle took us for a day-long sail ride. The hull cutting through the water not far from the craggy coastline, lying on the bow while baking in the sun, diving into the clear blue waters to cool off, and snorkeling in the salty sea was an experience I'll never forget.

I captured these moments, taking pics of the views, the horses, the filled to capacity pub watching Rogue on television, the sailboat and heavenly waters to post on Instagram. Sharing like that continued to increase my followers. But it was the photo Val took of us while we were riding on the motorbike that turned into another viral episode. We were cruising, not going very fast so that we could enjoy the view of the coastline as we rounded a turn. That's when she reached out with her mobile, and snapped a pic. It turned out gorgeous, I have to say. Neither of us were wearing helmets and we got a ton of shit for it. But we'd only been going a short distance to find a spot to park so we could dive into the sea. Val looks beautiful and free, though, with her long hair blowing in the breeze and a small smile on her face as she leaned her cheek against my shoulder. I had on sunglasses and a relaxed smile, my white T-shirt lifting in the breeze to expose a little toned skin. With the stunning coastline in the background, it was an unforgettable shot. I still love to look at it, as it captured the fantastic, free time we had together.

But the next day was our final together. Val had committed to helping her uncle with the last tourist group he had of the season and then would return to Barcelona. I had my own plans of returning to Dublin to sort out my next move. Our parting was bittersweet, but oddly mature. Neither of us got emotional about it. Turned out, we were both realists. We knew the score. This was a lovely little internet/summer romance and we took it for all it was worth. We had true fondness for each other and were genuine in suggesting that we meet up again during her school breaks. At the same time, there were no expectations. We wouldn't go back to texting and talking constantly like we had leading up to our meeting; it would be more sporadic, and that was okay.

Val did come to Dublin during her spring break. We did a bit of recreating our motorbike explorations, this time doing a full loop around Ireland. It was a fun adventure and we had a grand time together, but I think we both knew there was a little something forced with it. By then, I'd gotten Owen to really commit to our band and we'd brought Sadie on board. My future was taking shape and it was all about music. Hers was still based in Barcelona with her studies.

When I saw her off at the airport, I left not feeling sad or disappointed, but inspired to write a song about how precious timing is between people in a relationship. It's one of the songs we've played to great response in the handful of open mic nights we've done.

That's as far as we've gone officially with performing. But when I get back to Dublin, we've got that mini-tour of sorts lined up. Sadie and I worked together to get us booked into those clubs, never mentioning my connection to Rogue. It'll be a true test of both our talents and our ambitions. And I can't wait.

But first, the opening dates of Rogue's South American tour.

"What do you make of it, then?" Da asks, hands on hips as he surveys the stadium spread out before us in a daunting display of possibility.

I could revert back to the version of me who was instinctively critical of him. I could "jokingly" question whether they'd even fill the place. But I've let that all go. It wasn't an instant change after my trip with Conor, but more of a gradual one. He got me thinking about whether what I expected from my father was fair or even realistic. I came to accept that while my father did make some pretty epic mistakes, he was never after hurting me. I'll never know the full story of what went on between my parents. I know that he hurt my ma deeply, but I also know that he isn't a bad guy. He's just a man like any other, struggling to get it right—and moving in the right direction.

So, instead of some snarky comeback, I say, "It's incredible."

He puffs up with pride. I never really thought that it might matter to him to hear my appreciation for what he does. Silly, I suppose, when you think of it. Most men take pride in what they do. Why would he be any different? But when I came back from Barcelona, we had a good talk. It started with me gushing over their anniversary gig. I spent a half-hour breaking down all the ways I found it brilliant, including his part. That was the way that we opened up to each other again, the way I felt as close to him as I had those many years ago when we'd just sit and watch Doctor Who together. We ended up going to a pub that night. Just the two of us. Not only as father and son, but as friends. We talked and drank until they kicked us out. Or rather, they would have kicked us out had it not been for the fact that my da is Martin Whelan. At any rate, it was late when we left. We didn't go home and fall into bed, though. No, we kept our newfound connection going by jamming together for hours more.

From then on, we had an easy time in each other's company. I sought his advice on my music, and he gave it, careful not to be heavy-handed with it.

Conor had come back from our trip inspired to move in a new direction with the band and they burned through one new track after another, writing and recording their next album in record time. It includes the first-ever song written and sung by the man himself called "Coming Home." It was the second single and has been racing up the charts, with talk that it could rival "You're My One" in popularity.

When my da suggested I come along for the tour, I was thrilled. My ma never let us travel with the band once we were out of diapers and could process what all the scene entailed. I've seen Rogue play at some hometown gigs, but I can't say I was ever fully invested. Not like I am now. So, I jumped at the chance to follow along, but made the call to keep it to just a few dates because I have my own music to focus on. I think that short commitment actually pleased my da more than if I would have stayed on.

"Wait'll you feel it in here." He taps his chest with a fist. "It's the most addictive feeling in the world."

"What? The crowd going crazy for you?"

"Well, that," he concedes, "but more so that connection you feel with the audience as you produce the music that reaches their very core and they react with a kind of ecstasy."

I can't say I've gotten to that point in my few live performances. An open mic night, after all, isn't generally a rockin' crowd. But I know that'll come. I *know* it.

"Must be the most beautiful madness you can ever experience," I say.

He nods approvingly. "Wouldn't trade it for the world."

I stand taller and realize I'm now the same height as my father. Glancing over at him, I recognize some of the same features as well, though my build is muscular, it's not quite as ripped as his. There's just the hint of gray hair at his temples and wrinkles at the corners of his eyes, which would make him look distinguished, were it not for the tattoos that creep up his chest and onto his lower neck. The father I used to have trouble respecting is a badass. He plays bass for Rogue, for fuck's sake. He sleeps with a beautiful, world-famous actress. But most importantly, he's the one who has been there for me, pulling me out of my own way more times than I can count, patiently waiting out my fits of rebellion until we could get to this point of peace.

We spend another minute looking out at the empty stadium that will soon be filled to capacity. Then, he slaps me on the back.

"Come, let's go see what Sophie's planned for us."

Sophie and her kids are traveling with the band through the summer, as are Felicity and her kids. Sophie has arranged some sort of pre-show party that is suitable for the young ones. The after-party will be of the wilder sort. I smile, realizing I'm looking forward to both in equal measure. It's good to be around this group of people again, reminiscent of my younger years where everyone was always laughing, breaking out into song or dance, and the chatter never stopped. That I get to carry on in this tradition as an adult and something of an equal just makes it all the more satisfying.

I'VE GOT a smile glued to my face as I watch from the side of the stage that night. The band came in hot, playing tight and with enthusiasm. It was like they knew this was a whole new chance to enjoy themselves and all they'd accomplished and there was no way in hell that they were going to let it slip by.

It's especially fantastic to see Conor so completely engaged. At least, in his cool and controlled way, that is. He's got that strut as he makes his way across the stage or jumps off from a floor speaker. But he's also got that small smile of his. The one that is as much his signature as the pocket chain he still wears from time to time.

There aren't many people who truly know how close Rogue came to ending. Conor could have walked away from it all.

He chose, instead, to buy himself some time away from everything to reevaluate. I'm just lucky that I got to go along for the ride.

Lost in these thoughts and nodding unconsciously to the beat of one of their new songs, I barely register Conor's strut moving beyond his usual stopping point. He calls my name but the roar and chants of the crowd nearly drowns him out.

I snap out of it when Randy, his guitar tech, hands me my Telecaster. The one Conor bought for me in Paris, the one I've earned callouses from and fallen asleep with after obsessively playing. The one I still plan to repay him for.

"What's this?" I shout, looking from one man to another.

Conor leans in close. "Help us out with this one. We're doing 'Day's Done.' I'll even give you room to add to it like you did that time in Paris."

My eyebrows come together with incomprehension.

"Think about it, Donal," he tells me, a gleam in his eye. "But think fast. This is the chance of a lifetime. Let's go chase an adventure together."

I laugh. "Where have I heard that before?"

"Well?"

There's only a half-second of thought before I raise an eyebrow and tell him, "Give no fucks, yeah?"

He nods in that commanding way of his, and before I know it, he's back on stage and Randy is getting me connected to a wireless battery pack for my guitar.

"You're good to go. Knock 'em dead, kid," Randy says.

I take two deep breaths.

And then I walk out onto the stage just as Conor is using his mic to introduce me to the audience as a guest musician.

Me.

And I'm fucking ready for it.

The crowd is ready for it, too. They scream and chant and shine brilliantly under the lights.

This. Is. Epic.

The future is wide open.

My future is wide open.

The End

FOR A STEAMY VACATION/FAKE fiancée stand-alone romance with a guaranteed HEA, check out my book HULA GIRL.

COMING HOME
LYRICS BY CONOR QUINN

You held my hand
Sheltered me from the rain
Silence was a command
I didn't know how to explain

I'd fall at your feet if I were there
Caress your alabaster thighs
Stroke your hips, breasts, and hair
Take your lips with mine, make you sigh

Remember when I said you are the light?
It's been that way since before we spun the Eye
I promise you everything will be all right
I promise you this love won't ever die

So, this is happiness, my felicity
This is passion, my purpose
This is what's meant to be
All I need is the four of us

Coming Home

Four is the number of my life
Four brothers, family is four
Four decades and many more
Forever yours, forever yours

[Final chorus x3]
Remember when I said you are the light?
I promise you everything will be all right
I'm coming home, honey
I'm coming home to you
I'll always come home to you

ACKNOWLEDGMENTS

Thanks, as always, goes to my insanely patient family. They give me not just time to write, but endless support in all other ways, too.

Many thanks to Karen Cimms, Jennifer Hayes, and Samantha Richman for reading early and giving me invaluable feedback.

Thank you, Roxane Leblanc for your proofreading wizardry - and for always finding time for my projects!

Thank you to all you wonderful readers who took a chance on an unknown, unproven author (me!) and kept going with me and the Rogue boys on this journey.

ABOUT THE AUTHOR

Lara Ward Cosio is the author of contemporary romances that are raw, realistic, sometimes funny, and always feature swoon-worthy men and strong-willed women.

If you enjoyed this novel, please share your thoughts in a review on Amazon or Goodreads

To learn more about the Rogue Series, visit:
LaraWardCosio.com

Subscribe to my mailing list here:
Sign Me Up

Fans of the Rogue Series can find like-minded friends on a Facebook page called Rogue Rockers - join us!

ALSO BY LARA WARD COSIO

Tangled Up In You (Rogue Series Book 1)
Playing At Love (Rogue Series Book 2)
Hitting That Sweet Spot (Rogue Series Book 3)
Finding Rhythm (Rogue Series Book 4)
Looking For Trouble (Rogue Series Book 5)
Felicity Found (Rogue Series Book 6)
Rogue Christmas Story (Rogue Series Book 7)
Problematic Love (Rogue Series Book 8)
Rock Star on the Verge (Rogue Series Book 9)

Full On Rogue: The Complete Books #1-4
Rogue Extra: The Complete Books #5-8

Hula Girl: A Standalone Romance

Printed in Great Britain
by Amazon